Turning Season

Turning Season

a novel

✳✳✳

by Melanie Lageschulte

Turning Season: a novel
© 2020
by Melanie Lageschulte
Fremont Creek Press

Kindle: 978-1-952066-00-9
Paperback: 978-1-952066-01-6
Hardcover: 978-1-952066-02-3

Cover photo: Dudarev Mikhail/Shutterstock.com
Cover design: Melanie Lageschulte
Author photo: © Bob Nandell

Web: fremontcreekpress.com

Also by Melanie Lageschulte

Novels:
Growing Season
Harvest Season
The Peaceful Season
Waiting Season
Songbird Season
The Bright Season
The Blessed Season (coming fall 2020)

Short fiction:
A Tin Train Christmas

* 1 *

Melinda didn't have to check a calendar to know September had arrived. The sun appeared just a moment later every morning and, over the past few weeks, its once-harsh rays had slowly mellowed into a warm glow. And while the rolling fields around her acreage were still cloaked in drought-dimmed shades of green and brown, summer would soon step aside and autumn would arrive with its signature hues of red, rust and gold.

This morning brought another, immediate change: When she opened the porch door, a crisp breeze darted around the farmhouse and pushed her back inside. With a faded sweatshirt settled over her tee shirt, she was finally ready for chores.

The squirrels were already at work, even though the eastern horizon was still a shade of pink, searching for first-fall acorns under the oak tree behind the house. Melinda's barn cats, Sunny and Stormy, waited on the picnic table, eager to accompany her across the gravel drive to the barn. Her boys were also very focused ... on the bucket of warmed gravy in her hand.

"It's going to be another gorgeous day," she told the cats while handing out a few pets. "We've got a clear sky, a nice breeze ... Those geese last night were really something, huh? The first ones I've seen heading south. And I love the sunshine as much as anyone else, but I really hope we get more rain yet this week. The garden could really use it."

Stormy and Sunny had already vacated the table's worn boards and started for the barn, their tails held high with anticipation. With her nearest neighbors more than a half-mile away, Melinda was now talking only to herself.

Or maybe she wasn't. Her eight sheep were clustered on the other side of the pasture fence, awaiting their breakfast, and one of them soon let out an indignant bellow.

"Yeah, Annie, I knew you were listening. You might like a little rain, too, to get that pasture grass growing again." A lightning strike sparked a fire in the field behind Melinda's farm just a few weeks ago, and the blaze had burned a portion of her pasture before it was extinguished. She'd feared it would be spring before the meadow began to recover, but tiny shoots of pale green were already pushing up through the scarred dirt.

A series of barks echoed from the windbreak, and then a brown-and-white flash slipped around the machine shed and barreled toward the barn.

"Hobo, there you are! You're just in time to help with chores."

Sunny and Stormy had reached the barn's concrete stoop, and flattened their ears in irritation when they saw Melinda set their bucket down and wrap her arms around the dog.

"When you went out this morning, I told you to stay close." Hobo yipped and wriggled, ignoring the warning in her voice. While he spent a great deal of time in the house, he loved the freedom that came with being a farm dog. "We're pressed for time today; I've got to get those treats ready to take to work, remember? And if you're gone too long, Grace and Hazel will miss their papa."

Maybe that wasn't true, as the house cats followed their own agenda of snacking, sleeping, and stalking birds through the living room's picture window. But Hobo had taken the girls under his paw when they arrived at the farm, two sickly, orphaned kittens Melinda had been determined to save. She still often found the three of them snuggled in Hobo's bolstered bed.

Stormy and Sunny were soon settled in the grain room with their breakfast. Hobo completed his regular inspection of the barn's main aisle while Melinda fed the sheep their morning rations. As she started for the far corner of the yard, she could see the hens strutting about in their coop's run, enjoying the sun's earliest rays as they began a new day.

Yes, Melinda was the only person at this little farm, but she was certainly never lonely. At least, not anymore.

Those first days and weeks had been terribly difficult, filled with too many kinds of loss and too much change. She'd been downsized from a prestigious job at a Minneapolis marketing firm, and the loss of her dear cat, Oreo, had made her charming apartment too empty to bear. When Uncle Frank suffered a heart attack and the family's business needed another pair of hands, Melinda had come home to northern Iowa for what was supposed to be a temporary stay. But a "for rent" sign on the blacktop brought her down this gravel road, where she found an elderly bachelor farmer seeking someone to rent his acreage and look after Hobo and his other animals.

Maybe it had been too much to take on, especially for a single woman who'd been away for twenty years, but Melinda Foster recognized the lifeline tossed her way and reached for it with both hands.

She'd arrived with little more than a stack of storage totes and flagging spirits, her weariness matching the weathered white paint that tried to cover the farmhouse's narrow-plank siding. Her days were soon filled with her new job at Prosper Hardware, and learning the ways of country life.

The farm was hers now, thanks to Horace's guidance as well as his willingness to accept a below-market offer, and she'd put down new roots with a fresh perspective and a grateful heart.

With her chores completed, there was just enough time to take a quick shower, reach for a clean shirt and jeans, and pull her wavy brown hair into a low ponytail. Her own breakfast took priority over bothering with makeup on this hectic morning, and it wasn't long before her gray hatchback was pointed toward Prosper, a pan of apple-pie bars hitching a ride in the passenger seat.

A little rain would do wonders for more than her garden. Gravel dust coated her car, no matter how carefully she navigated the road's packed-down tire tracks, and threatened to obscure her view at the two rural crossroads that stood between home and the county highway. By this time of year, the rows of corn stalks should be high enough to bring her to a full stop at those intersections, but the drought had kept them stunted and short.

It wasn't long until the co-op's tall towers appeared on the horizon, the concrete structures backlit by the sun as it lifted higher into the clear sky. Prosper Feed Co. was the town's most-visible structure, marking the west edge of a four-block Main Street capped by a lone water tower on the east end. In between sat an efficient grid of homes, a brief business district where some storefronts had been vacant for years, an elementary school, three churches and a cemetery.

Prosper was home to only two hundred residents, but most of them were proud of their tiny community. Just before the county highway bumped over the railroad tracks and passed the co-op, a wooden sign adorned with a nostalgic painting of Main Street greeted visitors with the town's motto: "Prosper ... The Great Little Town That Didn't."

Many mornings, Main Street was mostly deserted at this hour. But the parking spots in front of Prosper Hardware were already taken, as were those across the street near city hall and the next-door library. Nancy Delaney, the town's clerk-librarian and its only full-time employee, was at the curb, waving vehicles around the corner to city hall's back entrance. Melinda acknowledged Nancy's grin and thumbs-up with an energetic wave, as the minor traffic jam signaled the activity taking over the council chambers would be a success.

More than forty cats were on the list for the monthly spay-and-neuter clinic, a new initiative helmed by Karen Porter, one of Prosper's two veterinarians, and Josh Vogel, who had a practice in nearby Swanton. Melinda handled publicity for the events and, when Aunt Miriam could spare her from Prosper Hardware, liked to walk across the street and snuggle a post-surgery patient or two. The wait list for the reduced-fee services was now so long that two events would be held in both October and November, as the unpredictable winter weather would shut the program down until March.

Melinda waited as one woman, balancing two rocking cat carriers, carefully made her way across Main Street. An empty-handed man got behind the wheel of his truck and gave Melinda a gleeful wave before he pulled away. She laughed and returned his greeting, understanding the relief and triumph she saw on his lined face. Getting any cat to the vet was hard enough. But strays and barn cats? Several distractions had to be deployed to trick them into a crate, and they had to spend the night in lockdown so they didn't eat anything before surgery. Many farmers and colony caregivers preferred to bring several cats to one clinic, just to get the howls and hisses over with. The one-day record so far was ten, held by Gertrude Millard, who cared for a large pool of strays on the edge of town.

"Gertrude was really a good sport when I approached her about the first clinic." Melinda rolled past the post office, then turned south on Third Street to reach Prosper Hardware's back lot. "We've helped even more of hers since then. If we can get the last six, her colony will be done! The kittens will be easy, but the other two? I'm afraid we're going to need chicken baby food, humane traps and lots of prayers."

Prosper Hardware had been in existence almost as long as the town itself. Melinda's Shrader ancestors opened the store in 1894, and Aunt Miriam took it over a few years after she married Frank Lange. The business had carried a diverse inventory from the start and, with other retail outlets at least ten miles away, its bare-necessity food and clothing departments were still its biggest sellers.

The commotion at city hall had pushed the coffee-group members' vehicles behind the store this morning. Auggie Kleinsbach's truck was right by the back door, as he prided himself on being the first to arrive. The long-time owner of Prosper Feed Co. was also a former Prosper Hardware employee. That was forty years ago, when Auggie was in high school, but he still had a set of keys to the store.

Uncle Frank's car was already there, although Melinda wished he'd taken the opportunity to walk the few blocks from the Langes' Victorian on Cherry Street. Frank's health had prevented him from returning to the store full-time, but his cardiologist continued to insist Frank fit in bouts of exercise whenever he could. Jerry Simmons' SUV was next in line. A retired school principal, Jerry was nearing the end of his first term as the little town's mayor.

Melinda parked on the far edge of the gravel, near the pop machine. Grandpa Shrader had rolled it out of the shop and chained it to an oak tree several decades ago, when Prosper's only grocery store closed. Bill Larsen, Prosper Hardware's only other full-time employee, would keep the case stocked until the first frost forced it to be emptied for the winter.

That day was still several weeks' away. But as the refreshing breeze threatened to pull the foil sheet from her pan of bars, Melinda found herself looking forward to when the weather would turn. It was a little early to break out the sweaters and the slow cookers, since afternoon highs had only dropped into the low eighties, but fall had always been her favorite time of year.

No matter the season, the coffee group's seating arrangements never seemed to change. Auggie always stationed his metal folding chair closest to the store's right-side picture window. Enjoying a cup of brew and gabbing with his friends were his main priorities, of course, but he didn't want to miss anything of interest that might appear along Main Street. The chair closest to the vintage sideboard would be occupied by George Freitag, a retired farmer who'd moved to town with his wife, Mary, a few years ago. Since George was in his early eighties, that post put him near one of the floor's generous registers as well as the coffee pot.

John "Doc" Ogden, Karen's business partner, sat next to George, and Frank usually wedged himself in by Auggie. Jerry gravitated to the middle of the pack, which was fitting, as he often had to moderate a heated discussion. Usually the last to arrive, Bill popped in a chair wherever there was room. Melinda always ended up behind the antique oak showcase that served as the store's counter, as she needed to reconcile the register and tidy up before the door opened at eight.

The comforting aroma of fresh-brewed coffee was already wafting down the store's main aisle when she came in from the back. Frank and Jerry were stretched out in their usual seats, quietly fueling up for the day, but Auggie's chair was empty. He was pressed to the window, his head swiveling with bird-dog precision as he studied the hustle and bustle across the street.

Jerry sat up and adjusted his purple ball cap. Along with being mayor, he was one of the local high school's biggest fans. "Hey, you brought treats!"

"Apple-pie bars." Melinda set the pan on the sideboard's metal counter and reached for the stack of paper plates kept behind one cabinet door. "Maybe it's a little early, but I'm in the mood for fall. They just sounded good."

Auggie's brown eyes lit up behind his dark-rimmed glasses when he spotted the pan, but he quickly turned back to the window.

"Oh, look at that one!" He pointed out the humane trap one woman carried. "That guy's got a really long coat, brown with white. He's a big boy, for sure. Bet he's never gone for a ride before."

Melinda and Jerry exchanged amused glances. Auggie had always claimed to not care much for cats. But a few months ago, he was adopted by two former strays that now presided over the co-op's front counter.

Jerry helped himself to a square of apple dessert. "I'm glad the clinics are so successful, but they're just one more reminder that we need a real community center. Performing veterinary procedures in the scrubbed-down council chambers is far from ideal."

Uncle Frank, who served on the city council, rose to refill his cup. "You're right. But what's the answer? Other towns have tried all sorts of things, from reclaiming rundown properties to erecting new buildings on vacant lots."

Auggie shook his head as he reluctantly took his seat. Cats were fine and all, but there was important community business to discuss now. "We've got the first. But we all know the drama that comes with property changing hands."

"And none of the latter." Jerry gave the idea more consideration as he chewed. "Or at least, no empty lots owned by the city. There's only a few, and they're all on residential streets."

"A community center means congestion," Frank warned. "Who'd want to live next door to that? But it's an issue we have to face, sooner or later. I heard Jake plans to address public use of city space within his mayoral platform."

The rest of the guys groaned. Jake Newcastle was another member of the council, a guy in his thirties already serving his second term. He was brash and outspoken, and well-known in the community since he was the high school's assistant wrestling coach as well as its physical education instructor. Jerry was well-liked in town, but Jake was determined to knock him off his post in November's election.

As Melinda poured her own coffee, she wondered how to encourage her friend. Because all of the sudden, Jerry looked rather defeated. "Insisting the city create a policy is fine and all," she finally said, "but with so little public space to fight over, it makes Jake look short-sighted. Why don't you add a discussion item to the next council agenda? Beat him at his own game?"

George shuffled in, looking a little winded. Parking in the lot made a long walk for someone his age.

"Whew, it's almost cold out there! I might need to pull out the long-sleeve shirts soon. Do you think Doc will give up those khakis and light-colored tees? Makes me do a double take, every single time. Never seen him in anything but jeans until this summer."

"Never seen it so blasted hot, either," Auggie reminded George. "A man's gotta dress for the job. I'd rather Doc look like a preppie than have him keel over when he's out on a farm call."

"Especially when he's one of our first responders," Jerry added. "We need all the volunteers we can get."

Melinda reached for the dust cloth and wiped down the counter, where two stuffed-fabric pumpkins were already on display next to the register. "Jerry, there's another plank for your platform. How about a plan to recruit more firefighters and EMTs? Public safety is a major issue for voters."

"I'll add it to the list." Jerry crossed his arms. "This platform's going to have so many planks, I could just about build us a community center from scratch."

Auggie twisted in his chair, his eyes wide.

"What?" Frank nudged him and chuckled. "See a ghost? It's a little early for that. Give it a month, maybe. But I have to say, I can't wait to get our Halloween decorations out at home. I'd love to add one of those inflatable pumpkins, but I don't know if Miriam ..."

"Now, that is just eerie." Auggie hurried to the door. "Here we were talking about the emergency crew, and I swear, Tony's truck just pulled up. I thought he had to be in Swanton before eight, you never see him in town this time of day. What's going on?" Tony Bevins worked at a bank, since his role as Prosper's emergency management chief came with only a small stipend.

Jerry joined Auggie by the windows. "Hey, he's got Doc with him. Guess Tony's having coffee with us this morning. Good thing we've got extra chairs."

Doc and Tony wore big grins as they wiped their shoes on the mat.

"I don't have long, I have to get to the bank." Tony's ruddy face was alight with ... something. Maybe excitement? "But I wanted to tell everyone, right away. Melinda, take a seat."

"Me? What ..."

Auggie eyed Tony and Doc. "You're smirking like crazy. Both of you. What's the deal? Spit it out, already!"

"Hobo's a hero!" Doc hooted and clapped.

"Well, yeah." Frank frowned. "Everyone knows that. He saved Melinda's farm, saved the whole township from ..."

"No, no, for real!" Tony shoved his phone into Melinda's hand. She blinked twice, trying to process the email on the screen. Happy tears sprang into her eyes.

"Wait ... are you serious? Hobo's getting an award?"

A national organization had chosen Hobo to receive one of its highest honors, which was granted to animals showing bravery during emergencies. A certificate and medal were on their way to Prosper, and the group would make a one-time donation in Hobo's name to any non-profit that helped animals in need. Melinda would choose which one.

Doc rubbed his hands together. "We were talking about Hobo, after the fire. I told Tony, it was worth a shot."

"I filled the form out online right away." Tony grinned as he accepted Jerry's high-five. "The paperwork and the rest of it will come later this week."

Uncle Frank clapped Melinda on the shoulder. "Looks like we've got another agenda item for next week's meeting. So, how does Hobo handle crowds?"

She cringed, thinking of Hobo's first trip to the senior-center apartment Horace shared with his older brother, Wilbur, in Elm Springs. That visit had probably been Hobo's last.

"He's ... unpredictable. But if I bring him in the back door, and we can be in and out in ten minutes, I think we can manage it. Oh, this is so exciting!"

Jerry pulled his phone from his pocket. "Tony, send that to me, will ya? I need to get Hobo on the website right away, people will love it. It's the kind of news this town needs these days. The drought's broken, finally, but it's going to be a lean harvest."

He turned to Melinda, as he often did when he was unsure how to handle a public-relations situation. "Do you think it's worth one of those text-alerts? Or maybe not ..."

"An all-points-bulletin might be too much. A news-page update would do. I'll send you a photo to put with it."

"Wait, what's this?" Frank teased Jerry. "Are you going to post that yourself?"

"Well, Nancy's busy checking in cats, I don't want to bother her." He raised his chin. "Besides, I need to get better at this stuff. Jake's a whiz at it; I can't look like an old fart."

Auggie seemed poised to say something snarky, but Melinda cut him down with a look. "Just click here, and there," she told Jerry. "See? It's easy."

* * *

Thanks to Jerry's post, word of Hobo's honor spread fast. Every customer wanted to offer their congratulations, then linger at the counter as they reminisced about the special dogs they'd known throughout their lives. Prosper Hardware seemed more crowded than usual, even though this was one of the store's busiest times of the year, and Melinda wondered how many people had found an excuse to wander in so they could press her for details about the award.

Aunt Miriam arrived just after ten. She put off the accounting work waiting for her in the upstairs office and swept the oak floors instead, as the well-wishers had kept Melinda from completing that morning task.

"Hobo certainly deserves it." Miriam's short, gray curls bobbed in agreement as she tackled the dirty shoe prints at the end of the housewares aisle. "He saved your farm, and probably several others. Are you going to get him anything special to celebrate?"

"No way." But her face hurt from smiling so much. "He's got a big enough head as it is, I can barely get him to obey even the easiest commands. I'm glad the meeting is still a week away. We'll need all the time we can get to prepare for a room full of strange people and news media."

"News media?" Miriam raised her eyebrows.

"Jerry just texted. He called the Swanton newspaper, and they want to send someone. I thought Nancy could just take a pic with her phone, but sounds like there's going to be quite the fuss."

Bill came up from the back with an oversized cardboard box in his arms. He was in his mid-thirties, stocky and strong. The first was probably due to too many treats being offered on the store's sideboard; the second came from lifting lengths of lumber and sheets of plywood in the woodshop. Bill and his wife moved back to Prosper when they started their family, and he was known as a master craftsman who could translate any customer's idea into a completed project.

"I'm sure they'll want to know everything you can tell them about Hobo." Bill rounded the half-wall divider that made up the rest of the checkout area and lowered the unwieldy carton to the floor with barely a blink. It was packed with gloves, ranging from work gear to winter-worthy pairs. "You know, his favorite toy, his cutest habit ..."

"Well, he spends the nicer days outside, napping in the dirt under the picnic table, which isn't very glamorous." The rush had settled a bit, and Melinda came out from behind the counter to help Bill sort and stack the new arrivals. Gloves would be part of the sale that started tomorrow.

"Or, he's down at the creek, getting mud all over himself, and then tracks it into the house. And he chases rabbits, which I hate, but at least he's not motivated enough to catch one." She snorted. "Doesn't sound like much of a hero, huh? But he's got a loving heart, he's loyal and sweet, and he's a good friend to the rest of my critters, even the cats."

"I'd say that counts for something." Bill passed her a pack of cotton gloves. "And what he did that night, how he alerted you to the fire? He deserves that award, for sure."

He jerked his head toward the front door. "Hey, here comes Esther. You know, I happened to drive by her house the other day. She's got all her Halloween decorations out already."

Esther Denner was Frank and Miriam's neighbor, and retired from the elementary school's kitchen. She'd rushed to the store when Frank fell ill, then volunteered to help Bill keep the ship upright until things settled down. Now, she was Prosper Hardware's only part-time employee. Esther loved every holiday that came along, and Melinda suspected her first-in-town Halloween display factored into Uncle Frank's obsession with his own decorations.

"It's beautiful out there, isn't it?" Esther's pullover pushed the season, as it was adorned with falling leaves and black cats. Tiny metal pumpkins dangled from her ears, and she carried two large plastic bags overflowing with fall decorations. "Now that the heat's gone, I can't wait to change out that window display. We need to get things looking like fall around here, at least a little bit."

Bill smirked, but kept his comments to himself. Several pots of orange and purple mums were already parked in front of the store, and Aunt Miriam had retrieved her scarecrow from storage and wired it to one of the iron-and-wood benches.

Melinda went back around the counter and pulled out three large metal hooks. "Our first Prosper Hardware sweatshirts came in yesterday, and I want to put a few in the window. I'll attach these to the side wall, and put the merchandise on swivel hangers so they're easy to see from the sidewalk."

Esther clapped her hands. "That'll leave room for the seasonal kitchen towels to be draped over the dresser's drawer fronts. I think we should put a stack of those cozy fleece throws on top, and maybe some work boots in front."

"And a rake." Melinda gestured at the hardware aisle. "We just got some in."

"Well, then, I'm glad I dropped by the hobby store in Mason City and went a little crazy with those sacks of fake leaves!"

Melinda only smiled, as no one simply "dropped by" anywhere in Mason City. The regional retail center was a forty-minute drive from Prosper. One way.

Esther was already hurrying toward the door. "Just wait until you see what else I found!"

Bill rolled his eyes. "I hate to be such a downer, but promise me this place isn't going to start smelling like pumpkin spice. If she tries to put a bowl of potpourri on the counter, like last year ..."

"Miriam told her it was messy and made her throw it out, remember? We'll contain the decorations to the windows. And, well, maybe the aisles' end displays. Oh, and we'll put a wreath on the door ..."

"Watch out! Fall fever is contagious." Bill turned back to the box of gloves. "I'll just be over here, working, staying out of the way. Oh, geez, what does she have now?"

Esther's arms were so packed with yellowed cornstalks that she couldn't manage the door on her own. Melinda rushed over to help. "Where did you get those?"

"A farm stand, just outside of Mason City. They trucked them in, I'm sure, as the ones around here aren't turning yet." Esther laughed. "You didn't think I stole them, did you?"

"Oh, no, not at all." Melinda looked away. Last October, she'd briefly considered slipping into the cornfield behind her farm and swiping some authentic decorations, but had talked herself out of that idea.

"They were on sale," Esther explained, to herself as much as to Melinda. "I couldn't leave until I had a few armfuls. They look really clean. Just imagine how wonderful they'll look, framing everything out."

The stalks were tied in bundles with wire, then anchored to the corners of the display. Even Bill had to admit they were festive, and the rest were grouped in the other window, for symmetry's sake. Esther then mounted the ladder and tacked an end of a faux fall-leaf garland to one upper corner of the display window. "That's so exciting about Hobo! You must be so proud."

"For sure. But I think Jerry's going to have a public discussion about community space that night, which means the chambers will be packed. I'm not sure Hobo's ready to face such a crowd." She was trying to add another synthetic pumpkin to the pile started on the other side of the display, but it kept toppling off. Surely there was something in the fasteners' aisle that would anchor everything. After all, this was a hardware store ...

"I noticed the award comes with a sizeable donation." Esther had moved the ladder and was draping the leaf garland across the window. "Have you decided which nonprofit will get the money?"

"Haven't had a chance to think that through yet. It's going to be tough, there's so many worthy groups out there. Hobo didn't come from a shelter, so there's not one obvious choice. But he was a stray, just showed up one day in Horace and Wilbur's yard."

Melinda took a step back. The display looked great. She'd fix the pumpkins later, but for now, she could add the kitchen towels. Besides, another idea had just come to mind.

"You know, this isn't just about Hobo. It's the perfect opportunity to highlight shelter dogs, how they can be just as intelligent as any purebred." Melinda spoke slowly, a plan forming in her mind.

"Jerry's already alerted the Swanton newspaper, and they're sending someone. Hobo's going to have to behave himself no matter what, for even a few minutes. I wonder who else might show up, if I put out some feelers. Maybe the Mason City television station, or the one in Waterloo. Other papers ..."

Although he'd insisted he wasn't interested in the fall decorations, Bill had wandered over to give them a cautious nod of approval. And encourage Melinda.

"If some of the media's already coming, you might as well turn it into a media circus. Hobo saved your farm. And several others, thanks to his keen sense of smell and his bravery. He didn't need registration papers to do that."

Esther stepped off the ladder and reached for her tote bag. "I was at the superstore in Swanton when I saw the post about Hobo. Please give him these, from me." She pulled out a package of treats Melinda usually passed up due to their price. "And I think you should go all-out, call everyone you can think of. He's already a hero to all of us; you might as well give him a chance to help other dogs, too."

✳ 2 ✳

Sunny's golden eyes widened as he sniffed the pail of wild plums waiting on the picnic table. Melinda had hoped for at least two buckets from the patch down the road, but the drought had already done its worst.

"I'll be lucky to get a dozen jars of jam this year." She rubbed Sunny's fluffy orange-tabby coat, and he began to purr. "Besides, we have to share them with the raccoons and the birds and everything else that lives around here, so sometimes it's slim pickings, anyway. I'll make sure Horace and Wilbur and Ada get their share, though, no matter how small."

Ada Arndt was still the youngest of the eight Schermann children, even though she was now in her early seventies. She lived in Mason City, as did her son, Kevin, who was close to his two bachelor uncles and had visited the farm often over the years to help Wilbur, and then Horace, remain at home for as long as possible. Last summer, Melinda found instructions for the plum jam in the vintage recipe box tucked away in the kitchen and revived a Schermann family tradition.

Sunny sauntered to the other side of the picnic table and stretched out on its sun-warmed boards, but one eye remained partially open and trained on the lane. How did her animals always sense when something was about to happen?

This Sunday afternoon was about to change from peaceful to hectic, as Mabel Bauer and Angie Hensley would soon arrive for what was shaping up to become the rural neighborhood's annual canning bee.

Mabel and Ed lived just up the road, past the creek and through the first intersection. They were retired from farming, but had been generous with their time as well as their emotional support from the day Melinda arrived. Angie and Nathan's farm was just to the north and then east. Their young family included Emma and Allison, as well their little boy, Blake, who was about two months old.

Last year, the canning crew needed the help of Ada as well as Melinda's mom, Diane, to put up the bounty from the oversized garden Horace planted before he left for the nursing home. But between Melinda's scaled-back plot and the dry weather, the three neighbor ladies could handle things on their own this time. Mabel had a few pails of tomatoes left on her vines, and Angie promised a smattering of corn and peppers to add to the cooking pots.

With Sunny out of the way, Melinda placed a large plastic basin next to the plums' bucket and began to sort them carefully, enjoying the dappled shade of the maple tree as the cicadas buzzed their way through this warm afternoon. She'd picked the plums yesterday evening but, as the light had waned by the time she came up the lane, the dreaded job of checking them for bugs was put off until today.

Melinda had lost most of her city-girl revulsion regarding mud and dirt since she'd moved to the country, but insects were still a cringe-worthy threat, especially if they found their way into her house. The plums spent the night in the garage, as Melinda had learned her lesson about picked produce being unattended. A few weeks ago, she'd absentmindedly left a bin of tomatoes on the back step and came out the next morning to find the raccoons had ransacked the buffet during the dark hours. Tomatoes had been tossed in every direction, and many had a maddeningly small bite nipped out of one side before they were discarded. Several had been smashed on the sidewalk, and their pulp was smeared across the concrete and already rotting in the humid air.

Stormy soon trotted around the side of the house, his gray-tabby coat and white paws as immaculate as ever, but he only gave the plums a quick sniff before joining his brother in their favorite napping spot. Melinda assumed the cats were related, but their origin story was shrouded in mystery. They'd simply appeared in the barn, scared and shy, a few weeks before Horace left for Scenic Vista. And it had taken several weeks of effort for Melinda to gain their trust.

Hobo had accepted the announcement of his impending honor with barely a shake of his white-tipped tail, far more interested in Esther's treats than his sudden fame. He was nowhere to be found just now, but would come on the run the moment he heard tires rattling the driveway's gravel. Hobo was particularly fond of Mabel and Ed, who cared for the farm's animals in the days between Horace's departure and Melinda's arrival, and the couple were still her first call when she needed to be away from home.

Her neighbors would be here in a few minutes, and Melinda tried to focus on her task despite the distractions her charming acreage offered on a mid-September afternoon.

A sturdy windbreak of hardwoods and evergreens hugged the north and west sides of the property, and fields and pastures rolled away from the farmyard to the south and east. Songbirds were everywhere, trilling their notes from the acreages' plentiful trees and the perches of several feeders. Hardy perennials, planted by Horace's mother, still bloomed inside the concrete-block foundation that used to hold the summer kitchen. In the garden, the surviving plants held their heads high. The chickens scuttled in their run, and the sheep were lazily following the freshest blades of grass across their pasture.

Melinda saw so much simple beauty around her, but there was so much work to do. Advancing age and aching joints had made it difficult for Horace and Wilbur to maintain the farm as it had been in its heyday. The barn still stood square and strong, but its dark-red paint had weathered over the years. And this summer's extreme heat and lack of moisture hadn't helped.

The farmhouse's gray-green shingles were holding their own on the steep-gabled roof, but for how long? From the road, her cozy home looked to be a fresh, solid white. But the narrow clapboards were actually dull and faded, as was the gray-painted trim.

The same story was repeated on the garage, as well as the machine shed and the chicken coop. How many hours, and how many gallons of paint, would it take to get this place looking sharp again?

It would be spring, at least, before she could get the time and money together to make some major changes. But her farm was charming just as it was, and it was about to become even more beautiful. The place looked lovely in the fall, with the trees awash in vibrant colors, and the fields around it faded to a rich gold.

Barks coming from beyond the chicken house interrupted her thoughts, and she turned to see Mabel's car rolling up the lane. Mabel's white curls were carefully coiffed as usual, but she wore a ragged tee shirt and old jeans. Canning was a messy business.

"I brought all the tomatoes I have ready, they've really perked up lately." Mabel paused in unloading the backseat to return Hobo's excited greeting. "There's my boy! Who's the celebrity, huh? We're so proud of you!"

Melinda reached for a cardboard box packed with mixing bowls and faded kitchen towels. Canning day wasn't just an all-hands affair, it seemed to require every spare container available. "I'm picking everything I can. We've got a month left, if we're lucky. Great, Angie's here!"

Angie's auburn curls were wrapped into a casual bun, and Melinda was relieved to see Emma and Allison were dressed in old clothes. She had a fall craft project in mind to keep them busy, but it might get a bit messy. They were ready to explore, but didn't protest when their mom requested they

carry some of her supplies inside before they ran off to find
Sunny and Stormy, who'd decamped the moment their naps
were interrupted.

Blake wailed when the women crowded around. "He's
been fussy today," Angie warned Mabel when she offered to
give him a lift to the house. "You sure you're up for it?"

"Oh, I've dealt with several cranky kids over the years."
Mabel took Blake into her arms and ruffled his hair. "He's
going to be a ginger, just like you. I'm sure of it."

"Well, there's still a chance it'll change as he grows."
Angie rolled her eyes, but seemed secretly pleased. "Here,
Melinda, can you take his diaper bag? I swear, he needs an
entourage to carry his gear every time we leave the house."

"He's the first grandson on both sides," Mabel reminded
Angie. "I'm sure he'll never lack for new things."

"Between my dad and Nathan's dad, they're already trying
to get him to pick sides. Whether it's sports-team colors or
tractor-brand apparel, this guy is a clotheshorse."

The enclosed back porch was soon packed with buckets of
produce and tubs of clean jars. Mabel spread newspapers
across the kitchen table and stacked the towels on the
counter. "It's a pain to tote everything around, that's for sure.
But it's far more fun to can with friends when, well ..."

"When you can?" Melinda laughed.

"Exactly. I did the rest of mine last week. Even made
some apple-pie filling, which I haven't bothered with for
years. It's been a lean growing season, so I'm grabbing
everything I can save."

A sheet of old plastic covered the dining-room table, and
Melinda spread out the selection of still-green leaves she'd
plucked from the yard after high winds came through a few
days before. She retrieved craft paint and foam brushes from
a drawer in the built-in buffet, and added a stack of white
paper and a full roll of paper towels.

Angie popped through from the kitchen. "This looks like
fun! Let me guess, the leaves are flexible enough to hold the
paint without crumbling?"

"Exactly. You just brush it on, then use the leaves like stamps. The more you mix the colors, the better they look."

"I'll tell the girls to be careful not to spill the paint. You've only had that rug, what, since the spring?"

Melinda waved her friend's concerns away. The inside of her farmhouse was a little bit grand, in a quiet way, with oak floors, generous woodwork and built-ins, even a transom of leaded glass above the living room's picture window. But it had withstood generations of the Schermann family with a certain humble grace, and nothing was too precious for the knocks of everyday life.

"Don't worry about it. The paint's washable. And I got a rug with a tweed pattern on purpose, to hide stains. There may not be kids in this house on a regular basis these days, but I have three furry roommates. Two of which, I'm afraid, may think they need to help the girls."

The pitter-pat of little paws echoed down the bare oak stairs, and Grace and Hazel soon rounded the cased opening between the living room and dining room. Both had beautiful, long coats, with Grace's a riot of calico shades and Hazel's a brown tabby with white paws, but they were curious to a fault and had a knack for finding trouble.

"They're big enough to get on the table now, even if I push the chairs in," Melinda warned Angie. "If they get too nosy, I might have to corral them in the bathroom, but I'm afraid they'll howl something terrible."

"No one likes to be left out." Angie gave Hazel a pet. "I can't believe how they've grown."

"I was afraid they wouldn't even make it through the night. Doc and Karen were right, though; they bounced back, and then some."

Melinda called Emma and Allison in from the yard, and the girls were soon engrossed in their craft project. Angie settled Blake next to the kitchen's double window, near the pulled-out table, and Mabel brought in the bucket of plums. "Let's start with these. It's a small batch of jam, so it'll feel like we accomplished something, right off the bat."

Melinda handed out disposable plastic gloves to keep the fruits' dark stain off their skin. They had only a handful of plums pitted when Angie put down her knife. "OK, you have to promise to not tell anyone yet, as things are still very early, but ... I've got big news!"

Mabel raised her eyebrows and said nothing, although she looked about to burst with an unventured question. Angie burst out laughing.

"Thank goodness, no! I'm not pregnant again. Three's going to be enough. But, well, I guess you could say I've got another kind of baby in the works."

She leaned in, her hazel eyes alight with excitement. "I talked to Vicki Colton again yesterday. She loved the muffins and cookies I made for her, as a trial run. She's hired me to make all the baked goods for her shop!"

"That's wonderful!" Melinda would have patted her friend on the arm, but her gloves were covered in purple juice. "Vicki seemed interested when I gave her your info. But she hadn't said any more about it, and I didn't want to jinx it by asking."

Vicki was new to Prosper, having moved to the area when her husband was hired to manage one of the banks in Swanton. They'd purchased the vacant building next to Prosper Hardware, and Vicki's grand ideas for the unassuming space included a small tearoom along with a gift shop featuring homemade and artisanal goods. The business was set to launch next month, and Vicki had organized Prosper's first fall festival to coincide with her shop's grand opening.

Mabel passed Angie another bowl of plums. "This is just the break you need to get your side hustle off the ground. I knew you were a good cook, but that spread of dishes you made for your church's luncheon this summer? Everything was perfect, from the sides to the desserts."

"Well, I'm a long way from a full-time catering business, but it's a start. And with three little ones, maybe that's just as well. Vicki just needs pre-packaged sweets she can sell with the coffee and tea. But who knows where this will lead?"

The conversation turned to all the wonderful treats Angie planned to bake for the store's opening, from apple scones to her signature pumpkin-carrot bars smothered with cream-cheese frosting. The holiday season would come next, of course, which meant gingersnap cookies and cranberry-orange muffins ...

As Angie and Melinda ran through several ideas, Mabel became unusually quiet.

"What's the matter?" Melinda asked, then rose from her chair. "Want some coffee? It's strong, it'll perk you up."

"Oh, no thanks. I just ..."

"Out with it." Angie raised her paring knife. "Anything said around a kitchen table is confidential, as you know. What's going on?"

Mabel sighed and stared out the windows, but didn't seem to see the golden afternoon. When tears formed in her eyes, Angie and Melinda shared a look of alarm, but waited for her to speak.

"It's Ed." She put a hand over her face.

"Is he sick?" Melinda hurried back to the table, the coffee forgotten.

"No, no, thank God, it's not that. But I'm sick at heart, girls. He's talking about giving up the farm, moving to town. And I'm afraid he's serious this time."

"But you can't!" Angie's voice rose to almost a wail. Little Blake began to fuss in his swing, and she picked him up. "You can't move away!"

"Oh, I wish we could stay. I really don't want to go."

"Then don't!" Melinda's heart sank. "Who's going to help me?" She looked at Angie. "Who's going to help us? Things won't be the same out here ..."

"Both of you will get along just fine." Mabel tried to steady her emotions. "Angie, you grew up on a farm, and you and Nathan have been married for, what, seven years? And Melinda, you've got this country thing down pat now. You'll be fine."

Angie shook her head. "It won't be the same."

"Wait." Melinda held up a hand. "When? How soon? Oh, no, you don't mean before winter! That would be the time to leave, but that's only a few months and you can't ..."

"No, no, it won't be that fast. Although, that's what has Ed all upset. Last winter was terrible, the worst we've had in, oh, at least twenty years. We're in our early seventies now, we're not spring chickens anymore."

"But you grew up in that house." Angie tried another tactic. "And lived there nearly all your life! It's been in your family for generations. Do any of your kids want to buy it, at least?"

"No." Mabel's voice was soft and far away. "No, everyone's settled, living their own lives. Maybe it's just time to let it go. Either way, we'll have one more autumn out here." Her gaze turned to the windows again. "And the holidays, too. The soonest we could move, realistically, would be in the spring."

Angie and Melinda were now silent, numb with shock and despair.

"Oh, girls, it's going to happen, one way or another. If not next year, then the one after it." Mabel turned to Melinda. "You know, more than anyone, how hard it can get for elderly folks to stay on the farm. Ed and I watched Horace and Wilbur decline, and some of our other neighbors and friends. It's hard to leave, but staying too long isn't the answer, either."

Melinda searched for some counter-argument she could offer. "Horace wasn't that bad off, not really. Sure, things were a little rundown here. Why, they still are."

She gestured at the kitchen ceiling, where fine cracks snaked across the plaster. Gallons of paint and hours of scrubbing and sorting had made a big difference, but the house still needed so much time and attention. And money. "But he managed. And your house is so nice. You've already made so many updates ..."

"Yes, we have," Mabel admitted. "But as we get older, the upkeep will get harder and harder for us. And as for here, well, if Kevin hadn't come down from Mason City all the time,

Horace and Wilbur wouldn't have lasted out here as long as they did."

Angie sat up straighter. "OK, I see what you're saying. But Horace and Wilbur both hit ninety before they had to move away. You and Ed are so much younger!"

"True. But we're not talking about a nursing home. We'd just find us a little house, maybe in Prosper, or Swanton. A small yard. Ed'll have to sell his beef cows, but that can't be helped. We'll take Sammy, of course." Sammy was Mabel and Ed's dog.

Tears formed in Melinda's eyes. "I need you two out here with me."

Mabel reached across the table to squeeze her young friends' hands through their plastic gloves. "You'll be just fine. Both of you." She gave Melinda a sly wink. "Besides, you've got Chase to help you out these days."

Chase Thompson had grown up on a farm, that was true, but his time in the country was now limited to calling on rural clients for his family's aerial company. That, and the occasional nights he spent at Melinda's place. They'd been dating for three months now, but he was based in Meadville, an hour's drive away, and their booked schedules sometimes made spending time together a challenge.

They both could be more flexible, but Melinda pushed that thought away, along with the honest truth about Chase and country life: Despite his rural upbringing, her skills now outpaced his.

"Oh, Chase can do a little here and there," was all she said, "but that's not my point. It won't be the same when you two are gone."

"It never is. I've seen this rural neighborhood turn over several times through the years. People pass away, or move away."

She smiled at Angie, and then Melinda. "And then, someone new moves in."

Mabel picked up her paring knife. There was work to do, and the afternoon was ticking away. "We won't leave too soon, I promise. Spring is a long time off. You can't get rid of us that easily."

"You're right." Angie raised her chin. "We've got several months to change your minds."

"I'm all ears," Mabel admitted. "I could be persuaded to hang around longer. As for Ed? Good luck, dear, he's as stubborn as they come."

✳ 3 ✳

Melinda turned off Main and followed Second Street to the gravel alley behind city hall. She was driving Lizzie tonight, and Horace's old farm truck belched and growled as it lurched into one of the empty spaces by the limestone building's back entrance.

"Easy, girl." Did the truck need power steering fluid … again? "I don't like to take you far, but you've been pressed into service thanks to our friend, here. He's getting a big award, but he really doesn't like to ride in the car. Thinks that means we're going to Doc and Karen's clinic."

Hobo sat tall on the faded tweed seat, an old bath towel under his rump and his leash securely tied to one of the bench's metal posts. The rain tapping on the truck's windows was a welcome round of moisture, but had torpedoed Melinda's hopes to have Hobo spiffed-up for his big moment. His coat had been brushed until it gleamed, and she'd bought him a new red collar for the occasion, but the evening's expanding puddles and softened dirt would make it impossible to keep his paws clean.

Melinda cut the engine. Hobo raised his ears and barked, confused by the strange sights all around him.

"Just a minute, I'll come let you out." Melinda stroked his nose before she shut her door. She hurried around Lizzie's rusted front fender, trying to dodge the raindrops, and untied his leash. Hobo gamely jumped down when she asked him to, but he was more eager to sniff the strange ground than obey her request to go inside.

She was juggling her purse, the leash and the towel when city hall's back door popped open. Josh Vogel's brown eyes danced with laughter, and he held out a hand.

"I saw you guys coming. Here, give me his lead." Melinda was happy to oblige. "Doc's out on a call, asked me to wait in the back to see if you needed any help. Karen's not here yet."

"Thanks." Melinda wiped the rain from her face. "Well, I got him here. That was half the battle."

City hall was on the national register of historic places, which meant it retained many of its original features from when it was Prosper's first mercantile. Town leaders purchased it for a dollar many years ago, and divided it into a mix of odd-sized rooms and short hallways that tried to serve the community's needs. The back entrance had barely enough room to turn around, and abruptly opened into a tired kitchen. Melinda tossed the towel over a metal chair and stooped to examine Hobo's paws.

"Not too bad. But it's a good thing the council chambers doesn't have carpet."

"Can you imagine? We couldn't hold spay clinics in it, if it did. This linoleum is easy to sanitize, at least."

"So, that's why you're here. For the community-center discussion."

"Sure am." Josh handed her the towel. Hobo squirmed a bit, but then allowed one last wipe down. "We're the first regular activity that's asked for community space, so I thought there might be questions. And of course, Doc and Karen never know when they're going to get a farm call and have to duck out." Josh's practice in Swanton, which he'd purchased earlier that year from a retiring veterinarian, focused on small animals and stuck to regular office hours.

The battered metal door into the council chambers was closed, but Melinda could hear several muffled conversations already echoing behind it.

"Yeah, the place is jam-packed." Josh saw the concern on her face. "It's getting loud in there, sorry to say. Nancy had to get out more chairs. I heard her tell Jerry this is the biggest crowd they've had for a council meeting in years." He reached down to pet Hobo. "Most of them are here for the community-center discussion, but I noticed several out-of-towners eager to meet our hero."

Melinda's eyes lit up. "The Charles City paper sent someone, right? I know Swanton was coming, but ..."

"Oh, it's better than that." Josh grinned. "The Mason City television station, too."

"Well, I thought it was worth a shot. They covered the Fourth of July parade. And if it's a slow news night, this gives them a happy story to fill airtime at ten." She wrapped her arms around Hobo. "You're going to be on TV! Maybe we should run out back, just to be sure you won't need a potty break once the meeting starts."

Josh turned to go back into the chambers. "Nancy has a few seats saved for you, right in the first row. You won't have to walk Hobo through the crowd, and can duck out as soon as he's done. Good luck!"

Melinda's phone buzzed. "Chase is here," she told Hobo. "He's come to see you get your award. Isn't that wonderful?"

Chase soon came in the back door, his dark-blonde hair soaked with rain. Melinda stifled a giggle, as she knew how he fussed over his appearance most mornings. But he wasn't concerned about that right now, as he only had eyes for her.

"Hello there." He gave Melinda a lingering kiss. "Sorry I'm running late, our meeting went over and I grabbed a sandwich to eat in the truck. Hey, buddy!" He knelt by Hobo, who whimpered happily and licked Chase's hand. "Tonight's the big night, huh? He looks great, all brushed out and cleaned up. I like that new collar."

"Well, I decided he deserved one. But we'll change it when we get home to keep it clean, save it for special occasions."

Nancy came into the kitchen. "Hey, Chase. Glad you could make it." She beamed at Hobo. "He's the star attraction tonight, although I heard the TV crew asking the Swanton editor about the community-space item on the agenda. I'll go tell Jerry you're here."

After she left, Melinda looked at Chase. "Could you take Hobo home, as soon as he's done? I think I'd like to hang around and hear what everyone has to say about the community center ideas."

"Not a problem." Chase squeezed her hand. "We can hang out together later. I thought you might want to stay. This is a big deal for Prosper."

Chase held the door while Melinda ushered Hobo through. Other than the council's long table at the front of the room, the entire space was packed with filled chairs and more people standing along the walls. Hobo's arrival brought some of the conversations to an abrupt halt, and there were oohs and aahs and smiles. Someone began to clap, and Melinda felt Hobo stiffen on his leash. She widened her eyes at Jerry, who hurried over to place a calming hand on Hobo's back before he addressed the crowd.

"Everyone, we're about to get started. But please, no applause, even though Hobo certainly deserves it. He's used to running around a farmyard, rather than facing a bunch of strangers."

The room fell into an understanding silence. Melinda, Hobo and Chase settled in the front, but not before she spotted her parents and Aunt Miriam in the fifth row, beaming with pride.

Uncle Frank was already in his seat at the council's table, with Jake on the other end. Clarence Spencer, who was in his fifties and owned an auto shop in Swanton, sat next to Frank. The other two members were Lucas Phillips, a pharmacist in Swanton in his forties, and Walter Barnes, who had moved into Prosper when he retired from farming. Walter and Lucas had been chatting with members of the audience but now took their seats, as did Jerry and Nancy.

Jerry called the meeting to order, and then came the rustle of clothing and the squeak of metal chairs as the crowd stood for the Pledge of Allegiance. Hobo pulled against his lead, aiming for the closed door into the kitchen, then whimpered as the recitation echoed around the room.

"Just a few minutes and you can go," Melinda whispered. "Won't take long."

"I'll hold him." Chase offered to take the leash. "So you can focus on keeping him calm."

Tony came to the front of the room with a certificate in his hand and a shiny medal swinging on a blue cord. Jerry motioned for Melinda and Hobo to join them.

"We've got a unique honor to hand out here tonight," Jerry told the crowd. "Hobo is a very special dog. Just last month, he sounded the alarm when the cornfield behind his home was struck by lightning and caught on fire. He saved his home, and probably several others in Fulton township, as well."

Tony took the microphone. "Melinda Foster is Hobo's owner. Or should I say, his best friend. She was kind enough to bring him in tonight so we could extend our thanks in person."

Melinda brought Hobo forward and gently asked him to "sit," and she was thrilled when he did. But only for about ten seconds. And then, too distracted by the interesting smells all around him, he began to turn in a circle of discovery that brought laughter from the crowd.

"As you can see, Hobo's a busy boy." Tony pulled a folded scrap of paper from his jeans' pocket. "I've got a proclamation here I was going to read, but let's just say that Hobo, we are indebted to you and honor you for your bravery. Melinda, anything you'd like to add before Hobo says it's time to go home?"

She handed Hobo's lead to Tony and took the microphone. This had to be brief.

"I want to thank everyone for coming out tonight, and to ask all of you to support our local animal shelters. Many of you may not know this, but Hobo started out in life as a homeless stray." A murmur of sympathy echoed around the room. "To further honor his bravery, as well as homeless animals everywhere, I've decided to equally divide the award's monetary donation between the Swanton and Charles City animal-rescue organizations."

A few tentative claps began in the back of the room. Jerry looked to Tony for confirmation he had a tight hold on Hobo's leash, then turned to the audience. "Since Hobo's just about to leave, I'd say we can give that a round of applause."

Hobo began to bark, and the claps and cheers intensified. Feeding off the crowd's excitement, he wagged his tail with delight and tried to jump on Tony. Jerry attempted to slip the medal's cord over Hobo's head, but he wouldn't sit still. In the end, Melinda leaned in next to Hobo and held up the medal while Jerry and Tony barricaded the dog between them, providing a few seconds of organized chaos to gain some pictures and brief video.

At the last moment, Jerry crouched down and wrapped his arms around Hobo. "Thanks for coming to see us, buddy."

Melinda saw the Charles City newspaper's reporter grinning from ear to ear as he snapped away with his phone, and knew that would be the best shot of the night: Mayor Jerry Simmons hugging the four-legged hero, both of their faces lit up with joy.

And then Hobo realized Uncle Frank was in the room, right behind him, and rushed toward the council table so fast he nearly got away from Tony.

"I think we're done," Melinda told Jerry.

Chase left his seat. "I'll take him home. He'll be glad to go, I bet, take a few victory laps outside before you get back."

"I shouldn't be long. There's a pouch of treats in the cabinet next to the stove, if you want to give him a few snacks."

Diane moved up to take Chase's empty seat next to Melinda. "Well, that went as smoothly as one could expect, I guess. I'm very curious about this talk about a community center, and so's your dad." Roger offered a wave from where he sat with Aunt Miriam.

Both of Melinda's parents were now retired. Diane had been a teacher, and Roger had worked for Swanton's communications utility. They had lived in Swanton since their marriage, but Diane was still interested in the happenings in her hometown.

Jerry opened the community-center discussion with a brief rundown of the town's need for more public space. He cited the spay-and-neuter clinics as an example of programming that could be offered at such as site, along with holiday celebrations and programs for senior citizens. The center could also be rented for events, such as family gatherings, club activities and even wedding receptions, which would bring much-needed revenue for the tiny town.

"But we need to choose a location carefully," Jerry reminded the crowd. "Any facility we use, or anything we build, will have to meet regulations for those with disabilities and also be energy efficient. There needs to be ample parking, of course, and the site ideally would be in our business district, where its activities would not be distracting to homeowners."

Jake didn't even raise his hand before he interrupted. "But there's no empty lots on Main Street. We have to go outside the business district." A few claps echoed from the back of the room.

Jerry set his mouth in a firm line, and looked at the other council members. "Anyone else have anything they want to add before I ... finish what I was trying to say?" That brought a few smirks and chuckles from the audience.

Lucas leaned forward. "I suggest the council refrain from making any comments or suggestions at this time." He glared at Jake, who gave a smug smile but looked away. "This is a time for residents to offer ideas and suggestions. Nothing is being decided tonight."

"We're just getting started," added Clarence, who'd served on the council for nearly twenty years. "And remember, this issue came up a decade ago, and didn't get off the ground due to lack of financial support."

Jerry asked that anyone wishing to address the council simply raise their hand. Each person would get three minutes to speak, and Nancy would keep track of the time. She'd told Melinda they'd considered placing a chair up front for the speakers, since the city didn't own a podium, but Jerry decided he didn't want anyone to get too comfortable. It was going to be hard enough to keep things moving.

Several people showed interest in renovating a vacant building on Main Street. The former bank was mentioned several times, as was another empty space that housed the town's drugstore years ago. Other residents challenged those suggestions, worried about the buildings' conditions and the mounting costs of restoration. The idea was raised to renovate the second floor of city hall, which was now used only for storage.

A few residents echoed Jake's call for a new building. One possible site, an empty lot one block off Main, drew boos from a group Melinda suspected consisted of nearby residents. Someone suggested the city buy a slice of property from a field on the edge of town, and one man even threw out the possibility of adding on to Prosper's elementary school.

Over a dozen residents had already spoken when Melinda heard a rustling behind her and someone poked her on the shoulder. She turned to find an elderly woman with a narrow face giving her a warm smile. "Honey, can you hold my purse for just a minute? Got to get this cane in position before I stand up."

"Sure, happy to."

Diane motioned to Jerry, and he nodded. A man was just finishing his remarks, and this lady would be the next to speak.

"Do you need any help, Delores?" Diane asked.

"No thank you, dear, I'm still chugging away under my own power." Everyone else in her row got to their feet to let Delores pass by, and she started her slow approach to the council table.

"Who is that?" Melinda whispered to her mom.

"Delores Eklund. A retired teacher, taught English for years when the high school was still here in town. Her husband was an accountant, but he's been gone for some time now. She lives in the little gray house on the corner of Fourth and Maple."

Delores finally reached the front of the room, and the murmurs of conversation that began while she made her approach fell away to respectful silence. Melinda saw several people sitting up straighter, giving Delores their full attention, and wondered how many in the room had been her students. In a break with his plan, Jerry hustled to the side wall and came back with another folding chair.

"Oh, no, no, I don't need that." Delores waved him off. "Won't be up here long. But I do have something to say."

"By all means, Delores. You have the floor."

She took the microphone and raised her chin, unflustered by the crowd, then turned to face the council.

"I'm confident you all will make the right choices about the when, and the where, and the why, but it's going to take some serious money to get this project done."

"That's for sure," Jake piped up. "That's what I want to know, we should ..."

"Jacob Andrew Newcastle!" Delores pointed at him. "You will wait your turn to speak."

Jake turned pale as snickers bounced around the room, then his face grew red and he looked at the floor. "Yes, Mrs. ... uh, Delores. Please proceed."

Frank had put his chin in his hand, but Melinda could see he was really trying to keep a straight face.

"Now, as I was saying, this project is going to be very expensive. As many of you know, my family has been in Prosper for generations. I'll be eighty-nine next month, lived here all my life, and I love this community. So I guess now would be as good a time as any to donate to the community center, before I either drop over or lose my marbles."

Delores abruptly held out the microphone, which a startled Walter finally accepted.

"Here." She turned to Lucas. "You hold my purse steady, so I can get my wallet …"

"Oh, Delores, I appreciate your support." Jerry came around to the front of the table. "But we're not to that point yet. We'll have to create a strategic plan, then come up with estimates, start a fundraising committee …"

"Yes, you will." Delores' voice was clear and firm. "And you'll need to be a good steward, Mayor Simmons, as you always have been in the past. I expect my money will be used judiciously, as will other donations offered for the project. Oh, where did I put that … here."

She held up a folded check and placed it in Jerry's hand. "I made it out to the city of Prosper, I hope that was the right way to go about it."

Jerry looked at Nancy, who shrugged and gestured for him to take it. Delores was clearly going to make her contribution now, no matter what anyone said.

"Well, then, thank you, Delores, we'll get you a receipt." He unfolded the check and his eyes grew wide with shock. The slip of paper nearly fell from his hand.

"What is it?" Jake demanded.

"What's the matter?" Frank came forward and reached for the check. Delores was immovable, but a smile was already crossing her lined face.

"Oh, good God!" Frank gasped. "Is this …"

"A real check?" Dolores frowned. "Of course it is. You can call my bank in the morning, if you like."

Murmurs ran through the audience as people rose from their seats and tried to figure out what was going on. Melinda could see the sweat breaking out along Uncle Frank's receding hairline. "But it's for … Delores, this is for two hundred thousand dollars!"

The council chambers erupted into bedlam. Jake reached for the check, and a stunned Frank let him have it. Nancy pushed back her chair and came on the run. "Here, here, give it to me. Be careful with that thing!" She had to shout to be heard over the whoops and cheers.

Jerry suddenly found his voice. "Everyone! Please, calm down and take your seats!" Tony made a shrill whistle, and the room finally went quiet.

"What's the catch?" someone shouted from the back.

"An excellent question." Delores nodded her approval toward the man, who likely was another former pupil, then turned back to the city leaders now hovering around her.

"There are a few ... stipulations, should we say? And I want everyone in this room to hear this, so there's no mistake later on. Of course," she told Nancy, "there'll be a formal letter of instruction coming from my attorney in the morning."

"I'll be looking for it."

"This contribution is a considerable portion of what was going to be my estate," Delores told the room, which was now hushed and hanging on her every word.

"My father, and my grandfather before him, were the doctors in this town. They handled their financial affairs wisely, and my husband and I did the same. Area families provided the seed money for those investments, through the fees they paid to the practice, so it's only right that this money goes back to the community."

She turned to Jerry, who was now smiling broadly. "I was going to wait until I was dead," she explained, "but where's the fun in that? And we need a community center."

Delores looked each council member square in the eye. "But the catch is this: A final decision on the location must be made before the November election."

Clarence shook his head. "But that's less than two months away!"

"And that is exactly my point. There is no reason to drag this out. This town needed a community center years ago, and never got one. And I don't want my family's good name attached to any election-cycle empty promises. No, you'll get your ducks in a row, and work together on this like adults should, or I'll take back every penny."

Jerry and Jake gave each other a wary glance.

"You two, in particular." Delores gestured at them. "Promise you'll fight fair. Or better yet, don't fight at all. Do what's best for the community." Jerry nodded first, and then Jake quickly followed. Delores made them shake on it.

Someone started to clap. And then, the room burst into applause. Nancy, the first to regain her composure, reached for the microphone.

"Well, isn't this an exciting turn of events! Mayor Simmons, perhaps we should close the public comments for tonight and let this amazing news sink in? We can take this up again at the next meeting."

Jerry, still stunned, could only nod.

"We'll share more information on the city's website and social media channels when it's available," Nancy promised. "In the meantime, please give more thought to exactly what you'd like to see accomplished with this ... wonderfully generous donation."

Jerry ushered the council members back to their seats, and they moved on with their agenda while the residents started for the exits, laughing and shaking their heads.

Delores shuffled back to her chair, where her coat was waiting, and paused long enough to pat Melinda on the arm.

"My dear, your Hobo deserves that honor, and then some. I have to say, I'm glad you called the newspapers and the television station. Their presence means there should never be any doubt about my intentions."

Delores turned and, with a polite smile, shook the hand of the editor from the Swanton paper, who was trailed by the cameraman from Mason City. In a matter of hours, if not mere minutes, little Prosper was going to be much more than a speck on the map.

"Can you call Chase and tell him I'll be late?" Melinda asked her mom. "I have a feeling Delores is going to find herself the top story on the ten o'clock news tonight."

✳ 4 ✳

Melinda expected the guys to arrive early the following morning, eager to rehash Delores' astounding announcement, but Prosper Hardware was dark and the parking spots out front were still as empty as the rest of Main Street. She filled the coffeepot, then leaned against the sideboard for support as she sleepily waited for the brew's comforting aroma to waft through the store.

Chase might as well have gone home last night, given how little time they'd had together. She'd stayed in town for almost two hours after the meeting adjourned, helping Nancy and Jerry first answer the reporters' questions and then craft information to post on the city's website and social media channels. Melinda was always happy to put her communication skills to work for the greater good, but that wasn't the only reason she wanted to help. If she hadn't been so eager to drum up coverage for Hobo's medal ceremony, those reporters wouldn't have witnessed Delores dropping her bomb and handing Jerry that check. Word would have spread eventually, but Prosper wouldn't have found itself in the spotlight so fast.

Just as she'd predicted, the town's sudden windfall topped the late newscast. Photos of Delores and Jerry, her proud smile in clear contrast to the shock written all over his face, were posted everywhere within the hour. The editor of the Swanton paper was driving over this afternoon for a sit-down with Jerry, and planned to have an extensive follow-up ready for tomorrow's edition of the twice-weekly publication.

But Delores' generous gift promised to do more than bring outside attention to their tiny town; it was poised to ratchet up the tension between the two men tussling over the mayor's seat.

As soon as the council adjourned, Jake rushed over to the television crew and began expressing his preferences for the project. Jerry, who'd been too busy with the Charles City reporter's questions to put a stop to it, had been incensed by his rival's attempt to position himself as a spokesperson for the town. Nancy had wisely intervened. She gently downplayed Jake's pointed remarks with a comment that official statements from the city would be forthcoming, then later cornered Jerry and reminded him that Jake was allowed to share his opinions.

Delores' deadline loomed over everyone's heads, but at least the other council members weren't under any election-season pressure. Lucas and Clarence's seats were both up for renewal; but so far, no one had raised a hand to challenge either post.

Auggie's truck was now lining up with the curb, drawing Melinda out of her musings. He was out of the cab surprisingly quick for someone his age, and started for Prosper Hardware's front door with great speed given the early hour.

"I bet he hardly slept last night." She reached for another mug, knowing he'd be craving his first cup of the day. "He's always beside himself when there's any kind of news, and this is the sort of thing that'll have him spinning like a top."

Auggie slipped out of his canvas jacket and tossed it toward the hall tree. "This dang drought! I've had about enough. A guy came in first thing this morning, I barely had the door unlocked. Wanted bags of oats for his horses, like usual. But when I told him the price had gone up since he was in a few weeks ago, he was livid."

The coffee cup clanged on the metal counter as Auggie reached for the sugar. "I know, I know, there's plenty else to chew over this morning. But I gotta get this off my chest, first."

Melinda, who was barely awake and still trying to process this unexpected turn in conversation, only nodded and took a seat.

"I've never seen anyone get so pissed about a few bucks as that guy. I had to raise the price again, I didn't have a choice! My supplier's just passing on the hurt. I'm not Delores, you know; I don't have bags of money stashed under my house."

Melinda knew times were hard for local farmers. The rains were coming regularly now, but the damage to the markets was already done. Feed prices were expected to remain high until at least spring. "So, what happened? Did he buy any?"

"Finally! But not his usual load. Said he'd take his business elsewhere if I was going to gouge prices. I told him, good luck with that. Drive all the way to Swanton if you want, or over to Eagle River, burn all that gas. You'll find the same everywhere."

Auggie turned from the sideboard so fast Melinda was sure he was going to spill his coffee.

"But you know the worst of it? He upset Pebbles! She was stretched out on the counter, waiting for her admirers to arrive, and this guy starts yelling. Her ears went back, and she took off into the office. Probably still hiding there in the basket under my desk. Anyway, I told that guy, he'd better keep his voice down when he's in my shop."

The sleek gray cat had padded into Auggie's heart after her friend Mr. Checkers, a stocky buff-and-white tom, won Auggie over at the first community clinic. They both came from Gertrude's colony, and quickly became the co-op's furry mascots.

Doc came in just as Auggie finished his rant. "Someone giving your kitties a hard time?" He winked at Melinda, who was trying not to laugh. "Forget about Delores and her donation! What I need to know is: what did Mr. Checkers think about all this?"

"Oh, he was still enjoying his breakfast, over in the corner, and never even looked up." Auggie's outrage over the rude customer blinded him to Doc's sarcasm. "You know, I've never seen anyone, man nor beast, eat as slow as he does. One little bite of kibble at a time."

George came in from the back, a canvas tote draped over his arm. "Well, I brought the Charles City paper, just in case Jerry hasn't seen it yet."

"Oh, I bet he has." Doc took his usual seat. "I bet his phone hasn't stopped ringing, either."

"Well, I guess it's a big deal," George observed in what had to be the understatement of the week. "Jerry's got his work cut out for him, I hear. So does Jake. Melinda, I'm sorry I didn't make it over to see Hobo get his big award. I meant to come, but I fell asleep in the chair after supper, and Mary didn't wake me. I missed the whole dang thing!"

"It was a barn-burner, for sure." Auggie was quickly distracted by the container George handed to Melinda. "Hey, are those muffins?"

"That's why Mary forgot to nudge me," George explained. "She was busy with those. They're pear, not apple, for something different. We've got a tree in our backyard."

Everyone was gathered around the newspaper when Bill joined them. "Look at the expression on Jerry's face, that's classic! Hey Melinda, have we got scissors behind the counter?"

"Huh?" She yawned. "Oh, sure."

"I think we need to display this priceless shot." Bill ripped off a piece of tape and stuck the clipping to one of the sideboard's upper doors. "Here he comes!"

Jerry looked even more tired than Melinda felt. He was deep in discussion with Frank as they entered the store, and had his school windbreaker off before he noticed the photo.

"Gee, thanks. As if I could forget."

"Well, look at it this way," Frank reasoned. "At least

you're the one in the photo, representing the city at that historic moment. Jake was still in his seat, far out of range."

Auggie had another cup of coffee ready with lots of sugar and a little creamer, just the way Jerry liked it. He accepted it with a nod, then dropped into the closest chair.

"It all happened so fast. I was thinking, 'this poor old lady, she's probably got five bucks or something,' and I was hoping people wouldn't start laughing at her when I unfolded the check."

George passed him a muffin. "If nothing else, this'll motivate other people to step up. If they can see this thing will get off the ground this time, they'll be more likely to donate to the cause."

"I wish two hundred thousand would cover it." Jerry adjusted his ball cap and stretched out in his chair. "It will go a long way, sure, but depending on what's decided ..."

"I just can't believe it!" Auggie had a muffin in his fist. "Who would've thought Delores was packing that kind of cash?"

Bill raised an eyebrow. "Well, they always say, it's the quiet ones you have to watch out for."

Everyone stared at George.

"What? If I had that kind of money, I'd be in Florida within the month. Iowa winters don't get any easier when you're my age."

"Wait a second." Auggie crossed his arms. "That's what they say about serial killers, not little old ladies with investment portfolios."

Jerry gave the photo one more glance, then chucked it into the trash. "I have a feeling the fun is just beginning. I need all of you to spread the word: Anyone with ideas, which will be every person living within twenty miles of this town, should send an email to the city's main account. Melinda, I'm sure you'll get an earful today, and then some."

Jerry was right. Hobo's honor had been the buzz about town for several days, but he was quickly replaced in Prosper's lack-of-news cycle by Delores' contribution.

"It's like we won the lottery," one woman exclaimed as she reached for a hand basket. "The possibilities are endless!"

A grim-faced man dropped a packet of screws on the counter. "I still don't think this'll go anywhere. I'd like to see the day this town can agree on something. That deadline Delores set will come and go, and nothing will be decided. You just wait and see."

Frank lingered long after the coffee regulars scattered, curious to hear customers' comments and willing to take some of that burden off Melinda's shoulders. But he soon grew tired of questions he couldn't answer, and Melinda suggested he head home.

"Jerry needs to take the lead on this, and anything you say might get twisted around and spread as official word from the city. Besides, Aunt Miriam will be in at ten. I can call her down from the office if I get swamped."

"Sounds good to me." Frank couldn't pull his jacket on fast enough. "Besides, it looks like it's going to be a fine day. Maybe I can get most of my new Halloween decorations up this afternoon. Little Prosper might suddenly be flush with cash, but the rest of the world goes on as usual."

* * *

The debate about the community center's location spread far beyond Prosper Hardware. Around every dinner table, along every back fence, and up and down the bar at the Watering Hole, the town's only restaurant, ideas flew fast and furious. Two nights later, the members of the library's book club found it hard to set the topic aside long enough to focus on their September selection, a bestselling memoir chosen before the group adjourned for summer break.

Jerry hadn't exaggerated the project's importance to residents in the general area. With Swanton about ten miles to the southwest, and Eagle River even farther to the east, tiny Prosper remained a hub for the rural region around it. Bev Stewart, who lived northeast of town, was quick to share her thoughts.

"Well, it's about time!" She set a pan of pumpkin bars on the meeting room's table, then tried to flatten her short, white hair with one hand. An impressive gale had started up that afternoon, sending the first of the fallen leaves dancing down the sidewalks and rattling across the streets. "We need something like this, for sure. But a new building's just a waste of money. Why build something when there's empty storefronts available?"

Sam Hayward, who owned the insurance office next door to the library, was quick to reach for the first pumpkin bar. And add his two cents.

"You're absolutely right. That center needs to be right here, on Main. Vicki, don't you agree? I mean, you and Arthur are making quite the splash there, across the street. We need more revitalization, for sure."

Vicki smiled, but it took her a few moments to answer. "Well ... I don't know." She reached for the stack of paper plates. "I'm glad we were able to save a structure, but it's been a little scary. Every day, it seems, we find something else we didn't know about. There's an old pipe that needs to be replaced, or something doesn't have enough clearance for code or, oh, it never ends."

Given Arthur's management position at the bank, Melinda had assumed there was a generous well of money available to support Vicki's new business. She was always dressed in the sort of casual chic that came with a hefty price tag, and the highlights in her long brown hair were the kind that required a long-distance trip to a salon. But Vicki's wary tone made Melinda and Karen exchange concerned looks.

"Are you running into serious trouble?" Karen leaned across the table to accept a pumpkin bar. She was blond and petite, the last woman you might assume was a veterinarian adept at handling large livestock. "You'll be able to open on time, right?"

"One way or another, yes." Vicki was committed to this venture, and nothing was going to get in her way. "The fall festival's set for the second Saturday in October, we can't change it now. I will have the shop open by then, no matter what, even if the shelves are partially stocked and the floors aren't refinished. Oh, and I guess I have an announcement to make."

"So, you've finally decided?" Melinda was all ears. "What's it going to be?"

Vicki took a deep breath, then grinned. "Meadow Lane! Meadow Lane Gifts and Antiques."

"It's perfect." Nancy gave her approval. "I know you were really stressing over the name."

"Well, I had to just make up my mind. My sign guy's been nagging me to settle on something, so he can have it ready in time. So at least, the exterior's going to be fabulous on opening day, even if the inside's still a work-in-progress."

"Rustic chic is very popular these days, you know." Amy Westberg raised her cup of warm cider in salute. She taught at Prosper's elementary school, and her husband, Paul, was the pastor at the Lutheran church down the road from Melinda's farm.

"No one will know the difference, unless you tell them." Nancy added a plate of cheese and crackers to the spread. "But really, if you get in a bind, just spread the word. I'm sure you can round up a few pairs of hands to push the renovations through."

"People in this town love to help out," Sam said. "But they also love to give their two cents' worth, and then some. Just be careful you don't end up with too many foremen and not enough workers."

"I'm afraid that's what's going to happen with the community center." Nancy shook her head. "Everyone's going to have an opinion, and in the end, hardly anyone is going to be happy with what the council decides to do."

Shelby Dunlap was the music teacher at the elementary school and Amy's friend. As the youngest member of the group, she always brought a refreshing perspective to its lively discussions.

"I have to say, I'm rooting for city hall." Shelby tipped her head in the direction of the building next door, which was connected to the library by a cased opening. "I know it's really old, and the upstairs is just storage. But wasn't it used for something else, a long time ago? Wouldn't it be easy to just clean it up? I mean, the city already owns it."

"I've thought about that, too." Sam put down his coffee cup. "Way back when, it was a community hall, actually. There's even a stage, on one end."

"What's left of one, I'm afraid." Melinda had climbed the narrow, steep stairs only a few times, to help Nancy and Frank evaluate Prosper's meager selection of holiday decorations, and found the cavernous space to be dark, dirty and depressing. "Long ago, dances were held up there on Saturday nights. It's still mostly a wide-open room, and Uncle Frank's almost done sorting the city's old files. He and Jerry have brought down lots of documents and donated some odds and ends, but I guess there's still a lot of stuff that has to stay."

"Wouldn't be too hard to put up a few extra walls," Bev suggested with the air of a farm woman confident in her ability to swing a hammer. "Couldn't they create a storage room on one end?"

"I wonder, though, about the utilities." Vicki sipped her cider. "City hall's on the national register, wouldn't it be difficult to get any changes approved? And then, there'd need to be an elevator, and handicapped-accessible restrooms."

"Nancy, you're pretty quiet over there," Amy observed. "What do you think?"

"We want to hear your ideas as a resident," Sam said. "Not with your 'city' hat on. Or should I say, one of your many city hats."

Nancy stared at the table, and adjusted her glasses. Then she looked around at her friends, as if considering something. "Don't take this outside of this room, OK? I don't think city hall's the best place for the community center."

"You're right." Vicki quickly agreed. "It's a lovely building, but with all the historical requirements ..."

"Oh, it's not that." Nancy gave a rueful laugh. "I wish it was that simple. It's because ... I think city hall's haunted."

For a second, no one blinked. Except Sam, who had just picked up his second pumpkin bar. "Now, Nancy," he finally said, "that can't be. There's no such thing! That's just a bunch of ... I don't know, foolish talk. Your imagination ..."

"Is getting the better of me?" Nancy finished his thought with an edge in her voice. "No, no, it's more than that. You wouldn't believe the things I've ... experienced, let's call it."

"Tell me." Sam raised an eyebrow. "You've got the floor. Enlighten us."

Karen's blue eyes lit up with interest. "This is better than the book! It was fascinating, sure, but ... I don't know about the rest of you, but I want to hear this. And I think you'll feel better if you tell us what's been going on."

Melinda loved history, and old buildings, and city hall certainly fell into both categories. Come to think of it, the second floor did have a strange, disorienting feel, as if it belonged to another time or place. When she'd been up there, hadn't it occurred to her that she would never want to climb those stairs alone?

"If Nancy says there's something going on, I believe it." Bev's vote of confidence caused Nancy to relax back into her folding chair. "There's some things in this world we can't begin to understand. And in a building that old? Why, so many people have passed through it, you see, so many things have happened inside its walls."

"Like what?" Shelby was eager for details. "A murder? A fire?"

"Not as far as I know." Nancy sighed with relief.

"Wouldn't take something that big to keep someone hanging around," Vicki reasoned. "I've lived in old houses most of my life. They've all got their own ... personality, if you will. I've been fortunate to never experience anything odd, but I think it's possible."

"What have you seen, exactly?" Sam was still unconvinced. "What have you heard? More than a few mice,

I'd guess. But it wouldn't surprise me if there's a pack of squirrels up there, living in the walls. They're pesky critters."

Nancy glanced over her shoulder, through the meeting room's plate-glass window and out into the empty aisles between the bookshelves, as if seeking assurance no one was out there, listening. Melinda shivered and clutched her cup of cider.

"Well, I haven't seen anything." Nancy held up a hand, as Sam was about to interject.

"But that's not the point. I've felt something, more than once. I've worked for the city for almost ten years," she explained to the newcomers at the table. "And one afternoon, I hadn't been here, oh, two months I think, I was in the kitchen, warming my tea in the microwave. All the sudden, I felt like someone was standing right behind me."

"Who was it?" Sam smirked. "Was it Tony, or Jerry?"

Nancy rolled her eyes. "I turned around, and no one was there. But that was just the start of it. I've had that same feeling, several times since then. Sometimes I'm at my desk, or the front counter. Or in one of the back rooms, looking for a file. But the worst thing that's happened ... One day I had to go upstairs for something, I can't even remember what it was. No one else was here, but it couldn't wait."

The stairwell's battered door was kept locked and its base sealed by a stuffed fabric tube, to deter snooping visitors as well as the drafts that drifted down from the unheated second floor. Those were safety measures as well; even with two handrails, the steps were passable for only sure-footed adults.

Now that she felt safe sharing her harrowing story, Nancy's words came out in a rush.

"I unlocked the door and turned on the light. And then, I was partway up the stairs when there was this ... I don't know, it was almost like a sudden gust of cold air. It came straight at me! Came down the steps, then brushed right past my shoulder."

Bev put a hand over her chin. "Like someone was going down, right when you were going up?"

"Exactly. I felt it go by. And then it was just ... gone. I'd left the stairwell door wide open, of course. No way would I risk getting locked up there, by accident."

"Oh, Nancy." Amy patted her on the shoulder. "That's terrifying. What did you do?"

"Well, I went on up and grabbed what I needed, I guess. I had to. But coming down, my legs were shaking so much I was afraid I might fall. I've never been so glad to get back downstairs, lock that door behind me."

Sam was sympathetic, but still unsure. "Old buildings are drafty," he said gently. "That could explain a lot of things."

"But there's more! It's the ... the footsteps ... that really scare me."

"The footsteps?" Karen gasped. "Why haven't you ever said anything? You shouldn't have to face this alone! If there's ... something going on over there, it could be dangerous. People need to know."

"No." Nancy shook her head. "No, they don't. I understand what you're saying, but can you imagine if this got around? The place would be swarming with gawkers, those ghost-hunter people would want to come and spend the night, and all that. It'd be a circus."

Bev cut her eyes at Sam. "And some people would think Nancy's lost her mind. She's got enough on her plate, keeping this town afloat. She doesn't need to deal with that, too."

"I never said she was crazy. I'm just a skeptic, that's all."

"Tell us everything." Vicki turned to Nancy. "It won't leave this room." Even Sam nodded in agreement.

"I used to only hear the footsteps, oh, maybe a few times a year. But since Frank and Jerry have been sorting through stuff, it's gotten much worse. It's like someone's walking around up there, but it's usually only a short series of steps. And then, nothing."

"They don't seem to go anywhere?" Amy was perplexed. "As if they just ..."

"Disappear, yes. But this one night last month, I was still here after the library closed, everyone else was gone. I went into city hall, decided to straighten up the front counter. The footsteps were louder that time, heavier. It was like they started in the back and then moved to the front of the building, like someone was going to the windows to look out over Main Street."

"So they went on for some time, then." Sam sounded less sure of his convictions. "Not just a few seconds."

"Right." Nancy took a deep breath, but her voice continued to waver. "And then they paused, right over my head, and they started pacing, back and forth, again and again."

Vicki gasped. "Oh, Nancy! You must have been terrified!"

"I was. But suddenly, I was angry, too. I started yelling at, well, whatever it was, to knock it off. And then I said, 'you stop that, right now!' And you know what? It did. I ran back in here, grabbed my coat and my purse, and took off. I was so scared, I left all the lights on, not just the overnight ones. The next morning, Jerry beat me in here and wondered why the place was all lit up. I just told him I'd been distracted and forgot."

Melinda leaned down the table. "So he has no idea, at all?"

"Nope. And I'd rather he didn't."

Bev frowned. "What goes on around here at night, once everyone has gone home?"

"I'm not sure I want to know." Amy shook her head.

"OK, new book-club rule." Karen tapped a finger on the table. "At least one of us stays behind with Nancy until she's ready to leave. We lock up together, always."

Melinda glanced over her shoulder. "I'm no expert on this, but don't they say renovating old buildings can stir up things from the past?"

"She's right," Vicki added. "If city hall is haunted, tearing into it could give us much more than a community center."

Nancy put her head in her hands. "I don't know what to do. Maybe I can find a way to say something to Jerry without making a huge deal out of it."

"Maybe start it as a joke," Amy suggested. "See how he reacts."

Bev reached for the cheese and crackers. "In the meantime, let's talk about this month's book. If nothing else, it might take your mind off this mess."

The debate soon grew loud and lively, and Nancy's chilling tale was momentarily forgotten. Just before the club adjourned, suggestions for October's book were scribbled on paper scraps, folded in fourths and placed in an empty flowerpot reserved for just that use.

Since the memoir had been Amy's suggestion, it was her turn to draw. "Oh, dear." Worry crossed her forehead, but then she laughed.

"What is it?" Nancy reached for the slip of paper, sighed, and handed it down the table. "Well, this is appropriate, I guess. He's the master of modern horror, after all."

"I read that a few years ago, so I won't have to do it again." Shelby sounded relieved. "Couldn't sleep half the time, afterwards, but it was very clever. Who put that in the pot?"

Sam chuckled. "Guilty as charged."

"You?" Vicki pointed at him, but she was smiling. "And I thought you didn't believe in ghosts?"

"Oh, come on, I think it will be fun. Everyone says it's really good, I'm curious to see if that's true." Sam raised his bushy gray eyebrows and gave a wicked grin. "Besides, the timing couldn't be better, since it'll soon be the season when the undead roam the earth."

Nancy crossed her arms. "Well, unless I'm losing my mind, I'd say it happens all year long."

✻ 5 ✻

Hobo lifted his paws to the back porch's bench as soon as Melinda put down the cardboard box. This was his home, and everything needed to pass inspection.

"No, no, those are for Horace." Melinda gently pushed his curious nose away from the jars of corn relish, plum jam and canned tomatoes.

"You wouldn't eat any of it, anyway. At least, I hope you wouldn't, but we're not going to find out. It's a beautiful morning. Why don't you go outside and enjoy it?"

Hobo didn't need to be asked twice. As he pushed through his doggie door, Melinda added herself to the bench. Out in the back yard, the maple tree's turning leaves rustled in the soft breeze. Sunny and Stormy had set up a feline sundial on the picnic table's faded boards, content to do absolutely nothing until supper time. Why was it so hard to let herself do the same?

She was meeting Chase at an apple orchard at ten, and her route home would be adjusted to swing through Elm Springs to visit Horace and Wilbur. It would be a day filled with some of her favorite people, and a chance to travel the back roads and revel in autumn's golden glory.

This wasn't a day for work, it was a day for play. But there was a stab of guilt when she reached for her sneakers instead of her chore boots.

Her to-do list around the farm was too long, and there was no way to know how many picture-perfect days there'd be before the first snow. The chicken house needed to be swept and scrubbed, and fresh straw hauled from the barn.

All her lightweight chore sweatshirts should be washed (again) and most of them stored away. She needed to sort the stash of winter gloves and knit hats in the porch closet, make sure her insulated coveralls still fit and didn't need mending. While she was at it, she really should clear the entire closet out, sort through the flashlights and rubber boots and orphan tools Horace left behind.

All the front porch's screens needed to be swapped for storm windows, and an army of spiders must be conquered before she would bring the frames up from the basement. Did she have enough mousetraps? Come to think of it, the root cellar should be swept out, and its shelves wiped down. And she should get on that soon, as in a few weeks she'd be so busy clearing off the garden and raking leaves ...

"The work never ends around here, but it all can wait." Melinda pulled on her jacket, reached for her purse, and picked up the box. "It's forty minutes to the orchard, I'd better get going."

Her yard may have needed work, but it was dressed for the season. Pots of orange, yellow and purple mums were nestled by the back steps. A trio of pumpkins stood guard along the cinder-block foundation, their cheerful glow echoed in the faux-leaf wreath behind the storm door's glass.

Sunny was sound asleep, but Stormy lifted his head when she passed by. "You're in charge, Stormy," she called over her shoulder, "since you're sort-of awake. Who knows where Hobo ran off to? I'll be home by chore time."

With the canning jars settled on the floor of the back seat, she started down the lane. As the gravel popped and rumbled under the tires, her worries lifted away. She turned north toward the blacktop and, as she passed over the creek bridge, scanned the trees along the waterway for any sign of movement. Her search was worthwhile, as she soon spotted one of the eagles taking flight. Both of the youngsters had left the nest, although Ed, who'd been tracking the family closely for several months, claimed he'd seen them around. As she passed the Bauers' farm, Melinda couldn't imagine what it would be like when her dear friends moved away, too.

"Mabel was right. Everything changes, sooner or later. But I just can't believe Ed's really ready to move to town."

One of their sons and his family lived close by, and they were always willing to lend a hand. Their daughter and other son, however, lived farther away. Ed and Mabel had done so much for Melinda; she never could have made a new life in the country without their help. She wasn't a seasoned farmer, far from it, but she was willing to learn.

Could she help Ed around the yard, at least? Would his pride let her? Will and Helen Emmerson were close friends of the Bauers, but they were elderly, too. Angie and Nathan were always busy, and now Angie was trying to get her catering business off the ground.

Melinda was far from bored, herself. But Mabel and Ed were deserving of every moment she could spare.

The sweeping views soon pulled her thoughts back to the present. The fields were mellowing into rich shades of gold, and harvest was only a week or two away. And she wasn't the only one with her farmyard decorated for the season. Straw bales were stacked along several driveways, providing rustic podiums for rows of pumpkins.

One man was setting up an inflatable jack-o'-lantern on his lawn, helped (or hindered) by two boys and an eager dog. Pots of hardy mums provided splashes of rich color to many porches. A majestic hawk kept watch from the ridge of one road sign, his sharp eyes sweeping the nearby ditches for the twitch of an unsuspecting mouse.

Several roadside stands appeared along the way, beckoning with their stacks of pumpkins and very-last batches of summer's sweet corn. Some were staffed by farmers and their families, and others were simply wagons sporting "help yourself" signs and donation boxes. Melinda resisted the urge to stop. She had enough fall decorations at home, and there would be more for sale at the orchard.

The terrain morphed from mostly flat fields to gently rolling hills as she traveled north and east. At last she turned off the main highway, then followed a county blacktop to a sign that pointed her a half-mile down a gravel road. Apple trees soon lined both sides of her route and, as she reached the crest of a small hill, their stately rows gave way to a farmyard bursting with pumpkins and shocks of dried cornstalks. A friendly woman in a plaid jacket directed her into the parking lot, which was merely a mowed-down pasture.

The yard was filled with people, laughing and talking as they toted shopping bags packed with apples and packages of donuts. Children were everywhere, and many of them seemed determined to drag their parents toward a fun zone offering a merry-go-round and an inflatable swimming pool filled with corn kernels.

She spotted Chase on the wide porch of the metal-sided main building, where rustic wood-slat chairs invited customers to sit a spell and enjoy the apple farm's patchwork of rich fall colors. A large black cat was lounging at Chase's feet, but it scurried away when Melinda mounted the steps.

"I see you've made a friend." She gave him a quick kiss.

"No bad luck for me today." His blue eyes sparkled. "Not when I get to spend several hours with my favorite girl. They've got several friendly felines around here, made me think of your clinics. It's kind of a drive to Prosper, but I'm wondering if the owners might be interested."

A fat orange tabby loitered by the front entrance, and a long-haired gray cat held court on another porch chair. Three more felines sunbathed in the grass by the barn, where they collected squeals of delight and occasional pets from the children on their way to visit the farm's miniature horses.

"Actually, this family was one of the largest participants at the August clinic," she said proudly. "A few of their cats were already taken care of, but Karen and Josh helped the rest of them. I think there's eleven of them, total, and now, it'll stay that way."

"Forty minutes down, and forty back." Chase whistled. "I bet that was an interesting trip."

"People are coming from everywhere, now that the word is out. Karen had a call the other day from a woman over by West Union. She'll be at next week's clinic, bringing three or four. Sixty-five miles, I guess. A new record."

They strolled down one long wall inside the main building and up the next, breathing in the sweet air and sidestepping clusters of gleeful shoppers. Chase tipped his head toward two women shrieking with laughter as they filled a cart.

"It's like everyone's getting high on cider. But look at this selection! I don't bake, but even I want to rush home and try to whip up something."

The bins were filled with apples in every imaginable shade, from tart green to sweet red. Customers could grab a sack and hand-pick each fruit, or reach for the already-filled white paper bags that waited in rows on tables. The front corner had an impressive stack of field-run pumpkins, ringed with specialty squashes and other varieties that were best for baking.

Melinda slipped her hand into his as they wandered the displays. "This is my favorite time of year! The crisp weather, the way the light glows in the afternoons, the scent of burning leaf piles ... and of course, the pies, and muffins, and ..."

"Turnovers?" Chase pointed to the chalkboard menu set up next to the small kitchen in the back of the building. "Three for five bucks. We can flip a coin to see who gets a second one."

"Oh, you don't have to worry. I'm going to get plenty for myself, and a few more for Horace and Wilbur. I've got a cooler out in the car, and I intend to fill it up."

They enjoyed their treats and cups of fresh-pressed cider at one of the picnic tables overlooking the orchard. A team of draft horses soon appeared around the corner of the barn, pulling a wooden rack stacked with straw bales. Kids and their parents rushed over to pet the horses, then pay a few dollars to hop on board.

Chase gave Melinda a sly grin. "Hey, there's adults getting on, too. What do you say?"

They sat on one edge of the flatbed, swinging their legs in the brisk air as the driver clucked at his team and the wagon rattled into the orchard. They traveled the gravel path among the Jonagold trees, then passed a field of still-growing decorative squash and started down a gentle slope toward an iron bridge that spanned a gurgling creek. The team clip-clopped over the bridge, then promenaded through a grove of trees ablaze with orange and gold.

"Oh, this is just beautiful!" Melinda gasped. The horses turned out of the woods and followed the edge of a golden cornfield as they started back toward the yard. The sun was warm on her shoulders, but she snuggled close to Chase and he put his arm around her.

Suddenly, she was overcome with gratitude. *If I hadn't come back, if I hadn't found the courage to stay, I would have missed all of this.*

"What's the matter?" Chase leaned in, but he was laughing.

"Absolutely nothing. Right now, I'd say that everything is perfect." She gave him a quick kiss. One of the women nearby nodded her approval, but the kids were too busy pointing out a trio of deer on the far edge of the field to notice.

They bought sandwiches and apple cookies for lunch, then found an open table on the patio. When their meals were nearly finished, Chase's phone buzzed. A grin spread across his face when he read the text.

"Excellent! Did I tell you, one of my old crowd from high school's just moved back to Meadville? Sounds like everyone's getting together tonight for pizza at the place where we used to hang out."

"That'll be fun." Melinda's happiness for Chase was dampened by a pang of regret. Her high school friends were scattered and, even though they stayed in touch, she hadn't seen many of them in years. "It's important to keep those people in your life."

"For sure. Most of us went away for college, including myself. There's a few that are still around here, and I hooked up with them again when I moved back. We get together, when we can."

Chase shook his head as he looked out over the orchard. "I just can't believe I'll be forty in January. How did you survive it?"

Melinda snickered. She'd had her milestone birthday in March.

"I kept it low-key, I guess. Maybe that helped? But seriously, it's not a big deal. I used to think it would be. You know how when we were in our twenties, everyone had these lists of things they wanted to do in life. Forty seemed like it was the end of everything."

"But it can be just the beginning." His smile melted her heart, but then it vanished in a blink. "I don't know about you, but I still have some things to cross off that list. I'm happy with my life, but I don't know ... I guess I thought I'd be married by now, have kids. And working for my dad? That wasn't the plan, not at first." He hesitated for a moment. "Does it ... does it ever bother you that you haven't done everything you thought you'd do?"

Melinda was thrown by this sudden turn in the conversation. For one long second, as Chase waited for her reaction, she wondered if he was about to pull out a ring. Her stomach flipped over once, then twice, but she felt far from giddy. He wasn't planning something like that, was he? And not here, in front of a bunch of strangers! They hadn't been dating for even four months yet. Surely marriage wasn't that far to the top of Chase's must-do list.

And she wasn't ready. Far from it, actually.

Chase wasn't either. Thank goodness.

"Sorry to get so ... philosophical," he finally said, then grinned. "I don't know, maybe I'm just getting old. Time moves faster, every year that goes by, seems like."

Relieved, Melinda took a deep breath and a big gulp of her soda. "That's for sure. Actually, I used to worry about that, more than I do now. For the longest time, after I moved back, I was so focused on trying to figure out what to do next, if I should stay." She set it all aside with a shrug of her shoulders. "But then everything fell into place, and that was it. I guess I don't worry about things like that anymore. Does that make sense?"

"It does." Chase took one last sip of his coffee. "You're not searching anymore; you're where you're supposed to be, doing what you're supposed to do." He flattened his empty cup and stood up. "Well, I think it's time to get some carts. I need to run errands and do laundry this afternoon. The weekend always gets away from me when I'm having fun." He winked at her, and she reached for his hand.

Melinda's cooler was soon loaded with jugs of cider, as well as doughnuts and turnovers, and she picked up three sacks of apples. Although she tried to stick to her list, temptation won out in the end. The caramel apples by the register were smothered in dark chocolate and studded with nuts, and she couldn't pass up a trio of tiny gourds that would look lovely in a porcelain bowl on her dining-room table.

With a lingering kiss and a long goodbye, they parted ways with the promise to meet for dinner next week. She didn't have more than a moment to miss him, as he was right: The afternoon was ticking away, and she had a stop to make on the way home.

*   *   *

With two thousand residents, Elm Springs was much larger than Prosper. As Melinda cruised through its business district, she wondered how Wilbur, who was the first of the Schermann brothers to go to a nursing home, had decided on Scenic Vista. There were two facilities in Swanton, which was closer to the farm.

But as she made the last turn, Melinda thought she had the answer. Scenic Vista might have been twenty minutes from home, but it sat on the very edge of Elm Springs. Wilbur hadn't been able to stay in the country, but he'd wanted to still see it from his apartment window.

And while the brick-building campus was clean and the staff well-respected, Scenic Vista lacked the frills and perks of some other facilities in the area. It was a bargain, at least by comparison, and the frugal Schermann brothers had always saved every penny they could.

Wilbur moved to the care center when a broken leg didn't heal properly, and it became difficult for him to manage the farmhouse's stairs. But now, a few years later, dementia was his main health challenge. Horace, however, was still sharp as a tack. Farm life had simply become too much for him, and Scenic Vista offered around-the-clock support and three hearty meals a day he didn't have to cook himself. When Wilbur's roommate moved away, Horace came to Scenic Vista for an extended visit, then decided to stay.

Melinda was elated to find a parking spot near the front door, as it was the perfect day for families to bring their loved ones outside for a bit of brisk autumn air. She studied the backseat, trying to decide what to carry in first, and reached for a bag of apples and one jug of cider.

The lobby was decorated with mums and pumpkins, and several residents were gathered around a table in the front room, working a puzzle. Horace was expecting her, and they met up in the hallway outside the brothers' apartment.

"There's the farmer lady!" Horace's grin lit up his narrow, weathered face.

"You're looking well!" Horace was rather reserved, so she refrained from giving him a hug. Instead, she held up the bag of apples. "Cortlands, your favorite. And there's more, wait until you see what I brought."

Horace's blue eyes sparkled with anticipation. "Oh, I've been waiting for those." He shifted his cane to his other hand and offered to take the apples, but she waved him away. He was rather spry for someone in his nineties, but she wasn't going to let him risk a fall.

The brothers' recliners sat together in the cozy living area, facing a picture window that framed an idyllic scene of faded grass and flaming oak trees. Cardinals and sparrows darted among the feeders, and Wilbur could barely pull his gaze away to notice his guest. Melinda put the apples on the section of counter that marked the apartment's compact kitchen, and went over to pat Wilbur on the shoulder.

"Well, hello." Wilbur smiled broadly, but had no idea who she was. He still knew Horace, and sometimes Ada and Kevin on his good days, but those came less frequently now. "How's the weather out there?"

Once a farmer, always a farmer.

"Oh, it's a nice day. It's almost sixty. Only a slight breeze."

"It was beautiful when I went for a walk after lunch." Horace already had three apples out of the sack and was carefully washing them in the miniature kitchen sink. "Might get cool tonight, though. How's the garden holding up? Did you get another basket of tomatoes?" They talked on the phone at least once a week, Melinda seeking Horace's advice and Horace yearning to keep a connection to home.

"Sure did. I'm hoping for another one or two before frost. Speaking of tomatoes, I've got some more stuff in the car. I'll be right back."

Horace placed the corn relish on a shelf with a reverent air that made Melinda stifle a giggle. She couldn't stand the stuff, but his gratitude made all the work worthwhile.

"My, my, tomatoes, too. And plum jam!" His brow furrowed with concern. "I hope you've got enough jars out there, won't run out before the season's over. Don't want anything to go to waste."

"No, I'm good." In truth, several boxes of unneeded canning jars had been sold at the family's auction in the spring. Some old men collected farm implements; Horace's weakness had been glass jars. But he'd loved his garden and, being a child of the Great Depression, thrift was a habit he never was able to break.

Melinda pulled out a spare folding chair, and they settled

in with their snacks. "Well, I've got big news," Horace said after he'd enjoyed a few thin slices from his apple. Wilbur was still working on the corner of his turnover.

"Oh, really?"

"Yep. Maggie called, just a bit ago. Says Wendy's going to bring her up next weekend." All those hours of searching paid off when Horace was reunited with his long-lost love. After seventy years, they'd picked up almost where they'd left off.

"They're going to come for lunch, I put in a reservation for them. We're having meatloaf, I guess, but it's not too bad. My mother's was the best." Horace shook his head. "I tried to replicate it, you see, but never quite got it down."

"I'm sure it'll be fine. I bet she'll like your apartment."

Their conversation tripped a switch in Wilbur's mind. "Where is Mother? Did she go to town?"

"She's not here," Horace said gently. "But that's OK."

Wilbur turned back to the window. "Harvest is coming, we'll be in the fields within the week. We'd better check the tractor over tomorrow, give it a tune-up." He was often confused about the present, but what happened decades ago was still sharp in his mind.

"You're right," Melinda said. "Fall means lots of work around the farm. It's a busy time of year." She turned to Horace. "I've got so much to do, I don't even know where to start. I haven't had time to bring the front porch's storm windows up from the basement, even. And they'll need to be washed before I put them out."

"We tried storing them in the garage one year, to save the stairs. But then, one got broken. And the mice made a nest behind one stack of them, and ..."

Melinda shuddered. "That's the other thing. The spiders have been busy in the basement, they've got a whole series of webs going down there."

Horace chuckled. "Well, they eat the bugs, so I don't mind them much, but ... Mother was terrified of them, too."

"She tries to shoo them with a broom." Wilbur leaned over. "She's too scared of them to get close enough to stomp them out. They just scoot off and set up shop somewhere else. Father keeps telling her that, but she won't listen.

"There's one thing you could try." Horace chewed thoughtfully. "Grandma Schermann always said if you sweep during the dark of the moon, the spiders will leave for good."

Melinda snorted. "I wish."

"Did you get your hedge apples yet?"

"What?" She glanced at her plate. "Uh, I don't think so. Just these Cortlands, and the Jonagolds and ..."

"No, no, hedge apples. They're not really apples, you see. Osage orange, I think. They're bumpy and bright green."

"Oh, I did see those at the grocery store. With a sign that said 'not for human consumption' or something like that. I thought it was strange."

"Just put some around the outside of the basement's foundation. They'll keep the spiders away, maybe some of the mice, too. You'll cover them up when you put the straw bales around, but that won't matter."

Melinda sighed. "Oh, yes. I'll have to do the straw, too." Neighbor John Olson, who supplied her hay and straw, had brought over dozens of extra straw bales last fall to insulate the north and west sides of the house's foundation. Was there enough in the haymow for this year's project? Probably not. One more thing on the list ...

"There's so much to do before winter sets in." The yearning in Horace's voice brought Melinda's thoughts up short. He'd settled in here, better than Ada and Kevin had expected, but his heart was still at the farm. "It's always a bit of a race against Old Man Winter. But I'd say, that's part of the fun."

Melinda reached for her phone and scrolled through her files. "I know Ada printed you a photo I sent her from Hobo's ceremony, but Chase was able to get a bit of video, too."

Horace grinned proudly as Jerry praised Hobo's intellect and bravery, then laughed when he saw Melinda trying to keep Hobo in one spot. "Look at him! He's never seen so many people at once! But you managed him well, for sure."

Melinda then knelt by Wilbur's chair, and replayed the clip. His eyes widened with surprise. "Tippy? It's Tippy! What ... where was this at? Who are those people with her?"

Horace leaned over. "No, no, that's not Tippy. She's been gone a long time. That's Hobo."

"Tippy always likes to be in the middle of things," Wilbur continued. "She likes to ride in the back of the truck. Sometimes she'll get right on the tractor, ride out to the field with us so she can chase rabbits."

"Tippy looked a bit like Hobo," Horace explained to Melinda. "Brown coat, white paws, even had that white tip on her tail. That's where she got her name, you see. She was our dog when we were just boys. Spent more time in the house than what Father may have liked. But she adored Mother, and the other way around. She was a special dog."

Wilbur motioned for Melinda to play the video again, and she was happy to comply.

"How long did you have her?"

"About twelve years." Horace sighed. "She just got old, like everyone else, and then one morning, she didn't wake up." He turned away and brushed at his face with one weathered hand.

"Wilbur and I, we buried her out in the windbreak, there behind the chicken coop. Father said he was too busy and asked us to do it, but I really suspect he couldn't bear it. We were, oh, fourteen and sixteen. Practically men by then, you see. We got the job done."

Melinda felt sorry for her friend, but then another thought formed in the back of her mind. There was a grave on her property, and she'd had no idea. Tippy had been a much-loved member of the Schermann family, but something about it still made Melinda uneasy.

"So ... is there a marker somewhere?" She wasn't sure she wanted to know. "I haven't noticed anything. But then, I don't spend much time out there."

"No, but Tippy's just to the west of that really big oak." Melinda didn't know which one that was, but it was just as well. "The others are all to the north of her, there on the edge of the field. We tried to get some rows going, keep it tidy ..."

Melinda's mouth fell open. Horace chuckled.

"Where else would we go with them? You can't leave them just lying around, it's not right. Besides, it draws the coyotes and everything else."

Horace started counting beloved farm dogs on his fingers. "Let's see, there's Sampson, he was the collie we had right after Tippy. And then Petunia. Mother named her, it was her turn. And then Rascal, and Buck, then Laddie ... Marty passed away, oh, five years ago? We didn't have a dog for a few years after that, until Hobo just showed up one day. Oh, and we had some cats from time to time. They're out there, too."

So there wasn't just one grave. More like a whole cemetery.

Horace loved books, but his tastes ran more to Westerns than horror. He'd probably never heard of the terrifying classic Sam had selected for the Prosper library's book club. The one that now had a whole new meaning for Melinda.

"I guess I'd never given that any thought," she finally said. "But you're right, of course. You had to do something with them."

"Oh, don't worry about it." Horace brushed it all away. "They're buried down deep. We made sure of that. Nothing's ever going to dig them up."

Melinda decided she'd take her comfort where she could find it. She reached for her purse. "Well, I suppose I should get going. Maybe I can sort the storm windows tonight, at least." She wasn't going to feel much like reading. Or turning out the lights at bedtime, either.

"You'll get it all done." Horace's voice held a warmth and confidence that made her feel better. He'd seen ninety autumns come and go at the farm, and survived every winter that followed. "September's not over for a whole week yet. And it'll be November before the weather really starts to turn."

She paused in the doorway on her way out, soaking in the

warmth of the small apartment and the bright leaves dancing outside the picture window. Wilbur was already asleep in his chair, and Horace had turned his attention to the newspaper. A clock ticked quietly on a shelf, marking the minutes until it was time to head down to the dining hall for supper.

There was so much to do at the farm. That hadn't changed. But Melinda had been reminded how blessed she was to have those tasks ahead of her. They carried the chance to be out in the sunshine and the cool breeze, feel her muscles warm with effort. And even better, know the deep satisfaction that would come as every chore was completed.

Someday she would be in Horace's shoes, and fall would be only a beautiful scene outside a window. So for now, she would tackle each task with a grateful heart.

✳ 6 ✳

An angry wind scratched at city hall's windows, rattling their metal storm frames. A cold drizzle dripped from the heavy skies, weighing down the decaying leaves that tried to find shelter under trees and along foundations. Melinda was grateful to be indoors on such a dreary, blustery day. She looked at the dozing brown-tabby cat in her arms, a male who came out of surgery only minutes ago, and gently rubbed the little white patch on his chest.

"I bet you're glad to be inside today, too," she whispered, and cuddled him close. "You're warm and safe, and your life is going to be so much better now."

Three other women and one man made up the rest of cuddle crew, whose only task was to keep the cats warm until their temperatures could rebound from the anesthetic. This corner of the council's chambers was stocked with fresh towels, coffee, and cookies. Surgery stations were set up at the front of the room, and Karen and Josh were working their way through the forty-six cats on today's list.

There were so many unfamiliar furry faces, most of them marked with fear or annoyance, lined up in crates along the far wall. But Melinda knew the cat in her arms. Jackson was part of Gertrude's colony, and Melinda had deployed a mix of tuna and raw hamburger to trick him into a carrier yesterday afternoon. He and his friends were the last of that group needing assistance, and Melinda settled back in her metal chair with a mix of pride and relief. More would arrive, they always did, and Gertrude would welcome them with a big heart and a bowl of kibble. But for now, Melinda was going to savor this accomplishment.

The room was warm and surprisingly quiet, as most of the cats were too terrified to keep up the howls and wails that accompanied their arrivals earlier that morning. Melinda was feeling as sleepy as Jackson looked when an icy draft crept in from seemingly nowhere and bit her ankles. She shivered, adjusted Jackson's makeshift blanket, and glanced at the ceiling. Nancy's confession now loomed in Melinda's mind every time she entered city hall, but at least she never had to be here alone.

The source of the draft soon showed itself. Auggie clomped in from the kitchen, the building's stubborn back door finally closing behind him with a creak and a groan.

"Nursie Nurse reporting for duty." He removed his wool cap and shrugged out of his jacket. "Who needs a cuddle?"

"You can take this little girl." Norma Beecham, a vet technician from Josh's office, approached with a kitten wrapped in a purple fleece blanket. "Just finished her up. It'll be awhile before she's alert enough to go back in her carrier."

Auggie settled in the last vacant chair in the recovery area, the fleece bundle comically small in his meaty, weathered hands. Melinda leaned over for a better look, and smiled at the kitten's tortoiseshell markings.

"I'm glad you could help out today. I know harvest is ramping up, and the co-op's swamped."

"That's for sure. But Dan can handle it for a few hours, especially since this damp is slowing things down a bit. We've got our seasonal part-timers on the clock, too. Besides, Mr. Checkers and Pebbles will provide their usual entertainment."

"I didn't know you added staff. The human sort, I mean."

"We didn't. It's just our usual crew of retired farmers who can't stay away. Harvest rolls around and they get the itch, you know? I give them minimum wage, a hot lunch and all the coffee they can gulp, and they're good to go."

Jackson soon opened his golden eyes, and Melinda was sure he gave her a grateful look. But his expression quickly changed from sleepy to shocked, and his paws began to swat at the towel. That was the signal to return him to his carrier before bedlam broke loose. Another volunteer hurried over to offer her assistance.

"You're here all day, right? One of the other techs is going on break. Want to help Vogel while she's gone?"

Melinda wasn't qualified to administer rabies shots or anesthetic, but she'd become adept at holding less-than-accommodating patients while the professionals did their work.

"Sure. Might as well." She washed up at one of the portable sinks and started for the front of the room, dodging two other volunteers with carriers in both hands. Karen and Josh had small headlights strapped around their scrubs caps, making them look as much like miners as veterinarians. Their makeshift surgical suites also had lamps, as the council room's tired ceiling bulbs didn't provide enough task lighting for surgery.

"Hey." Josh's brown eyes lit up with welcome as he prepped his table for the next patient. "How's the cuddle crew holding up? Do they have enough cookies to make it through the day?"

"I think so." Melinda pushed up her sweater's sleeves and reached for a pair of plastic gloves. "But then, Auggie just got here, so you never know."

A technician came out of the bathroom with a humane trap covered by a blanket. The space was the best place in the building to administer anesthetic, as it was so tiny the frantic cats had no hope of escape. "OK, he's a lively one. But I finally got the shot in him. He's about out."

Melinda lifted the blanket. The cat was mostly black, with a small white spot on his chest. But his coat was dulled by age, and most of one ear was missing. "Oh, sweetie, look at you. You've had a hard life, huh? We're going to make things better." She lifted the sedated cat out with gentle hands, and positioned him on the exam table.

"Karen says you almost have that grant application ready." Josh was organizing his surgical instruments. "We should hear in January, right?"

"Yes, at the latest. The competition's going to be tough, but I think we've got a chance. I found a few more I think we should apply for. How are things at your practice?"

"Crazy-busy, but that's a good thing. The Swanton shelter's asked us to host adoptable cats at our building, and I'm seriously considering it. They'd provide the kennels and food, and we've got room there in the front corner of the waiting room." He gave her a searching look. "They need more fosters, too. I hear you're a pro with little orphans ..."

"Oh, I'd better not. If I bring them home, I won't be able to give them back. And I think I've reached my limit. If I don't restrain myself, I'll be the crazy cat lady."

"More like the cat whisperer, from what Doc and Karen say. You have a special way with them, that's for sure." Josh nodded at the cat on the table, then gave Melinda a smile so wide she started to blush. Then blush more, but this time from embarrassment. Josh was certainly handsome, but she didn't need to make a fool of herself. At least everyone around them was too busy to notice.

Josh leaned over before he fastened his face mask. "And besides, Prosper already has a crazy cat lady. Gertrude wears the crown well, don't you think?"

Melinda stayed on through two more exams, passing Josh instruments and supplies. She was in the kitchen, setting out the sandwiches that had just arrived, when her phone buzzed.

"Hey, how busy are you?" Doc sounded strangely distracted. "I got an emergency call, and two people are stopping in over the lunch hour to pick up meds. Can you come over and watch the counter until I get back?"

"Sure." Melinda was surprised, but glad to help. She'd

taken the day off from Prosper Hardware to volunteer, so she might as well be where she was needed most. Karen certainly couldn't go. "What happened? Is it serious?"

"Don't know yet. I gotta run. Can you come right now? I'll leave the back unlocked."

"I'm on my way."

Karen only had time to nod her thanks when Melinda stopped by her exam table. After swiping a sandwich, she hurried out to the parking lot. The vet clinic was less than two blocks' away, but it was too nasty of a day to walk.

She paused in the kennel room to greet the furry patients spending the day at the clinic, then went up to the lobby. There wasn't much to do. She straightened the front counter, then studied the tips list kept handy for this sort of situation. Doc's wife, Anne, was a nurse at the Swanton hospital, but her swing shifts sometimes allowed her to help at the vet clinic. Their teenage son and daughter did the same, but this was Melinda's first time.

A woman stopped in to pick up flea treatments for her dogs, and the phone rang twice. The clinic was otherwise silent, and Melinda's eyelids started to flutter as she stared out at the gloomy day. Maybe she should make sausage-and-potato soup tonight. That was one good thing about this weather; it was time for hearty meals again. And there would be lots of leftovers ...

Suddenly, she sat up. Was there a radio on in the back? Why hadn't she heard it before?

The sound was coming from Doc's office, where a public-safety scanner had briefly come to life, then went quiet again. He was a volunteer for Prosper's emergency department, and now she wondered what the real emergency might be.

"I just assumed there was a sick cow or something, but ..."

She leaned over the desk, and waited. Come to think of it, as she'd turned out on Main, had that been Bill's truck whipping out of Prosper Hardware's parking lot and heading west out of town? He was a volunteer, too. That was just before noon, even though Bill always preferred to take a late lunch. When the scanner stayed silent, Melinda decided to check another reliable source of information.

Aunt Miriam picked up the store's line on the first ring.

"Melinda! What is going on?" Miriam beat her to it. "Bill ran out of here a while ago, wouldn't tell me why. Is there a bad wreck somewhere? Anybody at city hall say anything?"

"I'm at the vet office, actually. Doc called and wanted me to come watch the counter, so I did. The scanner came on a bit ago, but I missed it."

"Hmm. That is strange. Well, I was going to leave at two, since Esther just came in, but I'll hang around longer if Bill's not back by then."

Melinda checked her phone for text alerts from any of the regional media outlets, but came up empty-handed. Nothing unusual on their websites, either. The scanner burbled once with a cryptic request for barricades, which was answered with only a "10-4" from someone else on the system. Maybe Miriam's hunch was correct, and there was a vehicle accident somewhere. Melinda sent up a few prayers and went back to the counter. As she was surfing on her phone, wondering if the other pet parent was going to stop in as promised, a text from Nathan, Angie's husband, appeared on the screen.

He was harvesting some of his rented land a few miles southwest of Melinda's acreage, and the photo snapped from his combine's seat showed several emergency vehicles clustered in a field about a half-mile away.

This doesn't look good. Heard anything?

Nope. But something's going on. I'll let you know what I find out.

Adelaide and Mason Beaufort didn't live far from the scene. Only seconds after Melinda sent Adelaide a text, her number flashed on the screen.

"Are you at home?" Adelaide, who always seemed to take things in stride, sounded anxious and upset.

"No, I'm in town. Nathan Hensley's harvesting not far from your place. He sent me a photo. Are there really emergency vehicles out there? Is someone hurt?"

"I'm not sure. It's maybe a half-mile from here, down past the crossroads. Mason's over at the window, watching. Something's wrong, but we don't know what."

Two sheriff's vehicles had passed by in the last half hour, Adelaide reported, and then an ambulance, but none had their sirens blaring or their lights flashing. Mason had been an on-call firefighter in Wisconsin, and this silent run had him restless.

"No, don't you dare go down there!" Melinda heard Adelaide say. "Honey, I know. They're trying to fly under the radar, so it's gotta be bad. Just calm down." She turned back to Melinda.

"Now he says, it looks like they're setting up barricades at the intersection, a bunch more trucks just arrived. Wait a sec. Oh, no, is that ..."

Adelaide faded away for a moment. Mason was shouting now, but Melinda couldn't make out his words.

"Melinda," Adelaide gasped, "the medical examiner just drove by! Do you know what that means? Someone is dead!"

* * *

Melinda hurried into the office, and turned up the scanner so she could hear it from the front counter. The radio's lack of traffic, along with Adelaide's report, told her everything she needed to know: Emergency crews had ditched their usual frequencies and retreated to channels not available to the public.

That explained Doc and Bill's strange behavior, too; Tony had obviously warned them to not say where they were going, or why.

She paced the floor, watched the clock, and wondered what would happen next. Adelaide called with an update: A sheriff's deputy had just knocked on the Beauforts' door, and told them human remains had been unearthed down the road, along the bank of the creek. A work crew had been in that pasture for several days, Adelaide explained, digging a drainage ditch. They found the body.

The officer refused to elaborate, but told the Beauforts to stay alert and not go outside after dark. Three of their neighbors reported similar visits from law enforcement.

"I asked him if we were in danger. He said he didn't know. Either we are, or we aren't! Why can't they just tell us what happened?"

Melinda's phone beeped, and she pulled it away long enough to check the text.

"Hey, I just got an alert from the Mason City station. Says the Hartland County sheriff just confirmed a body's been found. Press conference at four."

"That's almost three hours' away!"

"I wish Doc would get back! Maybe now that word is out, he'll be able to talk about it. If someone's already dead, I can't imagine what there is for him to do. I'll let you know if I hear anything else."

Finally, an hour later, she heard boots scrape the mat inside the clinic's back door. Doc was soaked and exhausted. "Sorry, Tony said we couldn't say anything. Thanks for coming down. The county started calling for extra hands, but wouldn't tell anyone why. Then we got out there, and ..."

He aimed for the kitchen, eager for a mug of coffee, and she trailed after him.

"Now, you didn't hear it from me." He put up a hand. "But the remains? They've got to be old. I overheard the deputies talking." Doc took a hearty swallow. "Man, it's damp out there. That wind cuts right through! And the mud ..."

"I got an alert, there's a press conference at four."

"I hope that clears up some things. Worst that could happen now, if it's not an active murder investigation, is paranoia. I can't remember the last time there's been something like this, everyone's going to be in an uproar." He looked at the clock. "Well, you might as well head back to city hall. I owe you one."

Word of the discovery spread fast, and the rumors were right behind. Melinda went up front to check on the cats too skittish to remain in the bustling council chambers, and found Nancy trapped at her desk. The phone rang just seconds after the alert was issued, and it hadn't stopped.

"They want to know if there's a killer on the loose." As if on cue, an unearthly howl came from one of the carriers. "What am I supposed to tell them? Lock your doors and crawl under the bed? More than one person has said they're glad they have a gun in the house."

Melinda adjusted the old sheets tossed over the row of crates, tried to make the terrified patients feel safe.

"We'll just have to stay calm and focused," Nancy said, as much to herself as to Melinda. "Karen and Josh are wrapping up in the back, and we'll need to get everyone settled and ready to go home. But people are going to be frantic, and ..."

The phone rang again.

"Dangit!" Nancy leaned over the desk.

"Prosper City Hall," she said sweetly, rolling her eyes. "No, I'm sorry, Mayor Simmons is out this afternoon. Yes, I'm aware of the situation. You'll need to call the sheriff's office, ma'am. They're in charge ..."

The process to check out the cats was normally a joyous one, as owners were reunited with their pets and the volunteers were showered with gratitude for their efforts. Over the past few months, Melinda had caught more than one burly farmer blinking away a tear as he collected his barn friends. People were relieved to know their cats had come through their procedures safely, and that the population explosions on their properties had been curtailed, or even stopped.

But today, the queue's mood was noticeably different. There was very little conversation, and all of it was strained. Melinda was glad the cuddle crew had already been dismissed, and Auggie wasn't there to stir the emotional pot. Most of these people lived in the country, off sleepy gravel roads and at the end of winding lanes, and they were already on edge.

Nancy clicked on the television just before four, knowing the press conference was at the top of everyone's minds. The event was at the county courthouse in Swanton, and the live feed showed a cluster of grim-faced officials several steps behind a podium. None of them, it seemed, wanted to get too close to the microphone.

A few groans echoed around Prosper's council chambers as the sheriff, looking uncomfortable and clutching a stack of papers in one too-tight fist, finally came forward.

"Just look at him," one farmer told Melinda. "He's scared to death. Worse than my tomcat when I trapped him in that carrier last night."

"Well, nothing like this has happened in years," a woman said. "His head's probably spinning."

"Somebody's dead," the man reminded her. "I feel more sorry for them than I do the sheriff. Don't they teach them how to handle this kind of thing in cop school?"

With only a few glances at the camera, the sheriff read his notes: A crew digging a drainage ditch uncovered the body this morning in a pasture southwest of Prosper. The remains appeared to have been there for some time. A wide perimeter around the scene had been secured, and would be patrolled around the clock until further notice. At this time, authorities didn't think anyone else was in danger. Those with information should contact the sheriff's department.

The reporters weren't satisfied.

You said the remains have been there 'for some time.' *Can you be more specific?* "I'm not at liberty to say."

When will you know more? "The remains are being transferred to a secure location, and extensive testing will be required. That'll take several weeks."

If this is an active crime scene, how do you know there is no further danger to residents? The sheriff hesitated, then turned to stare at one of the men in the back.

The other man came to the podium and introduced himself as a state-level law-enforcement official. "We feel rather certain that people in the area are safe," he finally said. "But this is an ongoing investigation. As always, residents should use caution and be aware of their surroundings."

Prosper's council chambers erupted in groans and jeers. Melinda rolled her eyes and shook her head. Those officials had just thrown gasoline on the fire of fear burning across Hartland County. Serious crimes were rare around here, but hadn't they had any crisis training at all? Her public-relations experience taught her long ago that message and tone made all the difference.

"Well, gee, I feel better," a woman said sarcastically.

"What's 'rather certain' supposed to mean?" one man grumbled. "It's a bunch of crap, if you ask me. I've been saying all afternoon, something shady's going on here. There's a coverup, I'm sure of it."

The guy next in line nodded in agreement. "You got that right."

Melinda tried to put on a smile as she handed one woman the rabies vaccination certificates for her four barn cats. The lady absentmindedly stuffed the papers in her purse, then leaned over the table.

"What if someone's still out there?" Her brown eyes were filled with worry. "There's miles and miles of fields going in every direction. And harvest's just getting started. I know we had a tough year, but the corn's still tall enough for someone to hide in."

"Even if they drove away from the scene, they could ditch the car and take off on foot." The man behind her shook his head. "They could be anywhere!"

Melinda had already wondered if someone could hide in the windbreak at her acreage. But it wasn't very wide and, since Hobo was keenly aware of any movement among the trees, she'd decided it wasn't likely.

These people were right, however, about the cornfields. They stared at her, waiting for some sort of answer. She tried to think of something that wouldn't escalate their fears.

"I'm sure if there was any immediate danger, they'd say so. All we can do is stay aware, like they said, just in case." But Melinda was already calculating how much longer she'd be needed at the cat clinic, and how quickly she could race through chores when she got home. Sunset wouldn't come until around seven, but it was such a dark, dreary day ...

Josh appeared at her elbow, a small paper sack in his hand. The next patron's cat had a minor respiratory infection, but thankfully was tame enough to be handled. Josh explained how to administer the medication, and waved away the woman's offer to pay for it. He paused to study the television, which was now streaming video of a once-lonely country road blocked with barricades and law-enforcement vehicles.

"Hey, don't you live out that way?" he asked Melinda. "Seems like your place can't be far from there."

"About two miles. One of my neighbors said it's been a zoo this afternoon. A deputy came to their door a few hours ago, and suggested they stay inside."

"I grew up on a farm, and I miss it. A lot. But this might be one of the few nights I'm grateful I live in town. Stay safe out there."

"I'll be fine; I've got Hobo the hero dog, remember? He barks all the time, even when he shouldn't, so I'm sure he'll let me know if something's not right."

The room slowly cleared out, and it was time to clean up. Melinda tried to shrug off her nerves, but didn't quite succeed. Chase would be off work soon; should she ask him to come down and spend the night? But she'd seen him just two days ago, and it was an hour's drive each way. And, if she remembered right, he had an early-morning meeting tomorrow. Living alone in the country meant taking the bad with the good; she'd just have to find the courage to face this fear on her own.

But it was a relief to find out she wouldn't have to. As she wiped down a table, her phone buzzed with a text from Mabel. It's the perfect night for chili. *Why don't you come over after chores? Ed can follow you home later.*

The volunteers worked quickly, the day's stunning news temporarily taking a backseat to packing away supplies and getting the council chambers back to normal. But instead of leaving as soon as their tasks were completed, the women clustered in the kitchen and engaged in mindless chatter until Karen and Melinda turned off the lights in the council room. The helpers were trying to put on a brave front, but their intentions were clear: no one wanted to go out to the parking lot alone.

Karen double-checked city hall's back door was locked, then studied the alley from one end to the other. "Phones down, eyes up, ladies. And I want all of you to text me when you're safe at home."

* 7 *

Lights were already shining through the windows of most of Prosper's homes, and the co-op still burned bright with the hustle of harvest. Melinda had already decided she wasn't going to be afraid. But as soon as she bumped over the railroad tracks and was out of town, the ominous skies and vast fields made her feel small and alone.

It was a blessing the crime scene was a few miles beyond her usual route; if she didn't have to detour around it, or catch a glimpse of the law enforcement vehicles crowded at the crossroads, maybe it would be easier to put the gruesome discovery out of her mind, at least temporarily. She passed the Emmersons' place, then turned south toward home. As the gravel rattled under her tires, her mind wandered from what had been found to who might be to blame.

Doc thought the remains had been there for decades, based on what he'd overheard at the scene. But if that was true, why hadn't the sheriff simply said so? It would have eased many people's minds, including hers. If whatever happened occurred that many years ago, it was likely the person responsible had moved away or was deceased.

She normally turned into her lane, then walked across the road to check the mailbox. But tonight, she pulled over as far as she could, powered down the window, and leaned out with a quick hand to grasp what was inside.

Its contents were just as she expected, a bit of comfort at the end of this wild, weary day: a few bills, a circular from Swanton's only grocery store, and the Swanton newspaper. The front page was filled with photos from a children's craft activity at the Swanton library, and an update on plans to improve parking around the town square.

"I suspect the next edition's going to be much different." She tossed the stack on the seat. "More like 'Body found in field,' or, 'Cops conduct murder investigation,' something like that."

A few lights were on in the house, as always, welcoming her home. So was Hobo, doing his happy dance there by the garage. Melinda tried for a deep, calming breath, but her eyes scanned the pasture and front yard as she crept up the drive.

"I need to relax. The headline I want to avoid is: 'Former city woman scares herself to death for no reason.'"

Hobo was in his usual good mood, and Grace and Hazel were also unfazed by the day's news. Each cat had staked out half of the knitted throw jumbled on the couch, and stirred from their naps just long enough to receive Melinda's pets and greetings.

She changed her clothes, returned to the back porch to pull on her boots and chore coat, and wrestled a headlamp out of the tangle of gear on one closet shelf. It wasn't a necessity yet, and wouldn't be until the days were shorter and chores were always done in the dark, but the idea of a hands-free flashlight gave her comfort tonight.

Hobo was already back outside, and Sunny and Stormy now waited with him on the sidewalk.

"It's been quite the day, huh? I'm glad we're just far enough away that you missed all of it. All those strange vehicles, and the commotion." She hugged Sunny and then Stormy, and held them a little longer than usual even though she was in a hurry. The community clinics were always a reminder of how far her own barn cats had come, from two scared ferals hiding in the haymow to the sweet boys who were now part of her furry family.

"We're going on lockdown as soon as chores are over. That means you two; no roaming tonight. And Hobo, you'll need to stay in the house while I'm gone."

The sheep were still scattered in the pasture, oblivious to the day's events, but came running when they spotted Melinda on her way to the barn. Her routine gave her a measure of comfort, but she still felt vulnerable as she crossed the wide-open farmyard. It felt good to place her hand on the door's weathered boards, lean against something sturdy, if just for a moment.

She reached for the iron latch, then stopped.

Oh, no.

It was possible. The barn wasn't locked. And the sheep's pasture door was wide open. She leaned over to study the cutout Horace made in the side wall for Hobo, then had to laugh at herself. "Anyone small enough to squeeze through there, I could take them down, easy."

She turned the latch and flipped the light switch, and Hobo ran ahead, unconcerned. Sunny did the same, and Stormy turned back only long enough to give her a look that said, "what are you waiting for?"

The sheep clustered at their troughs, calling and grunting, eager for nose pets and their grain. "I know, you want supper. But I'm sorry, I need five minutes. Hobo, we need to check the premises."

A pitchfork waited by the sheep's gate, and she used its tines to push the grain room's door wide. There was nothing there beyond the stash of junk in the corner, the dusted-over windows high in the outside wall, and two impatient cats. With Stormy and Sunny fed and no longer underfoot, she marched into the back half of the barn and flipped all the switches. Only when she'd confirmed the vacant stalls were truly empty did she turn toward the stairs.

Three bare bulbs flickered to life far above, and she heard the faint rasp of wings gliding through the shadows. "Those had better be sparrows," she told Hobo. "You know I don't like the bats, no matter how many bugs they eat."

It was a scene out of a bad horror movie, the wide-eyed woman armed with only a rusted farm tool, but she had to be sure. Three steps across the wide floorboards, she stopped and listened. The wind moaned around the barn's eaves, just loud enough she wouldn't be able to hear any movement behind the stacks of hay and straw bales. She gripped the pitchfork tighter and walked the loft from one end to the other, her headlight shining a sharp beam into the shadows while Hobo sniffed the corners.

Downstairs, the sheep were growing restless. Melinda counted them twice and swore under her breath. There were only six, which meant her half-grown lambs were still outside. Leaving Hobo to whine on the other side of the gate, she scooped corn into a bucket and ran out to the pasture.

Clover and her sister were still snacking on the south side of the meadow. Knowing the wind would carry her calls away, Melinda lifted her sweatshirt's hood and started in their direction.

She was really out in the open now, and the sky was fading fast. Blinking against the gale, she looked out over the rolling fields and tried to take comfort in the pinpricks that signaled the yard lights of her neighbors' farms. Their faint, faraway glows had always been a reminder she was never really alone out here, and help was just a call away.

She recalled what Mabel said a few weeks ago, about how their rural area had changed over the years. So many people had come and gone. But some of them stayed. Melinda recalled her summertime rambles with Lizzie, all the farmsteads she passed while delivering invitations to the women's luncheon at the church. The smiling faces she'd seen, the kind people she'd met. And then, there had been the places that seemed hostile to visitors. The ones with ragged lawns guarded by agitated dogs, and sagging, rusted fences pockmarked with warning signs. What if ...

Being poor wasn't a crime, and it certainly didn't make you more likely to commit one. A farm might be a bit rundown, but that didn't mean its inhabitants were violent or cruel. Melinda tried to push those thoughts away, and stop scanning all the people she'd met with such a judgmental eye.

But one face came to mind, and wouldn't leave.

Bart Wildwood was around eighty, and lived halfway between Melinda's farm and the church. She'd been overdressed for her errand, for sure, but her nice skirt and blouse were especially out of place in the Wildwoods' weed-choked yard. Even their house had seemed menacing, with its peeling clapboards, narrow windows and sharp-pitched roof. Melinda had been afraid to get out of the car, but duty drove her to knock on the kitchen door.

Bart had sneered at her greeting, mocked her errand, and snapped at Marge, his equally ill-tempered wife. Later, Mabel had assured Melinda that Bart was relatively harmless, despite his ill temper. He'd taken up the bottle when he was a teenager, and never let it go.

Maybe Bart wasn't capable of something so terrible. She should feel compassion for him; and especially for Marge, who apparently suffered from dementia. But with such a shocking discovery unearthed only a few miles' away, her unsettled mind couldn't help but search for answers.

The young ewes were right along the fence, pushing their smaller snouts through the grid to reach the unchewed grasses on the other side. The cornfield was just a few feet beyond the boundary. Its yellowed stalks rustled in the wind, creating enough noise and movement to easily conceal anything that might be hiding down the rows. She hung back, and shook the bucket.

"Girls! It's time for supper. You need to get inside, right now!"

The lambs quickly decided shelled corn was less work than foraging, and were eager to follow Melinda into the barn. Annie glared at Melinda when the pasture door's two halves were locked tight.

The machine shed's rolling door seemed undisturbed, but Melinda slid it wide long enough to be sure. Hobo was only interested in giving Lizzie's dusty tires a curious sniff, and

Melinda took that as a good sign. She studied the windbreak as she trudged toward the chicken house, the roaring northwest wind threatening to push her back, but didn't see anything unusual.

Melinda sighed with relief when she opened the chicken house's door and found only her flock. Hobo waited outside while she changed out water and added feed to the pans. On her way out, she pointed at her most-stubborn hen.

"Pansy, you're on guard duty. Any stranger tries to get in here, you peck their eyes out, OK?" The scar on Melinda's right forearm was a constant reminder of Pansy's past transgressions. "I know you've got it in you."

As Hobo ran ahead across the yard, Melinda was already looking forward to a few bowls of Mabel's chili. The chores were done, she'd made her security checks; all she had to do was change her clothes. There were still some oatmeal-chocolate chip cookies in the jar; maybe she should take some along? Mabel hadn't said anything about dessert, but she'd never let anyone push away from the table hungry. It would be polite to bring something, though ...

Hobo had already slipped through his doggie door, but Melinda stopped short at the top of the back steps. The storm door wasn't latched tight. She knew better than to leave it like that, as a strong wind like this one could wrestle the door wide open and warp its hinges.

How long had she been outside? Long enough for someone to ... Her heart pounding in her ears, Melinda shoved her way into the back porch and burst into the kitchen. Hobo looked up from his water bowl in confusion as she hustled for the basement door and hurried down the stairs, flipping on lights as she went.

Nothing, of course. But Melinda had been on edge for too many hours already. Not until she'd checked every upstairs closet, the front storage room and even under her bed, was she truly able to breathe easy. Grace and Hazel were waiting for her in the living room, their eyes wide with wonder about the commotion they'd heard up above.

"Sorry I had to tear the whole house apart, girls. I've never been so glad to know that I'm alone out here."

But someone was watching as she slipped out the back door just minutes later. Melinda gasped when she spotted a hulking, mysterious shape perched on the ridge of the machine shed's roof. And then it turned its head, and she saw pointed, tufted ears outlined against the wind-driven clouds. A great-horned owl. She should feel honored to spot such a striking creature, as they weren't plentiful in the area and conducted most of their business long after sundown.

But what if this was some sort of omen? She could feel its dark eyes follow her as she scurried from the house to the garage. If only it would hoot a hello, prove it was a regular owl and not something more sinister. But there was only the wail of the wind, and Melinda peered into the backseat of her car before she opened the door. Her car rolled down the gravel, shadows lurking beyond the headlight's beams. She stared straight ahead when she passed over the bridge, only slowing for the rural crossroads before putting all her focus on the welcoming lights of the Bauers' gray farmhouse.

She pulled up next to the garage and reached for the container of cookies. Just as she got out of the car, she spotted something out of the corner of her eye. A white blur, determined and mysterious, rushed at her from behind the shed. It widened suddenly and, even under the wail of the wind, she heard an unearthly hiss.

Melinda screamed. Her arms were full, and there wasn't time to fumble with the car door. She darted around the bumper, her only thought to run for the lights of the front porch. Just as she rounded the side of the house, she heard Ed's voice somewhere behind her.

"Hector, you leave her be! Melinda, come back!"

Breathing heavily, she peered around the corner. Her eyes tried to adjust to the gathering gloom in the yard. There was Ed, right under the yard light with ... what was that thing?

A goose, she finally decided. A monstrously huge, white-feathered goose who now honked his approval of whatever Ed was fishing out of his coat pocket. As the gander gathered his treat from Ed's outstretched hand, two smaller geese waddled out of the shadows and patiently waited their turn.

Mabel stormed down the back steps just as Melinda, her knees still shaking, shuffled up the sidewalk.

"Edward Bauer!" Mabel raised her voice above the gale. "I told you those crazy birds need to be locked in at night!" Even in the faint light, Melinda saw the frustration on her friend's face. "Oh, my dear, I'm so sorry. Hector loves to ambush people. He must have frightened you half to death."

"Well, I already was, before I got here." She let out a shaky laugh. "All I saw was this shape coming at me ..."

"He chased me around the garden today. Twice. I don't know if he thought I was going to attack his lady friends, or what." Then her voice softened.

"Ed was at the Eagle River auction barn two days back, it was open-sale day. These three came through the ring, and no one made a bid. He felt sorry for them, I guess. I about died when he drove in with those borrowed crates in the back!"

Mabel motioned to the couple's dog, who wagged her tale amicably while Ed directed the feathered trio toward the barn. "Sammy and Hector have reached some sort of truce, thank goodness. But I'm afraid it's going to be a long time before things settle down around here."

"That's an understatement."

Ed soon returned. "Sorry about the ruckus. Hector's all wings, no bite, but I can see why he gave you such a scare."

Mabel shivered and wrapped her cardigan closer as they started up the walk. "Well, I guess it's dangerous out here tonight, one way or another." She glanced around the darkening yard with a wary look Melinda recognized. "Let's get inside and warm up. The chili's almost ready."

* * *

Melinda knew the coffee group's morning forum would be an interesting one. But she never expected to find special treats on the sideboard.

"Doughnuts!" Two boxes of rolls waited on the metal counter, where the coffee pot gurgled away. Not only were all of the guys planted in their usual chairs, but a weary Aunt Miriam was also among the circle.

Melinda added her coat to the hall tree and dropped her purse behind the counter. "Someone was up pretty early to get over to Swanton and back. But I guess there's a lot to chew over today, we'll need the nourishment."

"I brought them." Jerry rubbed his stubbled chin and yawned.

"Actually, I got them last night, on my way home. Or maybe it was this morning, now that I think about it. Can't really remember. It was almost one when I finally got in."

"You came off great on the late news." Auggie pointed at his friend. "Nice job putting off that news crew. I really liked that comment about how you trusted local law enforcement to do their job, uh ... what did you say?"

"Expeditiously. I don't know, it just popped out. They were camped out in the lobby of the sheriff's office when I went out to pick up sandwiches for everyone, I had to run the gauntlet to get to the parking lot."

Ed had followed Melinda home, as promised. She'd checked the locks twice, then shoved a small end table under the knob of the rarely used front entrance and leaned a folded stepladder against the inside of the back-porch door. Either would make a terrible crash in an attempted invasion. Her fortress had been secure just in time for the ten o'clock broadcast, which featured more shot-from-afar video of the scene but no new information. Jerry's ambush interview had been the highlight of the piece, in her opinion.

"You did a great job. I liked how you worked in those safety tips off the cuff. Those are basic things, but people need to be reminded of them at a time like this. And it gives them something to do, which always makes people feel better."

She was glad to see Jerry getting more comfortable with public relations, as it would serve him well as he tried to fend off Jake for the mayoral post. But then, two major events in barely two weeks would give anyone a crash course. The buzz about Delores' check had already subsided, and Melinda suspected it would be forgotten for the near future. Who would have thought such a stunning incident would be upstaged by something like this?

Bill also praised Jerry's efforts, but wondered why the news crew was eager to put Prosper's mayor on camera. The crime scene was outside the city limits, so the county sheriff was in charge. "Did you just happen to be in the wrong place at the right time?"

"We're the closest town, so I guess they were looking for an angle. And I think the sheriff was sick of talking to them, to tell you the truth. He stayed holed up in his office most of the evening."

Frank was tired, but that didn't stop him from taking a satisfying bite from his doughnut. Miriam must have been exhausted, too, as she didn't say a word as her husband chomped down on the fried treat.

"Mmm, chocolate with sprinkles, my favorite." Frank brushed some crumbs from his chin. "The sheriff pretty much bombed at that press conference yesterday. It was the perfect chance to make everyone feel safe, and he blew it. He looked like a scaredy-cat up there, blinking under those bright lights, and then he wouldn't even answer all the questions! Made that other guy handle it."

Auggie snorted. "Yeah, that was some crime-lab official, up from Des Moines. Doesn't know the first thing about Hartland County. I bet it'll take them forever to do those tests, whatever they are. Meanwhile, here we sit, just waiting for the killer to strike again."

"Oh, come on." Miriam topped off her mug. "Sure, it's scary, but whoever's to blame could be far away by now. Or even dead themselves. Word is, that body's been there for some time. I heard it's nothing more than a skeleton."

Heads snapped up around the circle, but Doc just took another sip of his coffee. Melinda stared out at Main Street, where the sun was shining as if nothing had happened. She didn't know what Miriam had heard, or where, but she'd kept her word to not spread Doc's confidence.

"Is that true?" Bill leaned in. "Do they know for sure?"

Jerry hesitated, then yanked the City of Prosper cap off his head and tossed it on the floor. "OK now, this is not an official statement from the mayor, just my two cents. Miriam's right, as far as I know. They carted the body off right away, but that's what the guys on the scene were saying."

"So why isn't that public knowledge yet?" George was exasperated. "Wouldn't it ease people's minds to know the truth?"

Auggie made a noncommittal shrug. "Maybe they don't want the hype to die down. At least, not yet. All this fuss might jog someone's memory, or even bring the killer back to the scene of the crime, now that it's being disturbed."

Everyone stared at him.

"What? Don't you watch those investigation shows? In some cases, the killer actually wants to get caught. Or, they were obsessed with their victim, and can't let it go. Sometimes they're just passing through the area. Other times, though, it's someone local. Someone you know."

He looked from one face to the next for emphasis. "And it's always the last person you'd suspect. You never know who it might be."

Melinda thought again of Bart Wildwood, but stayed silent. She'd had nothing but a hunch last night, and one based only on fear and paranoia. And this morning, between the bright sunshine and Jerry's confirmation of the facts, the situation didn't seem quite so dark. At least for now.

George wasn't too concerned. "Mary was in a state last night. She kept waking me up, saying she'd heard this or that, and would I go check, just to be sure? Finally I told her, if the axe man's coming for us, well, we've had a good long life. Might as well get some sleep."

Jerry drained his mug with one final gulp. "There's a statement coming out at ten this morning. I hear they plan to admit the remains are decades old, at least, but who knows if that will calm everyone down? They don't have anything else to go on, yet; it might be some time before we hear more. Good thing it's slow over at city hall right now, since I need to get ready for my big interview."

"With who?" Doc wrinkled his brow.

"Some guy from the Des Moines newspaper's on his way up here. Wants to do a 'mood piece,' he called it, on how such a shocking discovery affects people in the area. He wants to talk to some rural residents, too." Jerry suddenly brightened. "Melinda, would you ..."

"Nope." She took a bite of her doughnut and shook her head. "I'm staying under the radar. Ed might talk to him, though."

"Just send him down to the co-op," Auggie suggested. "It'll be the hot topic for days to come. I'm sure he'll get an earful."

"Well, I better get across the street." Jerry rose from his chair. "Mind if I take another doughnut for the road?"

"Here, take a whole box." Miriam placed one in his hands, ignoring the look of protest on Frank's face. "You paid for them. Besides, you'll need to keep up your strength."

✳ 8 ✳

The match struck the first time, and Melinda quickly touched it to the stack of kindling. The blaze caught and spread, filling the farmhouse's living room with a cheerful glow. Rain tapped at the square windows above the bookcases, and its staccato was soon matched by Hobo's toenails clicking on the oak floorboards.

"Nice and cozy, huh? Better stake your spot before the girls beat you to it."

Hobo accepted her pat of affection, then stretched out on the floral rug. But Grace and Hazel, snuggled in Melinda's overstuffed reading chair, only looked up long enough to take in the fire's gentle glow and stretch their paws.

"Looks like everyone is settled in." Chase carried a ceramic mug in each hand. "This is the perfect night to be by a fire, that's for sure." He handed one cup to Melinda. "When you can microwave cider in sixty seconds, why bother trying to warm it on the stove?"

"Works for me." Melinda took a sip. "Mmm, this is fabulous. What did you put in it? I don't have cinnamon sticks or anything fancy around here, but something ..."

"Nope. Just poured it out of the jug there in the fridge. Must be warming it up that makes it special."

"I suppose." Reaching for a fleece blanket, she joined him on the couch. "Or maybe it's just the company." She kissed him tenderly, and felt a thrill she'd almost forgotten about until he came along.

"Do you think one throw is enough?" His blue eyes sparkled with humor when they came up for air. "I mean, you always hog the covers. There's another one here ..."

"I think we can share. Besides, that lavender one? That's Grace's favorite, and she's watching you." Melinda was right; the regal calico was evaluating the situation from the reading chair.

"My apologies, Princess Grace." Chase bowed his head. "It's right where you left it." He leaned back and kicked his sock-covered feet up on the coffee table. Melinda didn't mind, because she'd already done the same. "So, what's on your agenda for this week? Is everything ready for the fall festival?"

"Just about. Nancy and I have been trying to do as much as we can, since Vicki's still pushing to get her shop ready for its grand opening, and there's only ten days left. I really need to get some things done around here this weekend, but Jerry asked me to help hand out flyers at Friday's homecoming game, and this is the only weekend Susan and Cassie can come down this fall."

"Put them to work, then. If I remember right, they enjoy helping out." Melinda's longtime friends from Minneapolis had quickly learned a trip to the country wasn't all relaxing walks along the creek and wine on the front porch.

"Oh, I intend to." She glanced out the picture window behind the sofa, and laughed.

"What?"

"There's no moon tonight; based on what Horace said, I should be cleaning, not lounging. His grandma said if you sweep in the dark of the moon, it'll keep the spiders away."

"Hmm." Chase wasn't convinced. "What if they're already here? I'm sure they are. Will they pack up their itty-bitty suitcases and hit the road?"

"Who knows? But it's worth a try. Maybe tomorrow. Of course, if I swept more often, maybe they wouldn't take up residence at all."

"This is an old house." Chase draped an arm around her shoulders. "I don't think there's anything that's going to keep the spiders out. Or the mice, for that matter. You just have to pick your battles."

"I've got traps set where Hobo and the girls can't get to them, like under the sinks. But Hazel and Grace have caught more than a few in the basement." She shuddered. "The other day, I forgot to latch the stairwell door before I left for work, and I came home to find a, shall we say, 'trophy' proudly laid out on the rug in front of the stove."

"They didn't!" Chase was laughing heartily now. "They want you to know they're earning their keep! Well, at least they aren't leaving them on your bed."

"Funny you mentioned that, as I now check it carefully before I turn in at night, and when I get up in the morning."

The wind was out of the east, and cold air suddenly brushed the back of Melinda's head. With a sigh, she rose from the couch to close the picture window's curtains. But it wasn't just the drafts she wanted to shut out. While authorities had clarified that the unearthed remains had been there for several decades, a low-level tension still ran through the rural community. Melinda rarely gave it much thought during the day, caught up in her work and chores and activities, but once the sun went down, she preferred to be safely inside with the drapes pulled against the darkness.

But she didn't share those fears with Chase. "These old windows are beautiful, but they're so drafty. We got our first shipment of plastic sheeting yesterday, and I was the first in line to stock up."

"You've got so much to do." Chase's tone was sympathetic, if a bit smug. "This is why I live in town. I mow the lawn, and that's it. Sam, who lives across the street, said he'd do my leaves again this year. Didn't Nathan do yours last fall? He always took care of them for Horace. Why don't you ask him? It'd be one less thing."

"Nathan will be in the field for a few weeks yet, and Ed and Mabel need his help more than I do. Sure, it's a lot of work, but I've taught myself to drive the lawn tractor. I'm going to have John and his son help me stack the straw around the house, but that's it." She elbowed Chase. "It's been a while since you've tossed a bale. Want to join us?"

"Sorry, babe, I think I'll pass. We moved to town when I was in high school, and I never looked back."

He pulled his side of the blanket closer and glanced around.

"This is a great house, but do you really think you'll stay out here for good? I mean, wouldn't you rather be in town?"

Melinda bristled at the hint of dismissiveness in his voice. She'd given this plenty of thought, long before they met, and made her decision. And even then, Horace insisted she wait until spring before the farm changed hands. It had been a difficult winter, one of the worst anyone around here could remember, but she'd come through it more determined than ever to make this acreage her home.

"Which town?" she finally said. "Prosper's so tiny that once you go off Main, in any direction, you can catch a glimpse of a cornfield. Karen's house backs right up to one! It's not much different than being in the country. And Swanton ... well, that seems too big."

"Too big?" Chase's eyes widened. "Ten thousand people is too big? What's that make the Twin Cities then?" Like Melinda, Chase had attended the University of Minnesota.

"Way too big. I missed the city at first, but now ..."

Chase stared at her, like he couldn't believe what she was saying.

Melinda lifted her mug of cider and tried to steer the conversation in a safer direction. "I'm glad Cassie and Susan can come down this weekend, saves me the drive up there. I haven't bothered to attend Swanton's homecoming since ... maybe sophomore year of college? That was way back, before Prosper's district merged with Swanton. Things have changed, I'm sure, but it should still be fun. I hear Prosper will become a ghost town by six or so, as everyone will be at the game."

"Meadville's homecoming is Friday, too. I usually don't go, but I thought, this year, why not? A bunch of my old friends said they're going, and ..." He was quiet for a moment. "You know, five or ten years ago, I wouldn't have been caught dead at homecoming. High school was in the past; I was too busy looking ahead. But I have to say, now it sounds sort of appealing. Wonder what's changed?"

"We're getting old, honey." She kissed him quick and pushed her end of the blanket aside. "That's all. How about I make some popcorn while you start the movie?"

* * *

October slipped in the next morning on quiet feet, bringing sunshine and calm, cobalt-blue skies. The farmers took advantage of every hour of the fine weather that week, and combines rumbled through the fields long before sunrise and far after sunset. Prosper Feed Co. was already bustling when Melinda drove past just before seven on Thursday morning, and she expected Prosper Hardware to be as busy as it was the day before.

It would feel good to settle in one of the chairs around the sideboard for a few minutes of coffee and conversation, two things she could count on to start her day off right. But George decided to shake things up a bit.

"I got a surprise in here." He set a canvas tote by his chair before he removed his jacket.

"Is it nut bread?" Auggie, who'd been clocking marathon hours at the co-op since harvest began, was suddenly much more alert. "Or apple muffins?"

George shook his head. "Now, that would be something for all of us to enjoy. This, I think, is ... well, it's an acquired taste. Melinda, why don't you see what it is?"

"Pumpkin spice creamer!" Melinda set the cannister in a place of honor on the sideboard. "George, you remembered! Now, if I had some fresh whipped cream, I could almost imagine I was back at that little coffee shop down the street from my apartment."

"Whipped cream?" Auggie rolled his eyes. "I bet we've got some of that spray stuff at home."

Melinda added several hearty shakes to her mug. "Gee, thanks, but that's not quite the same. See, they have a machine that froths it, and then they put a design ..."

Auggie snorted. "Yeah, I've heard about that. Give me six bucks, and I'd be happy to whip the cream by hand. I would bet, though, that the atmosphere here is far better than any you'd find in some snooty big-city coffee shop. At Prosper Hardware, no one has to write your name on the cup."

"We know everyone," George stated matter-of-factly as he reached for the coffee pot. "And everything that goes on in this town, past and present."

"That's for sure." Auggie nodded. "Which is why this whole dead-body thing has me stumped. Lived here all my life, and I can't think of any unsolved murders in the area."

"I still can't believe it." George took his seat. "Just think, if that crew hadn't been working out in that field, no one would be the wiser. Or what if they'd been digging just a few feet over? Might have missed it entirely."

Auggie crossed his arms. "Makes you wonder what else we don't know about. I gotta say, this whole thing? It gives me the creeps, for sure."

Melinda studied her friend's weary face. Auggie tended to be a bit dramatic, but was he really that afraid? "I didn't know you spooked so easily."

"Well, don't you find it strange that this all is happening right now, here before Halloween? And that's not the half of it. There's a super blood moon coming later this month."

"Sounds terrible." George was trying not to laugh.

"Oh, mock it all you like. But it's a rare occurrence: a full moon that's closer to Earth than usual, which makes it larger and brighter; and then one night, there'll be an eclipse that turns it red. It's something that doesn't come around all that often."

"I tell you what's really scary." George leaned in, as if sharing a secret. "My second cousin's nephew? He's a deputy.

Spent a few nights out there at the scene, right after it happened."

Prosper Hardware was still in its early-hour state of quiet anticipation, and the three of them were alone in the store.

"He said it's beyond creepy out there, in that field. And once the sun went down? Forget it! They felt like they were being watched, he said, so, into the squad car they went. It took all his courage to take a bathroom break, if you know what I mean. Just think of it, the wind whistling in the trees, maybe some fog rolling in. And a black, gaping hole, where they'd just pulled out a body ...

The metal door between the store and the wood shop let out an unearthly screech, and Auggie nearly dropped his mug.

"Frank's gotta get those hinges oiled." He wiped his plaid shirt with a paper napkin. "It's enough to make you jump right out of your skin."

Doc and Jerry were in the lead, with Bill right behind. They were laughing and talking, as sunny as the brisk morning outside, and the mood inside Prosper Hardware changed in a moment. Frank had just pulled up out front, and soon poked his head through the door. "Hey. Someone come help me with something."

Jerry hustled out to the curb, and they lifted a wooden box out of the back seat.

"What's all this?" Bill wanted to know as Frank and Jerry settled the crate on the floor.

"Well, you know my work's winding down over at city hall, I should finish up the archiving this week." Frank slipped two fingers under the box's plywood lid. "But I've found something else to occupy some of my time."

Melinda was as curious as the rest of them. What was Frank up to now?

"Aunt Miriam said you've been busy out in the garage, but it was some big secret." Miriam had also complained about the noise and the mess, but Melinda kindly left that unmentioned.

"Oh, it was. Until today. Look what I've got here!"

Frank lifted an iron weathervane from the crate, and pushed the pivoting arrow into a gleeful spin.

"This is the first one I've completed." He gave the rooster-shaped cutout an affectionate pat. "I did it in glossy black, of course, but I can customize the finish and colors. I've got a barn design in the works, and cows, pigs and birds, too."

"Frank, this is incredible." George shuffled over for a closer look. "Where did you get the iron? And those directionals are really something, all that scrollwork ..."

Frank shrugged, but was nearly bursting with pride. "The letters come from kits you can get online. The rest of the iron all came from that big salvage yard up in Meadville. I haven't done much with metalworking since high school shop class, but it's been fun to pick up the torch again."

Jerry whistled as he held up Frank's handiwork. "It's sharp, for sure. What gave you the idea?"

"All those months away from the store last year, just lounging around the house, got me hooked on those sites where everyone's making stuff. You should see what people are up to, it's just amazing."

Auggie gave a grunt of approval when the weathervane passed into his hands. Melinda caught Frank's eye and nodded her congratulations. Auggie was hard to impress.

"It's kinda charming, with that chicken and all." He held it up. "I like the base design, too. Trouble is, Frank, you've got a lot of ironwork in here, and time to boot. That adds up. Who around here's got the cash to compensate you fairly? The drought may be over, but it's going to be a lean year."

"Lots of people would, I'm sure of it." George studied it next. "The weather is probably the biggest topic of conversation around here. These tell you at a glance which direction the wind is in, which often is a sign of what's coming." George started to chuckle. "Although, I think we all know where most of the hot air comes from."

He pointed the arrow squarely at Auggie. That brought a round of hearty laughter, even from the butt of the joke.

"I know Aunt Miriam's always looking for new inventory."

Melinda looked around the store, thinking. "We could make room over there, by the branded merchandise. Wait! Even better, can we get one installed on the roof? That'd really get people talking!"

"Folk art's always popular," Doc chimed in. "People like stuff that's handmade and unique."

Frank didn't answer at first, but he was grinning. "Actually, I've got a better idea," he finally said. "I'm going to approach Vicki about selling them in her store."

Jerry said what everyone was thinking. "What's Miriam going to say about that?"

"I don't think she'd mind. After all, this is my hobby, separate from our business. And besides, I think they'll be a better fit next door."

"Not only that, but I bet you could get twice as much," Melinda said. "Vicki's shop will cater to people eager to hand over their money for something unique."

Frank nodded. "That's what I thought. Our customers want items that are useful and affordable. Or, you know, just the basics and cheap."

Doc balanced the weathervane in his lap and gave the arrow a spin. "I'd love one of these for the clinic. It'd give it some much-needed charm. I think a general barn shape would be the way to go, however. I'd better not play favorites with my clients' critters."

* * *

"I'm sorry the microwave's not here yet." Vicki motioned for Karen and Melinda to take their seats around a wooden table in the front of her soon-to-be shop. "One day at a time! The break room's been an afterthought."

"Don't worry about it." Karen reached for her sandwich. "I'm just glad to be eating lunch indoors. Some days, I eat in the truck."

Vicki had invited her friends to bring their sack lunches along for a sneak peek at Meadow Lane. Since the thick plastic had come off the storefront's windows a few weeks ago, interest in Prosper's newest business had built to a steady buzz. Her hopes were high for a successful launch, but the littlest details were still keeping her up at night.

As she looked around, Melinda was amazed at how this dreary, empty building had been transformed. "You've got a week yet, I'm sure it will all come together. The painting's done, and that would be the worst of it. Once the shelves are fully stocked, you'll be ready to go."

The cinderblock walls were now clad in beadboard, which was painted a soft gray-blue, and toile curtains with a cream-and-blue pattern softened the edges of the front windows. A sturdy laminate floor with dark wood tones now covered the chipped concrete floors.

An ornate antique bar would serve as the store's counter, and its sections had already been pieced back together on the left side of the shop. The statement piece arrived only a few days' ago, hauled halfway across the state from a Dubuque architectural salvage firm, and caused quite the stir when its delivery temporarily blocked Main Street.

Open wooden shelves sectioned off the space and provided display areas for ceramic collectibles. The table the ladies were gathered around would soon hold a selection of soaps and bath products. Reclaimed bookcases lined sections of the walls, and padded chairs invited guests (Vicki thought "customers" a little too prosaic) to sit a spell and soak up the atmosphere.

"I love those handmade cards." Karen pointed to a nearby stationery rack. "They're so unique; you can't get them at the superstore."

"A woman over by Sioux City makes those," Vicki answered around a mouthful of her salad. There wasn't time to waste. "Aren't they divine?"

A half-walled section in the back was still under construction. The snack area's iron tables and chairs remained stacked in one corner, and the cabinet that would house the coffeemakers and trays of Angie's home-baked treats was not yet painted. It wasn't the grand tearoom Vicki envisioned, but it was a start. And something little Prosper hadn't seen before.

An oversized clock from an old train depot marked the half hour they'd carved out for lunch. Melinda glanced at it and reached into the tote bag at her feet.

"My mom sent this for you to look over." The herringbone scarf was knitted in two lovely shades of rose, and Vicki and Karen gasped in delight. "And it's not just any wool. This is the first yarn from the fleece of my sheep."

Vicki wiped her hands on the paper-towel napkin in her lap. "Oh, this is just lovely! And these colors, they're so soft. Who did the wool for you?"

"There's a place about two hours from here. They clean it, spin it, dye it. It's just incredible to see. My girls gave us just enough to get started, so Mom's going to source more small-flock wool from that place when she runs out. If you're interested, she can get a few more finished before the opening. Trouble is, given the costs involved, the retail price is higher than Mom had hoped."

She winced, then named the figure Diane had quoted.

"Not a problem." Vicki shrugged. "That's fair given what such pieces go for online, or in other shops like this."

Melinda was glad for her mom's sake, but wondered if a town this small could draw enough of the right clientele to support such a markup. Vicki was positioning Meadow Lane as a destination boutique, which was certainly spot-on. Its rural location meant few people would stumble across it while just passing through.

"Tell Diane I'll take five," Vicki said confidently, "if she can have them ready by next Friday. Otherwise, three is fine for now. I won't put out large quantities at once, anyway. I want each piece to shine, not be dumped in a pile like at a discount store."

"Frank's thrilled that you want a few weathervanes." Melinda pulled an apple from her lunch bag. "I don't think he even cares if they sell. He's just so proud they'll be on display."

Vicki looked up, thinking. "I'd love to hang them from the ceiling, maybe over by the window. That would save space on the shelves, and the arrows could turn freely. I was really impressed with his craftsmanship, and it's given me another idea. It would be fun to create a barn-board backdrop somewhere, to show off some of the rustic, outdoor items."

Karen shook her head with admiration. "How are you ever going to get it all done?"

"I'll find a way. I've always wanted my own shop, and here it is." She checked the depot clock, and reached for the rest of her salad. "OK, let's run through the plans for the festival. Nancy and I chatted this morning. I think everything is nearly ready, but we're running out of time."

Melinda and Karen were about to leave when Vicki jumped out of her chair and ran behind the counter. "Oh, I almost forgot, there's something else."

Vicki always planned everything to the last detail, which made Karen and Melinda exchange curious looks. Sure enough, she came back with a secretive smile on her face and a stack of something in her hands. "So, what do you think?"

They were signs. Yard signs, in fact. "Colton for Council" was emblazoned on both sides.

Melinda didn't know what to say. "Are ... are you serious? That's great, but ... it's past the deadline to get on the ballot, and ..."

"Oh, that doesn't matter." Vicki placed the signs on the table and reverently squared their corners. "They turned out great, right? So colorful! Look, I know I don't have much of a chance this time around, or probably any at all. But I thought, might as well. Actually, it was Frank who gave me the idea."

"He did?"

"Well, not directly, but ... see, he told me how he ran last year as a write-in candidate. No one else was on the ballot, I know, so he was a shoo-in. Clarence and Lucas both have a wide base of support, and for good reason. But they're both running unopposed, and I decided it could be fun to throw my hat in the ring."

"Wait a minute." Karen raised an eyebrow. "Marketing's not my thing, so I'll defer to Melinda on this one. But this will be great exposure for your store's opening."

Vicki winked. "Exactly. In fact, that's all I care about. This year, at least."

Melinda knew Vicki was right, her chances were slim. But still ... "What if you get elected? I mean, you've already got a full plate."

"Well, then, I'll happily serve the fine community of Prosper in an official capacity." Vicki gestured out to where the bushes and trees tucked along Main Street blazed with autumn colors. "Street repairs, sidewalks, updated utilities ... there's no end to the things this town could do!"

Melinda thought for a moment. "You know, I don't think there's ever been a woman on the Prosper city council. The school board, yes, but not the council."

"I'd say it's about time." Karen raised her soda bottle in salute. "If you win, you'll make history! Doc used to be on the council, but said it caused too many hard feelings among his clients. The human ones," she quickly added. "And most of them don't even live in the city limits! But everyone always has an opinion."

"I know, I know." Vicki sighed and dropped into her chair. "Arthur said the same thing. But I told him, in a town this small, everyone has to participate."

Melinda gathered her things. "Well, you've got the right attitude about it. I wish Jerry wasn't so wound up about the mayoral race, he's driving us crazy with his worries about Jake."

"Hey, there's another opportunity." Karen reached for her jacket. "If Jake becomes mayor, there'll be a special election to fill his council seat."

Vicki groaned. "As much as I'd like to get more involved, I hope that never comes to pass."

The rattle of the cart brought Hobo out of the windbreak. Sunny and Stormy were less enthusiastic, as the metal frame made a terrible racket as it bumped and thumped over the uneven yard, its wheels crushing some of the fallen leaves.

"What do you think I'm up to now?" Hobo didn't bark an answer, but his bright eyes said he couldn't wait to find out. The cart usually stayed in the barn, where it was primarily used for moving bales of hay and straw. "I want to get one more thing done before Susan and Cassie get here. I'm sure you'll be willing to help."

Even though the sun was still bright, a crispness had crept into the late-afternoon air. The metal bleachers at Swanton High School's sports complex would be cold tonight, and any breeze pushing off the nearby fields would make it worse. She should rustle up extra hats, gloves and scarves, just in case Susan and Cassie didn't bring enough gear.

The cart screeched to a stop at the northwest corner of the house, where Melinda's new rain barrel waited on its wooden stand. The growing season was nearly over, as the first frost might arrive any night now. Time to store the orange drum in the garage until spring.

"Stand back, OK?" she told Hobo. "Dad helped me get this up here. I'm not sure how best to wrestle it down, or which way it might go."

There was still a bit of water in the bottom. She unscrewed the lowest cap, and tipped the fiberglass barrel forward so it could drain. Hobo, who always loved a drink from the hydrant by the garden, edged over and stuck out his tongue. But he didn't stay for long.

"Kinda gross, huh? It's just stale, is all. But not what you're used to."

The drum was now lightweight, but still awkward and slick under her chore gloves. She bumped it down into the grass, then unscrewed the top to let out the last of the water while she took the stand to the garage.

Melinda and the barrel were just rounding the picnic table when she heard tires rumbling on the gravel road, and Cassie's cherry-red Escalade soon slowed to turn up the lane. Hobo was elated to discover they had visitors, and Melinda tried her best to match his enthusiasm. She wanted this weekend to be a relaxing visit with old friends; she just hoped she still had two when it was over.

While Susan reached out regularly, Melinda and Cassie had only connected a few times since their disagreement that spring. Life choices had been questioned and challenged, and Melinda cringed when she recalled how their relationships with men had factored into their hard feelings. She and Cassie had been close for almost twenty years, and Susan even longer. No emotional spat was ever worth jeopardizing such valued friendships.

Of course, it should help that both women had, in at least some small way, taken the other's advice. Melinda and Chase had been dating for four months now and, according to Susan's reports, Cassie had calmed down considerably since her divorce was finalized. She was no longer going out several nights a week, and Jim had dropped his threats to seek full custody of their children. For the first time Susan could remember, Cassie seemed genuinely content without a man in her life.

And happy to see an old friend.

"Look at you, farmer girl!" Cassie pushed back her

designer sunglasses and gave Melinda an unexpected hug. "Hard at work, even on this beautiful afternoon."

"I wanted to get some things done before you arrived, since I don't want to ask the two of you to work all weekend."

Susan came around the front of the car. "I don't care what we do, as long as we can spend time together." She wrapped an arm around Melinda's shoulders. "But Cassie's hoping we won't have to scrub the chicken coop. And I have to admit, that sounds like a nasty job."

"Don't worry, there's plenty to do around here that doesn't involve manure. Maybe a little raking, harvesting the last of the garden ... oh, and there's a new little bistro in Swanton, on the square. Lunch tomorrow will be my treat."

Cassie took a deep breath of the fresh air. "Is someone burning leaves? I love that smell!"

"Someone has a brush pile going, I think." Melinda pointed to the west as her friends gathered their overnight bags. "There's just enough breeze to bring it this way."

Cassie's long dark curls had disappeared, replaced by a sharp, stylish bob, but the shadows under her eyes were gone, too.

"I'm so glad you're here," Melinda told her as they started across the lawn. "And I love your hair. You look good," she said gently. "You really do."

"Well, I'm trying to be good. I just ... went sort of crazy for a little bit, you know?"

Susan pushed her short strawberry-blonde hair behind her ears, then stooped to greet Hobo. "We're a little early, I hope that's OK. We wanted to get on the road sooner than usual, since it's harvest time and we knew the farmers would be everywhere once we turned off the interstate."

"It's usually about forty minutes after that, but it took us over an hour," Cassie chimed in. "It was an exercise in patience, for sure."

"They've got about a week to go, Auggie says. Just go on in and get settled." Old friends were like family, and Melinda didn't need to play hostess. "I'll be in when I finish chores. Hazel will be happy to see you. And Grace ... well, she might sit in your lap if you pledge to worship her forever."

The high school's parking lot was mostly full by the time they arrived. Throngs of fans, dressed in Swanton's shades of purple and white, already swarmed the bleachers on the home team's side of the field. Timber Creek's supporters were decked out in red and black, and made an admirable show across the way. The districts had been rivals for decades, and Melinda felt a nostalgic thrill as Cassie locked her vehicle and they started for the gate. Friday-night football had been a highlight of her years at Swanton High School, and tonight promised to be a fun trip down memory lane.

"I'm going to get hot chocolate, first thing." Susan shifted the blanket folded over one arm of her peacoat. "I bet they have the real stuff. You know, the reconstituted kind we drank when we were kids."

Melinda laughed. "I'm sure it's still super-sweet, just the way we remember it. That sounds good, I'd like one, too."

She checked her tote again, just to be sure none of Jerry's flyers had fallen out in the car. Melinda had designed the pamphlets herself, after working with Jerry to refine his message, and then sent them through an online company to get them printed.

Cassie checked her phone. "We've got a half hour before the game starts. This might be a good time to hand out the flyers, as people are milling about. Otherwise, we might be in the way."

"I was thinking the same." Melinda texted Jerry. "He says he's just west of the concession stand, over here to the right."

Jerry was chatting with several other retired educators. He had on his usual spirit gear, but even in the dim light on the edge of the field, something seemed different.

And then, Melinda knew what it was. Under the rim of his cap, Jerry's salt-and-pepper hair looked darker than usual. Much darker. "Hey, what ..."

"I know, I know. It looks terrible! I followed the directions on the box, even." He glanced over his shoulder, as if worried someone might overhear their conversation. "Oh, why did I even bother!"

"Why did you?" Melinda was exasperated. "There's nothing wrong with your hair! So what, you've got some gray? OK, a lot. Who doesn't? You just need to be yourself, that's what matters."

"Hmm." He stuffed his hands in his pockets. "Seems you aren't above such tricks yourself, if I remember right."

"I just have a few, it's not ..." Melinda would lose this debate, so she stopped. "I get it, Jake's younger than you."

"Twenty years younger. Twenty four, actually."

Susan was still in line at the concession stand, trying to get the hot chocolate. Cassie joined Melinda and Jerry as they moved away from the crowd gathering in front of the cinder-block building.

"What's the problem?" Cassie frowned. "You have enough flyers, right?"

Melinda shook her head. "Jerry dyed his hair, just before he came over here,"

"Highlighted it." Jerry pushed his cap down as far as it would go. "The box said ..."

Cassie reached over and lifted the brim. "Well, it's ... very dramatic. Now, I need you to listen to me." Jerry was surprised, but all ears. "As soon as the game's over, go right home and get out the laundry detergent."

"What?"

"You heard me. The best stain-fighter you've got. I've done it before, it'll work. If it's a powder, mix it with some water, form a paste. Scrub and rinse, at least twice. It'll dull the color. And then, go heavy on the conditioner."

"For now, just keep that cap on," Melinda muttered. "A stocking hat would be even better, but you don't have time to run home." She reached into her tote. "Here, take a third of these. Susan and Cassie will help me hand out the rest."

"These look really sharp. There's just one problem. How am I going to know who's here from Prosper, and not Swanton? They'll all be wearing purple and white."

"You'll just have to ask." Melinda gave him a gentle shove. "It's the perfect ice-breaker. Besides, there's only two hundred people in Prosper, and I think you know most of them. Just chat people up. Remind them you're running for mayor, and give them the flyer. Easy-peasy."

"I wish Frank could help me. But Miriam says he can't."

Melinda almost said something, then decided it wasn't worth the trouble. She and Miriam had both reminded Jerry, several times, that Frank's role on the council meant he couldn't publicly endorse one mayoral candidate over the other. It was a fine line, since everyone in town knew Frank and Jerry were longtime friends, but Frank had to stay out of the fray.

The hot chocolate arrived, as well as a coffee for Jerry. Susan waved off his offer to pay her back, and he soon disappeared into the crowd. Susan worked at one of Minneapolis' most-respected marketing firms, and the small-town politics surrounding this situation had her concerned.

"I'm sure Jerry loves the help, but should you really be doing this? You don't own Prosper Hardware, but you're the face behind the counter now that Frank's basically retired. I just hope this doesn't backfire on the business. As they say, the optics aren't so great."

"I wondered about that, too," Cassie admitted. "Working behind the scenes is one thing; this is as public as it gets."

"I know, I know." Jake's pool of followers seemed rather small, but its members were die-hard and vocal.

She handed a large stack of flyers to each of her friends, and kept the smallest bundle for herself. "Why don't I take the crowd hanging around the north end zone? They look younger, less likely to care about such things."

Most of the flyers were distributed before kickoff, and Cassie and Susan said their inquiries were met with overwhelmingly positive responses. "People really like Jerry." Cassie punctuated her observations with a definitive nod. "So many commented on how fair he is, that he keeps the council on track and helps them build consensus on tough issues."

"Being a retired principal is in his favor," Susan reported. "Several people said they knew him personally, from when they were in school, or because of their kids. Educators are generally respected and admired. But then, you said this Jake guy is a teacher, too."

"He's the phys ed instructor and a wrestling coach. He's a loudmouth, but he plays it well. The people who like to stir up trouble, be the dissenting voice in the crowd, love his approach."

"Is he really that big of a threat?" Cassie wondered. "Does he have the numbers to win? I would think the community-center debate should work in Jerry's favor. If he can get the council to come up with a plan, shouldn't that cement his re-election?"

"I would think so. But Prosper's so tiny. All it would take is for every Jake supporter to show up at the polls, and too many of Jerry's to stay home, and who knows what might happen?"

The score remained close, with Timber Creek holding a narrow lead at halftime. Both sides of the field were fired up, as bragging rights for another year were at stake. Swanton's marching band performed several numbers, then ended with a rousing rendition of the district's fight song that had supporters on their feet and singing along. When it was time to announce the homecoming court, Melinda and her friends gave up their bleacher seats and hurried down to the wire line to support Nancy, since her son was a senior and one of the king candidates. Amy and Paul Westberg soon joined them.

"It's not the end of the world if he's not chosen," Nancy told her friends. "I just hope he doesn't end up disappointed."

"High school's just the start of life," Amy said. "But at that age, everything is a big deal, right?" Everyone nodded and rolled their eyes.

The members of the court stepped out on the field. Melinda was glad the crowd cheered for all of the boys and girls, since in the end, this was merely a popularity contest. Some of the king candidates, like Nancy's son, were in their football uniforms, and the rest wore dress slacks and sensible sweaters. The girls, however, had cranked the glamour up to ten.

"Look at that one, in the teal dress," Cassie hissed. "I hope she doesn't have to bend over, we're all going to get a show!"

"When did the dresses get that short?" Susan wondered. "I would have been grounded for leaving the house looking like that. And no coats! It's cold out here!"

Several faculty members, all of them wearing Swanton spirit gear, soon joined the court on the field. Melinda and Nancy groaned.

Susan leaned over. "Let me guess, Jake's out there. Which one is he?"

"On the far left, short dark hair." Nancy pointed him out. "I know he's on the homecoming advisory committee this year, but ... oh, I hope no one hands him the mike."

Melinda glanced at the scoreboard. Halftime was ticking away. "If he doesn't know when to shut up, and embarrasses himself, that'll make Jerry look that much better."

The principal made a few remarks, then handed the program off to the committee chair, who was one of the science teachers. She'd barely finished her opening comments when Jake snatched the microphone.

Amy sighed. "Here we go."

Melinda searched the crowd for Jerry, but didn't find him. She hoped he was at the concession stand, or somewhere else he couldn't publicly react to what was about to happen. Frank and Miriam were in the stands with Diane and Roger, and she saw Miriam put her hands over her face.

"Thanks, everyone, for coming." Jake flashed his trademark grin. "Homecoming is a special night. It's a time to look back, remember all the good times, and meet up with old friends."

Jake stepped out of the cluster of teachers and positioned himself in front of the court. He was just getting warmed up.

"He always does this," Nancy explained to Cassie and Susan. "He just can't help himself."

"But homecoming isn't just about the past. It's also a time to appreciate how fortunate our school community really is. And that includes our top-notch sports teams!"

That brought a roar of approval from the home crowd. Melinda stifled a laugh. The football squad wasn't exactly having a championship season, but Jake knew what people wanted to hear.

"We also have a winning team of teachers at every level of the district, from kindergarten to those leading the advance-placement courses at the high school."

"I thought he was running for city council, not school board," Cassie whispered to Melinda.

"And our district needs to stay strong. We need to deliver a solid education to all students, at all levels, while keeping property taxes low." That brought another wave of cheers from the crowd.

Jake nodded and grinned. He was on a roll, and ignored the grim faces of his fellow educators as well as the homecoming candidates' anxious smiles.

"That promise needs to extend to our district's communities as well. Low taxes, good roads and updated infrastructure benefit everyone, and add value ..."

"Who's gonna be king and queen?" someone shouted from the bleachers.

Melinda felt the tension rolling off Nancy. She was trying to catch Jake's eye, implore him to stop for his own good.

"Come on, announce the winners!" one man yelled from farther down the wire. The ripple of applause in the bleachers soon ebbed away into jeers and a few sarcastic whistles.

"Quit stalling!"

"Halftime's more than half over! Get on with it!"

The principal marched over to Jake, who was now rambling on about how community spirit and team spirit were one and the same, and wrenched the microphone from his hands.

"Thanks, Jake, for that ... inspiring overview." Snickers were now echoing through the crowd. "And now, the moment you've all been waiting for. It's time to recognize our homecoming court!"

Nancy's son wasn't named king, but she was too incensed about Jake to give it much thought.

"I can't believe this!" she fumed. "Sure, I get along well with Jerry, but I'm all for other people wanting to serve. I just wish someone else had stepped up. If Jake gets in, he's going to drive me crazy."

Susan tipped her chin at two women walking past. They were laughing at Jake, mocking his attention-grabbing speech. "See? Give that guy enough rope, and he'll find a way to hang himself with it."

"I'd say the score is: Jerry, one; Jake, zero." Cassie reached for the rest of the flyers. "Let's get these passed out before the players get back on the field. Although I have to say, after that debacle, Jerry may not need our help to win."

Swanton pulled out a victory in a nail-biter fourth quarter, and the ladies found themselves energized by the home crowd's high spirits.

"Normally I'd be ready for bed about now," Susan admitted as they started for the gate, "but after that? I'm wide awake."

Melinda gave her friends a sly grin. "Well, I'd thought of somewhere we could go after the game, just for a drink or two. But I didn't know ..."

"I'm in!" Cassie crowed. "I'll stick to soda, but we have to go! Girls, do you remember what it was like in high school? The end of the game was just the beginning of the fun."

"Oh, yes," Susan said. "My hometown is so small, we couldn't really cruise the strip. We had to drive to the next town over for that. Or we ended up in a field somewhere, with a case of beer somebody acquired under suspicious circumstances."

"Swanton doesn't have a glittering nightlife," Melinda warned her friends. "We're a million miles from Minneapolis. But there's a cozy bar just a few blocks off the square. No live music," she added apologetically, "but ..."

"Sounds perfect to me." Cassie unlocked the car. "Somewhere warm and quiet is much more my speed these days."

* * *

The small bar was fairly crowded, but they scored a booth along the far wall and settled in. As they warmed their hands and gave their waitress their drink orders, more revelers streamed through the door.

"Looks like an informal alumni reunion," Susan observed. "But it's homecoming, so people like to come back for that. Melinda, see anyone you know?"

"I don't think so. Most of the people I was close to in high school moved away, too. I met up with a few friends last Christmas, when they were still in town, but that's about it." She picked up the menu.

"I heard they have great food here, not just pretzels and peanuts. Oh, wow, chili cheese fries!"

"Let's do it." Susan reached for her purse. "If I take an antacid now, it'll kick in just in time." She shook her head, but she was smiling. "How sad is that? Chili cheese fries and a beer, and I'm living on the edge. But you know, I don't miss high school, as fun as it was."

"Me, neither." Cassie leaned over the table. "And, as we know, you make special friends past high school, too. Ones you just might have forever."

Melinda turned to Susan. "Sophomore year in college; I can't believe how long ago that was! And Cassie, I remember the first day we all worked together, when you asked me to invite you to lunch so you wouldn't have to eat alone."

"And that was that!" Cassie smiled. "Oh, we thought we had the world on a string. We had real jobs, ones we had to dress up for. Some of us even had our own apartments, no more roommates. I felt so grown up."

"Those were great times." Susan sipped her beer, which came in a bottle. "You know, I don't think I've had this brand in at least fifteen years. Maybe it's not as bad as I remember."

Melinda took a swig of hers. "Oh, it is." She pointed her bottle at a booth across the way. "But if you want to order it in bulk, they'll bring you a dozen in a bucket packed with ice."

While Susan and Cassie debated if they needed one order of fries or two, Melinda slipped out of the booth. The football game was fun, but the restrooms were tolerable at best. Had they always been that gross? Maybe she'd become picky over the years. Or maybe, she was just getting old. Either way, she hoped the bar's bathroom was in better shape.

She didn't have to wait long and, thrilled to find hot water flowing at the sink, was smiling as she made her way back to their table. It took so little these days to make her happy, and the evening was certainly looking up.

"Melinda! Melinda, is that you?"

She turned this way and that. The bar was packed now.

"Melinda, over here!"

Jen Fuller, who was Jen Collins these days, was in a crowd over by the pool tables. They'd been in debate together in high school. Melinda couldn't easily recall all of her extended social circle from back then, but Jen came into Prosper Hardware on a regular basis. She worked as a nurse, and her husband, Steve, was a sheriff's deputy. Since they lived in Prosper, he often drew the assignment to drive through town a few times a day, since the little community didn't have its own police department.

"Hey, Jen!" Waves of nostalgia had been washing over Melinda all night, and she greeted the couple warmly. "Hi, Steve! It's been crazy for you lately, I bet."

"It's been nuts. First suspicious death in over three decades. Well, I'm off for another. Honey, you want one?"

Jen declined, and Steve started to edge through the crowd. "I'm letting him blow off some steam tonight. He's been putting in some terrible hours lately."

As they chatted, Melinda began to sense someone was staring at her. The bar was crowded, and she brushed it off. They stepped to the side, trying to stay out of the traffic lane, but the feeling persisted.

And then, she saw him. Over in the corner, with another crowd of revelers. He looked older, of course. Why wouldn't he? But that face. Melinda would know it anywhere.

Jamie Kellerton, her first serious boyfriend. They broke up at the start of senior year, and avoided each other as much as possible after that. She hadn't seen him since ... the summer after graduation? No, wait, she'd run into him somewhere, when she was home from college. Maybe at the grocery store. It was all so long ago, she couldn't even remember.

At one time, he'd been a major part of her life. Sadly, maybe even its center. But they'd been young, and ...

He was coming her way. What would she say? Thank goodness for Jen, who had her back to Jamie and was telling Melinda about her kids. At least she wouldn't have to face him alone.

"Hey, I thought that was you." Jamie's eyes were as blue as ever, but there were light flecks in his brown hair, especially at the temples. And he had a beard, even though it was short and well-groomed. Those lines around his eyes; when had that happened?

Then Melinda caught herself. She had them, too.

"Hey, Jamie." She managed a smile.

Jen caught on quick. "Oh, I bet it's been a while. Well, I might just ..."

Melinda gently pinched her arm. Jen stayed.

"So, what are you doing these days?" Melinda tried to keep up the friendly charade. She'd forgotten, or actually, had made herself forget, how it all went wrong. Jamie had claimed to have the flu, then went to a party without her and made out with another girl from their class. Or, from what Melinda later heard but Jamie always denied, did much more than that.

"I'm still running my bike shop, over by the fairgrounds." Jamie shrugged, but she could see he was proud of his business. He'd gotten his first motorcycle just a few months before they'd started dating.

"That's great." She stalled for time and hoped for an easy exit. Jen was wide-eyed and silent. "So, you're here with some friends, then?"

"Sure am." He tipped his head toward the corner. Melinda saw a few faces that might be familiar, but couldn't be sure. "But I'm not here with anyone, not really. I'm divorced."

That wasn't what she meant. Not at all. What game was he playing? In a second, she was incensed. He'd always been full of himself. Why hadn't she been able to see that? She could have saved herself so much heartbreak.

"I moved back from Minneapolis last year." She wasn't about to dignify his comment with a response. "I'm working at Prosper Hardware, and I bought a little acreage."

"I always knew you'd make something of yourself, find a way out of this town." Jamie took a swig from his beer, but then he smirked.

Melinda felt the sting of what he didn't say: She'd done well for herself. But then, she'd ended up back here, just like him.

"I have to go." She patted Jen on the arm before she turned away. "Nice to see you."

By the time she made it back to her booth, her temples were throbbing and her hands were shaking. Suddenly, she was so angry. She wished they'd never set foot in this bar. The humiliation was back, as sharp as ever.

"What happened!" Cassie stood up. "Did one of those rednecks grab your butt or something? This place is packed, but that's no reason to ..."

"No, no." She dropped into the booth, and told them everything.

"The nerve!" Susan set her bottle down with an angry thud. "Forget him! He did you a favor, way back when. If he hadn't cheated, if you'd stayed together, would you have gone away to college like you did?"

"You're right. I'd like to think so. But who knows?"

Cassie patted Melinda's hand. "Hey, you know what? He sounds like a jerk, but I actually have so much to thank him for. I can't imagine what my life would be like without either of you in it."

"I thought it would be fun to go to the homecoming game." Melinda put her hands over her face. "You know, step back in time for a while. But I didn't expect this."

"Nostalgia is a dangerous thing." Susan shook her head. "The bad sometimes shows up, one way or another, not just the good." She pushed the platter of chili cheese fries toward Melinda. "Here, soothe yourself with some of these. They're fantastic."

* 10 *

Lizzie coughed and sputtered, and Melinda gave the old truck a little gas, just in case. The tractor ahead of her was pulling two gravity wagons heaped with corn, and she was trying to maintain a safe distance. Lizzie was ancient, but she didn't like to idle for very long.

"Easy, girl. Harvest is the only time there's a traffic jam in this town. We'll get the oats and chicken feed, and get home."

One of Auggie's seasonal helpers finally waved her through the co-op's entrance and to the left, away from the line snaking toward the scales. As she eased the truck into one of the few open spots in the gravel lot, Melinda silently thanked Horace for insisting she take Lizzie as part of the acreage's sale.

Her hatchback could only haul two fifty-pound bags at a time, but Lizzie's spacious flatbed meant Melinda wouldn't have to come back to the co-op until harvest was over.

Prosper Feed Co. always put her in a good mood, even when it was crowded. There was that comforting, yeasty smell the moment she opened the door, and the rotating gaggle of gossiping farmers lounging by the corner coffee pot. The aisles were packed today, but Dan, Auggie's assistant manager, still found a moment or five to shoot the breeze.

Melinda ripped a preprinted sheet from the thick pad on the counter, and started to write down her carry-out feed order. Pebbles soon jumped up to supervise. "Hey, girl." The sleek gray cat batted at the pen, then rolled over for a belly rub. "It's busy today, huh?"

Just as Melinda completed her list, Auggie popped out of the office. "Hey, I didn't know you were coming in. What do you need?"

"Everything, and lots of it. I hope to not show my face in here again until harvest is over. This place is a madhouse."

Auggie was on his way over to chat, but he was stopped by first one man and then two others. All of them wanted to debate prices and pick Auggie's brain about the futures market. He kept smiling and sidestepped most of the men's complaints and questions, but there was an uneasiness Melinda had first noticed about a week ago. He'd been quieter than usual at the store in the mornings, and she'd chalked it up to the full-throttle pace of harvest. But was something else going on?

When Auggie finally made it to the counter, he leaned on it for a moment. His brown eyes were weary behind his thick-framed glasses, and he seemed to be turning something over in his mind.

"Hey, do you have a minute?" His voice was strangely cheerful given his obvious exhaustion.

"Sure. I'm already going to get home later than usual. But I think the bags of feed will smooth over any hard feelings."

Auggie surprised her by suddenly lowering his voice. "There's something I want to talk to you about." He took a deep breath. "I'd really appreciate it."

Whatever it was, it had taken Auggie a great deal of courage to ask her for help. Her mind raced with questions, but there were too many farmers gathered around to ask them.

"Absolutely." She picked up her ticket. "This can wait."

Melinda assumed they would go into the office. But Auggie aimed for the side door instead.

"Out here," he said over his shoulder, suddenly in a hurry. "Let's go."

It was a gloomy afternoon, and a gust of sharp wind hit them as soon as they stepped outside. The roar of the tractors and trucks idling in line assaulted Melinda's ears, and she had to shout over the racket. "Auggie, you're scaring me! What's going on? Are you OK?"

His only answer was a flick of the wrist, urging her to follow him across the gravel. When they reached the last row of grain bins on the west edge of the lot, he finally stopped.

There was nothing beyond the bins but miles of empty fields. Their brisk walk had Auggie panting with exertion.

"What are we doing way out here?" She pulled her sweatshirt's hood up against the chill. "Your jacket's not warm enough; why didn't you grab a cap? It's damp, and no day to be ..."

"Shhh. Wait." He pointed. "Over there. Do you see it?"

Behind the last two bins was a ramshackle shed. Its rolling door sagged on a rusted metal track, and there were cracked panes in its dirty windows. Unruly weeds, now brown and dying, slumped along the cinderblock foundation.

Melinda couldn't figure out what they were looking for. And then, there it was.

A white cat with striking black patches in its fur was watching them from behind the far corner of the shed. Its coat was long but far from luxurious, and its white paws, underbelly and chest were scraggly and stained with dirt. The cat's cautious face carried a unique mark: a black spot right under its nose, as if it sported a moustache. The distinctive feature was a charming quirk, but the fear in the poor feline's golden eyes told Melinda this animal was in distress.

"Oh, no, look at him! I mean, I assume it's a male. Here, sweet kitty."

The cat vanished as soon as she took a step. Her hands were cold, and she stuffed them in her pockets. "How long has he been out here? The poor thing! I get the feeling he's come a long way."

Auggie didn't answer at first, and she was stunned to see the tears in his eyes.

"Come a long way? Yeah, I believe he has." Auggie's chin trembled. "Do you think it's possible for animals to ... to travel through time?"

Her mouth fell open. The cat hadn't shown himself again, but she knew he was still there, behind the shed.

"I want to tell you something. You gotta promise, now, that you won't tell the guys. Tell anyone, for that matter." He shot her one of his looks, and she nodded. None of this made sense, but Auggie was clearly serious.

"Just let me get this out, OK? Don't interrupt." He crossed his arms over his chest, maybe out of defensiveness as well as to keep warm.

"When I was a kid, a little boy, I got a cat for my birthday. I'd wanted one, for so long, and Mom and Dad kept putting me off. We already had a dog, you see, but I wanted a cat so bad."

Auggie had always insisted he wasn't "one of those cat people," even though he'd been a loyal companion to many dogs over his lifetime. So when Melinda convinced him to help at the spay clinics, and he was adopted by Mr. Checkers and Pebbles, everyone had a good laugh and chalked it up to Auggie softening in his advancing years. That, and the co-op having a serious rodent problem.

"So, I got this kitten." Auggie sounded far away. "The cutest thing, black and white, fluffy. And he had a little patch on his face, just like ..."

He pointed toward the shed. As if on cue, the cat showed itself again. A chill ran down Melinda's spine.

"But that was, what, fifty years ago? You can't ..."

"Listen. I named him Chaplin. Charlie Chaplin, see, for the moustache. We did everything together. He slept on my bed, followed me around the yard, even rode in a little wagon. We were best friends. Then one night, a few years later, he didn't come in. I couldn't sleep, I was just sick with worry. In the morning, Dad had something to tell me at breakfast: Chaplin had been hit by a car, the paperboy found him. He was gone."

Auggie was crying now, tears running down his wind-chapped cheeks.

"I'm so sorry. I didn't know."

"That's not all of it." He glanced at the cat, who was still as a statue, its golden eyes fixed on Auggie's tear-stained face. "I cried and cried. Mom wanted to get me another cat. I said no. No one could take Chaplin's place! And then, a few weeks later, I was walking home from school and came around the corner. We lived over on Second and Oak, by the way, and ... there he was."

"Who?" Melinda was afraid she knew the answer.

"Chaplin." Auggie wiped his face with the back of his hand. "Chaplin came back."

A strange pattern emerged over the next decade, one so astounding Melinda could hardly breathe.

The second Chaplin lived a few years, just like the first, but was fatally wounded by a mean dog from the other end of the block. A month went by; another eerily similar stray showed up on the Kleinsbachs' back stoop. This one had seven happy years with his family, then died in his sleep without warning.

Only a few weeks passed before a neighbor knocked on the door, carrying a half-grown, black-and-white kitten they'd found wandering the alley. Long hair, moustache, the whole works.

They already had three cats at home; would the Kleinsbachs be kind enough to take the poor thing in? And look, he's so similar to Auggie's other cat! How strange ...

"We had three years, that time; but he found some poison one day. I don't know where the stuff came from, but that's what the vet said. Chaplin was suffering, it was too late, we did what we had to do."

Auggie was sobbing now. Melinda wrapped an arm around his trembling shoulders and guided him toward the nearest storage bin, trying to get him out of the cold wind. When she turned back, the cat had vanished again.

"So, that time, how long until ..."

"That's just it." Auggie put his hands over his face. "I waited, and I waited. We all did. How long would it be this time? When would he come back? But he didn't. He never did! All I wanted was for him to come back again. Why didn't he? What did I do wrong?"

"Auggie! You didn't do anything. He ... I mean the cats, they just ..."

"No!" He shook his head. "No. There was only the one. All of them, they were one and the same. I'll swear on it. That face! And here he is, after all this time. Where has he been? Why is he back now?"

Melinda didn't have an answer for any of it. Maybe it was all a coincidence, or maybe there was something going on that defied logic.

But one thing was clear, at least: This mysterious creature was clearly a living, breathing cat. It wasn't a ghost, an apparition, or a trick of the eye. It needed help, and something had to be done.

"This cat's had a hard life." Or maybe several. "But there's shelter in that shed, it's not much, but there's mice all over the place. Any stray would linger here, if they could. How long has he been around?"

"Five days." Auggie sniffled. "I've been bringing him food and water, but he won't come to me, I've tried."

"Well, maybe that's the answer." Melinda almost laughed with relief. "I'd say that's a good sign he's not Chaplin, then. You know Gertrude feeds those strays behind her house. It's not too far from here, if they follow the railroad tracks. There's always kitties coming and going. What are the odds he belongs there? Maybe this is all just some sort of ... misunderstanding."

Auggie said nothing, and Melinda sensed he didn't want there to be an easy answer. Only the one he desperately wanted to be true. "I'd know him anywhere, like I said. All these years, and I'd know him anywhere."

Melinda gently steered Auggie toward the main building. The rush of harvest went on around them, shouts and laughter and diesel exhaust, the groan of the scales and the roar of the grain dryers that ran all day, all night.

"You've been working too hard. Not enough sleep, too much stress. It's your busiest time of year, and it's been a hard one, as you've said. Whatever is going on, promise me you'll try to throttle things back a bit. Can you go home early, get some rest?"

"Rest? We've got at least a week yet! And Dan ..."

"Can manage on his own, with all the extra help."

"Fine. But I'm not crazy, dammit. I thought you, of everyone I know, might understand. Say you believe me."

"OK." She nodded. "OK, I believe you. Now, let's get inside where it's warm."

Auggie's face was red and his eyes were puffy. Dozens of sharp-eyed farmers were waiting in line with their loads, and several more were loitering at the counter inside. Every one of them would see Auggie was upset, and there would be questions. And gossip. Melinda nudged him to the back door.

"Here's what we need to do. You go straight into the office and compose yourself. I'll ask Dan where the cat food is, and I'll take some more out there. I'll tell him you feel sorry for the cat, and you got a little upset."

"But not that it's Chaplin."

"No, none of that." It wouldn't do any good to debate Auggie's assumption. It was clear his mind was already made up. "Dan's a cat person, he'll understand. And if anyone else notices, they might rib you a bit, but they never have to know what's ... well, what's going on."

Auggie's blotchy face raised a few eyebrows. But Dan fell in line, just as Melinda had hoped.

"Yeah, he's been worried about that new one out there." Dan rubbed his coppery beard. "We're probably feeding raccoons, too, putting kibble in that shed, but who cares? We've already got two cats, what's one more? I'd like to see him move inside before winter, if he decides to stay. But then, some of them are born to ramble. Maybe this is just one stop on his journey, you know?"

Melinda only nodded. If Auggie's hunch was correct, Dan was closer to the truth than he realized.

Then Dan laughed. "Can you believe Auggie? Never saw him give one whit about any cat, not before Mr. Checkers. And now, look at him! These two have him wrapped around their paws, and another one's trying to move in! The cat food's in that tub over there. I'll ring your order up while you're gone."

Melinda filled plastic containers from the kitchen with kibble and water and started across the lot. There was no sign of the cat. The old shed's door was still cracked open, and she pushed it wide enough to slip inside.

Chaplin, as she already thought of him, was simply a cat in need of help, but she was still relieved when she couldn't spot him in the gloom. The shed was packed with junk and dust, and she sneezed. She found the other dishes, swapped them for the full ones, then looked around and listened.

He was in here now; she felt like she was being watched. And then she spotted two golden orbs behind a pile of rusted metal buckets.

"I don't know who you are," she whispered, "or why you've really come. But that old man you've seen around here, the one outside just a few minutes ago? Inside that gruff shell is a sad little boy. I don't know if it would be better for you to stay or to go, but please, he can't get hurt again."

She rolled the door back, leaving a slim gap for the cat to slip through, and hurried back to the office. The afternoon was waning, and heavier clouds were piling up on the horizon. All the feed needed to be unloaded before the rain came. But now, she had one more stop to make.

"Gertrude surely has seen him. It's maybe three blocks to the co-op, a straight shot down the tracks. I bet he's one of her boys. He has to be."

Melinda had visited Gertrude's colony several times, between delivering bags of food from Prosper Hardware and escorting the cats to the community clinics. She'd never noticed one with such striking markings, but surely ...

"Black and white, you say? With a little moustache?" Gertrude frowned and closed her ratty sweater against the chill, then picked up the orange cat mewling at her feet.

"And fluffy, longhaired."

Gertrude sighed. "No, dearie, I don't have anyone quite like that. The closest would be Moo, and she's right there, up on the porch." Moo's black-and-white coat was too short, and she bore no other resemblance to the mysterious Chaplin.

"But ..." Melinda grasped for an answer. "Anyone in this neighborhood have a cat like that? Maybe he's lost, or ..."

"Not as far as I know. One like that? He'd stand out for sure. Oh, the poor baby, someone probably dumped him out. And the weather's turning, too." She hugged the orange cat close, and there were tears in her eyes. "Tell you what, if he shows up here, I'll give you a call."

* * *

The bags of feed made it inside the barn just before the skies opened. Melinda ran back to the house for her wet-weather gear, and spent a miserable half hour doing chores in the cold rain. The warmth of the kitchen felt good when she came in, and the chicken simmering in the slow cooker was comforting, too. It was a little early in the season to turn on the furnace, but it was the perfect night for a fire.

The flames dancing in the hearth not only took the edge off the chill, but their bright glow made the house feel cozy, too. She tried to focus on transferring the chicken and broth to the stove, and adding the noodles she'd rolled out that morning. There was fruit salad, and a few cookies still in the jar. It was the perfect supper for such a damp, windy night, but Melinda's heart remained heavy as she feasted at the kitchen table. Her thoughts kept traveling to Chaplin, huddled in a dirty corner of that rundown shed. And to Auggie, and the grief he'd carried for decades.

She couldn't even escape her unease by diving into a good book. The book club's latest selection was meeting its reputation for being a riveting read, but its themes were just too close to home tonight. The story unfolding on the pages was filled with deceased animals coming back to life ... in the most-terrifying of ways.

"I can't believe Sam picked this one," she told Grace, who had grudgingly made room for Melinda in the reading chair. "Guess he thought it would be great fun, huh? A good scare just in time for Halloween?" She snapped the book closed and added it to the top of the bookcase behind her, out of sight. "I've had enough scares for one day, no thanks."

Hobo was sprawled out on the couch, snoring lightly, one of his front paws twitching in his sleep. She wondered what he was dreaming about. Hazel camped on the rug in front of the fireplace in a Sphinx-like pose, her golden eyes staring into the flames.

What did she see? Or, like Hobo, were her thoughts far away, somewhere Melinda couldn't follow?

What if it's true? Auggie was so certain Chaplin had come back to him. Said he'd know him anywhere.

Melinda's throat tightened and her eyes brimmed full. Now that she was home, alone with only her animals and the rain running down the farmhouse's windows, she could reflect on her own loss.

Oreo had left her so suddenly. His coat had been black, with white feet and a bit of white on his chest and stomach. It was a common pattern, yet it was all his own. She understood what Auggie had said. She'd know Oreo anywhere, too. He'd been gone less than two years. But if she lived to be ninety, Melinda would never forget him.

The tears were rolling down her cheeks now, and she didn't try to brush them away. Oh, what she wouldn't give for a few more moments with him! What if she'd arrived home sooner, if they'd made it to the emergency room ten minutes earlier? Could they have saved him? And the seizure ... had she missed something, some warning sign? What if ...

"Stop. You have to stop this." She put a hand over her face. Grace stared up at her, her green eyes glowing in the low light. "It won't bring him back. He's gone."

But then ... she'd seen Oreo, she was sure of it. The very next night, she woke up suddenly in the wee hours and, overcome with grief, was unable to fall back asleep. She padded down the hall, aiming for the kitchen and a glass of water, then spotted a familiar, shadowy figure right where Oreo's dishes had once been.

There was no doubt in her heart, either that night, or this one. Oreo had simply looked at her, and she'd felt this wave of love rolling toward her, there in the dark hallway. And then she blinked, and he was gone.

Auggie was wracked with guilt. Melinda understood that, too.

She felt it keenly now, and not only about her lingering heartache over Oreo's death.

I thought you, of everyone I know, might understand, Auggie had said. *Say you believe me.*

She had, of course, but she could have said so much more. Although Oreo had arrived in her mind at that very moment, she'd kept the incident to herself. Somehow, she had to share it with Auggie. It would ease some of his pain. And maybe hers, as well.

The saddest part of Auggie's story was that an indoor-only home would have prevented many, if not all, of the events that triggered so much grief and loss. But that was decades ago, and times were different. Cats were allowed to do as they pleased, and their kingdoms expanded far beyond the safety of their family's home. Even now, as much as she loved Sunny and Stormy, Melinda knew they would never be content living inside the house.

Hobo enjoyed rambling about the farm, too, and had always had his freedom. She couldn't imagine trying to curtail that now. As long as her dear boy stuck close to home, and came in when she asked, she'd do her best to set her worries aside and put his happiness first.

And right now, he seemed perfectly content.

Hobo was still fast asleep, his fuzzy head perfectly positioned on one of her chic throw pillows. As she watched the firelight dance over his face, her mind turned to another beloved pet who'd passed away.

Wilbur had been so certain the dog in the video was Tippy. Horace admitted that Tippy and Hobo bore a passing resemblance to each other, but Melinda hadn't given it much thought, too distracted by learning there was a farm-dog cemetery in the windbreak. But now ...

Hobo's arrival at the farm had been a mysterious one. When Horace and Wilbur discovered a small pup under the lilac trees one spring morning, they called everyone in the neighborhood. No one admitted to leaving the little dog in the Schermanns' yard. He'd just ... appeared.

Just like Chaplin.

No, it wasn't the same thing. Not at all. If someone in the area had dumped a dog, they'd never admit it. And it was just as likely, probably more so, that the offender had no ties to the neighborhood. But Melinda thought again of Tippy, of her grave out behind the chicken house, and Wilbur's instant recollection despite his dementia and advanced age.

Of what Auggie had said about Chaplin, and what she knew to be true of Oreo.

I would know him anywhere.

A gust of wind rattled the metal storm windows. Melinda shivered, and pulled her fleece blanket closer around her shoulders. Grace, annoyed with her nest being disrupted, jumped down to join her sister on the hearth. Melinda leaned over and petted Hobo until he stirred, until his brown eyes focused on her face.

"I know you're Hobo. You're your own dog, and you're one in a million. Tippy was too, I guess, and I think she'd be glad to know she was never forgotten. Chaplin would have felt the same. Or, maybe he feels that way now. Or ... oh, does it really matter? That cat needs love, and Auggie has plenty to give. That's what's important. Some things defy logic. Some mysteries aren't meant to be solved."

The mantel clock chimed, and Melinda jumped. It tolled eight times, marking the arrival of a new hour. After the last note died away, she sighed and reached again for her book. The club's meeting was less than a week away, and she was only halfway through.

Grace and Hazel were still as statues on the floral rug, their eyes trained on the fire popping in the hearth. "Girls, I need to ask you something: They say cats have nine lives. Is that true?"

Neither acknowledged her question. And what they saw inside the flames, Melinda couldn't begin to guess. Maybe it was better if she didn't know.

* 11 *

The brim-full bucket of water threatened to pull Esther off balance, but she still hummed a happy tune. Prosper's first-ever fall festival would kick off in under an hour, and her high spirits were matched by the bright apples screen-printed on her sweatshirt.

"Coming through! Can't have a bobbing contest without water." The two women at the counter gave Esther a wide berth, and a man studying the rack of work boots just inside the front door offered to give her a hand.

"Thank you kindly, but I can manage." A galvanized wash tub waited next to the sideboard, a generous sheet of plastic already under it to protect the store's oak floors. Just as she emptied her bucket, Frank came down from the office with a gigantic bowl of gleaming, washed apples.

"How much is enough?" Esther asked him. "Will two more buckets do, or will we need a third?"

"Let's do three. The little kids won't have to lean over so far. We certainly don't want anyone to lose their balance and topple in."

"There's plenty of towels, if they do." Aunt Miriam breezed by with a stack of fall linens in shades of rust, brown and gold. "Not these, of course, as they're the fancy ones I ordered special for today. Melinda, what do you think? Should I display them at the register, or the first end cap?"

"Maybe the end cap." Melinda gave the second woman her change, and came around the counter to help. "We've got those extra bags of candy stacked on the counter already."

Prosper Hardware was always packed on Saturdays, but the store was charged with anticipation this bright, cool morning. It was one of those picture-perfect fall days, and Melinda hoped this new event would prove to be as wonderful as the weather.

The ribbon-cutting for Meadow Lane was set for ten o'clock, and several other activities were planned throughout the day. In addition to apple-bobbing at Prosper Hardware, children could step across Main Street to carve pumpkins at the library. The Watering Hole was getting in on the fall fun, too, selling fresh caramel apples along with the restaurants' much-loved cinnamon-sugar donuts. A special Saturday edition of the farmers market was already in full swing at the city park, with vendors offering pottery and fall decorations along with pumpkins, apples, and other late-season produce from local gardens and orchards.

Diane and Roger soon arrived, ready to help out on what promised to be one of the store's busiest days of the year. While most of the area's residents were intrigued by Vicki's new business, Melinda's mom was especially curious about how Meadow Lane would be received.

"Just think! One day soon, I could be walking down the street here, or in Swanton or Charles City, and see a woman with one of my scarves draped around her neck." Diane reached for a stack of returns waiting under the counter. "Of course, maybe they won't sell, especially at that price ..."

"You know they will." Melinda patted her mom on the arm. "Vicki knows the market, she's done her research. She's on top of this, just like everything else she does."

"Well, I can't believe what she put on my weathervanes." Frank rolled his eyes, but Melinda could tell her uncle was secretly delighted. "Are they really worth that much?"

"To the right person, they would be. They're statement pieces, for sure. And the holidays are coming ..."

"Oh, yes, they'll be here before we know it." Frank thumbed through the rack of Prosper Hardware-branded merchandise and pulled out a sweatshirt. "Here's my size. Melinda, put it on my tab. Haven't bought one of these yet, but today's the perfect day to wear one."

"That'll look nice on you, dear." Miriam paused to peck her husband on the cheek. "Speaking of the holidays, Vicki hopes to call a meeting of the business owners in a few weeks. Says she has some ideas for expanded promotions for the end of the year. I'm curious to see what she has in mind."

"Probably several things, but I bet most of them will be good." Frank snipped the tags off his new sweatshirt. "She's driven to succeed at everything she does, that's for sure."

"Colton for Council" signs had popped up in several yards over the past few days, giving Vicki the additional exposure she wanted in advance of her store's opening. A press release on her candidacy was shared with the local media and, true to what she'd told Karen and Melinda, Vicki did have a list of priorities she'd champion if elected. Her announcement had turned heads in Prosper, especially among female residents eager to see a woman finally get a seat on the council, but whether she'd gather many votes in next month's election remained to be seen.

Lucas and Clarence didn't seem too concerned about their new challenger. Melinda assumed they were simply complacent. But according to Frank, Clarence was rather weary of serving on the council, since he'd been on the board for so many years. And Lucas, in his usual easygoing manner, said he was happy to let the voters make their picks without any grandstanding on his part.

If only the mayoral race could be as drama-free as the council election. Jake had doubled his efforts since his awkward showing at the game, and was now going door-to-door hawking his yard signs to residents. Jerry, true to form, took a laid-back approach. A stack of signs was always on his front porch, with a note that encouraged supporters to grab extras and pass them on to family and friends.

Jake's support, therefore, was currently more visible, although Melinda had noticed a few yards sporting banners for both candidates. The conversations around those dinner tables had to be very interesting. But based on residents' reactions at the mayoral forum the other night, Jerry seemed to hold the lead, at least for now. As expected, the community center issue had dominated the debate. Delores' donation was certainly generous, but estimates showed it could fall a bit short depending on which option was chosen.

With so many residents divided on that issue, as well as who was most worthy of serving as mayor, Nancy came up with a plan she hoped would bring everyone together: Posters and donation boxes for the community center project were quickly created, and delivered to the town's handful of businesses and public spaces just yesterday evening. The displays would make their debut during today's festival.

Aunt Miriam had placed Prosper Hardware's on the far end of the counter. "I've never seen this town so divided. Something has got to give." She adjusted the sign, and gave Melinda a hopeful smile. "And I hope that'll be everyone who comes through the door today."

While Frank and Esther put the finishing touches on the apple-bobbing station, Roger helped Bill stock shelves and Diane reached for the broom kept inside the front door.

"I love to see the resurgence of this little town. Vicki's new business, all the activities ... but we need that community center. The council chambers just isn't big enough to host public events."

"Well, there's always a chance the center could end up across the street," Miriam reminded her sister. "Revitalizing the upstairs hasn't been crossed off the list, at least not yet."

Nancy hadn't shared her supernatural worries with Jerry. Even if he believed her, what could he do about it? And he'd look like a fool, or worse, if he passed those concerns on to the community. As mayor, he couldn't vote on the plan, but was still expected to provide guidance and suggestions to the council. Some people would say he was crazy; others would claim Jerry was attempting to sway public opinion. And with a contested election looming, both were dangerous.

There were risks for Nancy, as well. Even if people took her concerns seriously, it could jeopardize her standing in the community. She was the city's only full-time employee, and some residents already felt she had too much influence due to her dual role as city clerk and librarian.

Nancy was staying silent, and for good reason. But Melinda saw an opportunity to speak up.

"City hall's just such an old building," she reminded her mom and aunt, in a voice just loud enough to catch the ears of several shoppers. They were already listening, even though they pretended otherwise. "It has a certain charm, sure. But I can't imagine what it would cost to make the necessary upgrades. And being on the historical register, I think it would be so complicated to get changes approved."

"That's for sure." Miriam took the bait. "The paperwork alone would be a nightmare. And poor Nancy's got enough on her plate, as it is."

One woman paused to admire the autumn kitchen towels Miriam had just set out, then inserted herself into the conversation. "Why, the elevator alone would drain a large portion of Delores' donation! We had to put one in at the Methodist church a few years ago, and the cost was staggering."

Another customer gripped her handbasket tight, and frowned as she peered across the street. "I don't know, it's certainly a pretty building, but something about it's always given me the creeps."

Eyebrows went up all around, but the woman only shook her head and started for the grocery aisle. Melinda was dying to hear the details, but knew she needed to let the conversation drop. Had the woman seen something, sensed something? Maybe Nancy wasn't as alone in her fears as she'd suspected.

* * *

Main Street was soon flooded with cars and pedestrians. Many of the visitors were families, with young children in tow. And as the clock ticked toward Meadow Lane's grand opening, a crowd gathered in front of the building next door. Melinda slipped out and found Angie near the shop's entrance.

"I've been baking for days on end." She yawned and brushed her auburn curls out of her eyes. "I don't know what I would've done if our parents hadn't been able to take the kids so much. Between wrapping up harvest, and trying to get everything just right ..."

"I'm sure it'll be fine. Those carrot-spice muffins you brought over the other night? Those were amazing."

Just like the shop's interior, the outside of the concrete-block building now bore no resemblance to its past life. It was painted a soft blue, and crisp white trim had been artfully arranged around the plate-glass windows to create cottage-like charm. Navy shutters let the rust-red front door take center stage. A wooden wheelbarrow was parked by the entrance, and its bed overflowed with pumpkins and colorful squash.

Vicki soon appeared in the doorway, and was met with a round of applause. Arthur was right behind his wife, as was their college-age son.

Jerry stepped out of the crowd, microphone in hand. "What an exciting day this is! Meadow Lane will bring jobs to our community, revitalize Main Street, and draw people from around the region. This could be the start of a whole new chapter in Prosper's history. With greater activity in the downtown, and a community center in the works, Prosper's future is brighter than ever."

That brought a round of thunderous applause and a few whistles from the crowd. Jerry seemed pleased, but looked to Melinda for approval.

She gave it with a small nod, and the mayor beamed. Jake was there, as expected, and she'd cautioned Jerry to choose his remarks carefully. Anything that could be construed as a campaign message would cause Jake to charge forward and insist on equal time to speak.

Vicki's comments were enthusiastic, if brief. She thanked the community for its warm welcome and continued support, then took a moment to recognize Angie for her contributions. It had been years since Prosper had welcomed a new venture along Main Street, so there'd been no thought to securing an oversized pair of scissors, or roping off the entrance for dramatic effect. Nancy simply snapped a few photos, as did the editor of the Swanton newspaper, and Jerry declared Meadow Lane open for business. After another round of applause, Vicki reminded everyone that coffee, tea and cocoa waited inside, along with special coupons and door prizes.

"I'm glad Vicki has this shop," Angie told Melinda as they took a step back, away from the throng of eager shoppers aiming for the door. "She misses her son terribly, now that he's off at college. I can't imagine! Thankfully, my own empty nest is years' away."

"She's certainly making the most of her free time. I have a good feeling about this place. It's going to put Prosper on the map, I'm sure of it."

* * *

Uncle Frank was crouched next to the tub when Melinda returned, helping the littlest customers snag apples from the cold water.

Miriam was at the register. "I don't know who's having more fun; Frank, or the kids."

The children shrieked with laughter as one little boy surfaced with his prize, his entire face wet and his tee shirt nearly soaked. One of the moms nearby chided the kids to keep their voices down, but Miriam brushed it aside. "Oh, I don't mind. They're enjoying themselves, and that's what matters."

The pumpkin-carving activity at the library started at two, so the apple-bobbing wrapped up soon after lunch. Esther bucketed away the water, then Roger and Bill carried out the plastic sheet while Frank carefully mopped the floorboards dry. "I think we have ourselves a new tradition. Honey, don't you agree? And it wasn't as messy as we thought it might be."

"A little old-fashioned fun is good for kids." Miriam gathered the damp towels and stowed them in a large plastic bag. "They loved it. I think we fared better than Nancy and her volunteers will, over at the library. Carving pumpkins is fun, but that's as sloppy as it gets."

"All in all, it's been a great event so far." Diane had her arms full of more Prosper Hardware sweatshirts and tee shirts, as those were some of the day's bestsellers. "Word is the farmers market is packed, too. I'd say today's been an incredible success."

Roger added more caps to the display. "Great weather, big crowds, lots of positive feedback ... everything's gone so smoothly. If I didn't know how hard so many people worked to make this happen, I'd say it's almost too good to be true."

Uncle Frank soon propped open Prosper Hardware's oak door to let a refreshing breeze drift through the screen. Melinda was adding more work boots to the rack when she heard a shrill scream over the buzz of conversation outside.

"What is that?" Miriam frowned. "Did you ..."

Another scream. There was a girl on the sidewalk in front of the library, her hands and face covered with orange pulp, wailing with all her might. Two boys ran out next, shepherded by a harried volunteer wearing a goo-stained painter's smock over her clothes.

More than a dozen children soon poured out of the entrance. Many of the kids were crying; others, including some of the older boys, were shouting and laughing, and a few were trying to run back inside.

Melinda's phone buzzed in her pocket. It was Nancy, and she sounded out of breath. "I hope they can spare you for a few minutes. We need your help!"

* * *

Prosper Public Library was normally an oasis of calm. But not today. Books were tossed randomly in the aisles, and the potted plant by the circulation desk was crumpled on the floor. The temporary tables in the children's area were covered with newspaper and coated with orange pulp. Half-carved pumpkins waited impatiently, their grins lopsided or missing, and one unfortunate orb was smashed on the wood floor, its seeds spilling everywhere.

Nancy was in the third row, her old tee shirt and jog pants speckled with chunks of pumpkin. She gripped a broom in her hand.

"What happened?" Melinda glanced around. A few other volunteers were trying to contain the mess.

"That!" Nancy pointed her broom up and over. "That's what happened!"

And there, between the top of one bookcase and the ceiling, crouched a very angry squirrel. Melinda's arrival was met with a glare of triumph, and a round of scolding chatter.

She wanted to laugh, and almost did.

But it wasn't funny.

Oh, yes it was!

"What are you going to do with him?" The giggles wouldn't hold back for much longer. "How did ... oh, no! He ran down the tables, didn't he?"

"He did more than that!" The squirrel squawked again, and Nancy waved her broom in warning. "Hey, you stay up there! Don't you dare come down until we can get someone to catch you."

"Doc's on his way." One of the volunteers popped around the stacks. "I told him to come in the back, so he doesn't have to haul a live trap through that crowd." She pointed at the disgruntled squirrel. "Little fella, you've caused enough trouble already."

Several people were pressed to the library's front window, trying to figure out what would happen next. Most of the parents and children had left, but Melinda saw one dad still trying to comfort his teary daughter.

Another volunteer came through the opening into city hall with a large plastic tub in her arms. "What are we going to do with these half-finished pumpkins? Most of those kids are so traumatized, they won't want to come back for them, much less finish their designs."

"Dump them in the park after the farmers market wraps up," Melinda suggested. "The deer will find them. And the other critters, too. They'll have a feast."

"I don't think you deserve any!" The second woman addressed the squirrel, whose chatter had become more agitated when the tote appeared. "Oh, you think I'm going to try to catch you with this? No way, I'll leave that to the pros."

The ladies gathered up the pumpkins' remains and the pulpy newspapers, then wiped down the tables. Melinda soon heard laughter echoing through city hall. Then Doc appeared, trap in hand, with Tony and Sam in tow.

"I don't know what's so funny," one of the volunteers scolded the men. "Just look at this mess!"

"Oh, come on." Tony grinned. "This is the best call our crew has had in months! Beats a dead body in a field, right?"

Nancy shook her head. "Perspective is everything, I guess. Sam, what are you doing here?"

"Oh, I've got special hours today, for the festival. I happened to be out back when Doc came. Thought I'd lend a hand." He held up a container of roasted peanuts, and gave it a shake. "I love these things, always have some in my desk."

"The perfect bait." Doc positioned the humane trap in the aisle and set the spring for its door. "Here, Sam, fill this dish up. Nancy, how about you lock the front door so this little guy won't get disturbed? If we clear out of here, I don't think he'll be able to resist."

Doc offered to hang around for a bit, just out of sight in city hall, and listen for the snap! of the trap's door. Tony was helping a neighbor with his farmers market booth, but told Doc to call him if relocation turned into a two-person job.

"I wonder where he got in?" Nancy ushered everyone else through city hall and into the kitchen. "As far as I know, our back door hasn't been propped open today. And I can't imagine a squirrel would dash in when a person was coming and going."

"I'll take a look around," Sam offered. "Might be a small hole somewhere."

"Might be?" Tony laughed. "In here? I bet there's more than a few. Wouldn't take much for a squirrel to squeeze through."

Melinda and the other women began to slice the pumpkins into deer-friendly sections while Nancy gathered up the garbage. When they were nearly finished, Sam returned. "Well, I think I found the spot. Looked like the smaller storage room's door was cracked open, so I poked around. Back behind those file cabinets? There's a hole in the plaster. Maybe two inches, but that's enough."

Nancy's shoulders slumped. "So that means ..."

"Yeah," Sam sighed. "He came down through the wall, so there's at least one route they have going through here. They must be sneaking in upstairs somewhere, maybe in the eaves." Sam suddenly brightened. "But Nancy, this is really good news!"

"Why?"

"Because that means you don't have to worry about ... you know." Sam raised his arms menacingly and made a poor stab at an unearthly moan.

The other women stared at Nancy in confusion, then back at Sam.

"Oh, just ignore him." She gently shooed the volunteers toward the back door. "Thanks so much for your help, ladies. I'll let you know when the suspect's been caught and released."

Nancy's cheeks were flushed when she returned. "Everyone at book club promised to not say a word about that to anyone!" She pointed at Sam. "That includes you."

"Sorry. I couldn't resist. But, seriously, that could be the answer. And if there's one squirrel, there's bound to be more. Well, I better get back. See you at book club, if not before."

Doc soon let out a whoop, then a smattering of applause echoed down the hallway.

"The squirrel must be in custody." Melinda wiped her hands on a towel. "I'll get back across the street. Do you need help taking the pumpkins to the park later?"

"Oh, no thanks, I can manage. Thanks for coming over, though, in our hour of need. I know the store's packed today, and I'm sure you've got plans with Chase tonight."

"He's busy. You know how this time of year is, everyone's running every which way. A family thing at his grandma's this afternoon, and something with friends tonight."

That wasn't a lie, but it wasn't the whole truth, either. Family came first with Chase, which Melinda understood. But then he'd wanted her to drive up to Meadville when she got off work, even though she'd be exhausted by the end of the day, and she'd refused.

Nancy, who now seemed lost in her own thoughts, suddenly crossed her arms.

"Sam might have a point. But I know what I heard, what I felt. And that was no squirrel."

"What are you going to do?"

"I don't know." Nancy shook her head, then started laughing. "But maybe one part of my problem's been solved. When word spreads that a pack of squirrels is camped out inside city hall, people might start looking elsewhere for their community center."

Melinda thought she'd had her biggest surprise of the day, but found another one when she stepped out of city hall. A glossy-black touring bus had found its way to Prosper, and was now parked along Main Street.

Diane was at Prosper Hardware's register, and her smile stretched from ear to ear.

"What's going on?" Melinda pointed out the window. "Where'd that come from?"

"Vicki put her shop on the list for a regional craft tour that's happening today. No one got back to her, to confirm she'd made the cut, so she'd forgotten about it. But she did!"

"They rolled up just ten minutes ago." Aunt Miriam's arms overflowed with more seasonal textiles from the storage room. "Vicki said she's going to suggest the ladies check us out, too, before they leave! Let's put out every festive fall thing we've got, and maybe they'll clear the shelves before the afternoon is over."

She winked at her sister and niece. "Happy Halloween, girls, and Merry Christmas, to boot!"

* 12 *

Adelaide was waiting inside the back-porch door, and gave an enthusiastic wave when Melinda pulled up next to the carriage house that now served as the Beauforts' garage.

"This must be good." Melinda returned the greeting as she reached for her purse. "All she said was she had something interesting to share with me. Wonder what it is?"

Prosper Hardware was always closed on Sundays, and Melinda was especially glad this time around. Yesterday's festival had been a great success, but she was tired today, and couldn't find the energy to tackle her autumn to-do list around the farm. Adelaide's call had been a welcome distraction. When it came down to scrubbing the root cellar or having tea with a neighbor, the choice was easy.

The Beauforts' farmhouse was an impressive mix of Victorian and Queen Anne styles, a full two stories plus a steep-pitched attic. Porches with ornate spindles jutted out in every direction, and there were too many windows to count. But while the front of the house was painted in lovely shades of lavender, the rest of the clapboards were in various stages of restoration and repair.

Along with the former carriage house, there was a strong-shouldered barn, several outbuildings, and a vintage picket fence surrounding a generous garden. The place was teeming with life, from the goats and pig rooting around in the front pasture to the beehives sequestered behind the garden. One of the Beauforts' chocolate labs greeted Melinda when she got out of the car.

"Isn't it a beautiful day?" Adelaide's long gray hair was secured in a neat braid, and her blue-plaid shirt was faded but clean. "So glad you could make it! Mason went to Swanton for some power tool he couldn't live without until tomorrow. He said to tell you hello."

"That lattice under the front porch looks like it's new." Melinda slipped off her jacket and added it to the hooks inside the door. "He's really making progress around here."

"That's for sure. Winter's coming, so he'll have to move his handiwork inside soon." Adelaide gestured at the kitchen's high ceiling. "There's always plaster to patch, or woodwork to strip." She went for the kettle as Melinda settled in at a small round table by the windows. "At this rate, the house might be totally finished in a decade or so."

"It's so lovely. I know you said a very prosperous farmer built it, and it shows. So, when it's finished, what are you going to do then? Take up fishing, or go south in the winter?" Melinda's comments came with a smirk, as she knew her retired neighbors weren't ones to sit still.

"Actually, we've got an even better plan." Adelaide brought the mugs and a plate of oatmeal cookies to the table, then leaned over as if sharing a secret. "Imagine this place as a bed and breakfast."

"Oooh! Yes, I can see that!"

"But, we're going to do it one better." Adelaide raised an eyebrow. "It'll be a working-farm retreat. They're getting popular. People can just hang out if they like, of course, and we might try to cater to artistic types ... writers, painters, even quilting groups. The best part is people will not only see where their food comes from, but they can help make it, too."

"You'll put them to work, but they'll pay to do it." Melinda reached for a cookie. "That's genius!"

"They can help milk the goats, make cheese, gather honey and eggs. Nothing too taxing, and I doubt anyone will want to fork manure out of the barn. Just the sort-of-fun stuff. That's a good year out, for sure. But a girl can dream, can't she?"

Melinda decided that when she was closer to sixty than forty, she hoped she felt like a girl. Adelaide made the future look bright.

"Anyway, that's more fun for later." Adelaide passed a bowl filled with packets of flavored tea. "This whole situation down the road has really raised my interest in the history of this area. I was in Swanton the other day, and I decided to pop in at the historical society's library. And I found something good."

"Really? I love local history, and that place is fascinating. You could get lost in there for days! Or at least, I could." Her cookie dropped to her plate, as Adelaide was nearly bursting with some sort of news.

"Does this have anything to do with the body they found?"

"Well, I don't know for sure. But what if it does? The site was crawling with law enforcement for several days, as you know, but things died down. And then, a few days ago, we noticed they were back! Oh, just a truck or two, not anything that would draw a lot of attention. But word is they're digging out there again."

Adelaide quickly answered the question Melinda was about to ask. "None of the neighbors know what they're looking for, or if they've found it yet."

She went to the counter and came back with a file folder. "But it got my gears turning, so I decided to snoop around in the archives. Right around that bridge, where they found those remains?" Adelaide was whispering now, even though they were alone. "There was a little town! Well, maybe that's not the right word. But there used to be a house, on the west side of the road, and a post office operated out of it for almost ten years in the late eighteen-hundreds."

"A post office?" Melinda blinked.

"Yes! I found mentions of it in a few books." She reached into the folder and pulled out several photocopies. "Hawk Hollow, it was called. And, this is even better, for a while there was a building across the road with a general store and creamery. The store was closed by 1900, but the creamery went on until, oh, I think the forties or so."

"Hawk Hollow." Melinda picked up a print of an old map. "What a great name! There was a little creamery not far from my Grandma and Grandpa Foster's farm, over by Swanton, for several decades, too. They said there used to be creameries all over the countryside to make it easier for farmers to process their milk. When you traveled by horse and wagon, getting to an actual town took far longer than it does today."

"Exactly. And there's more: a family named Peabody once owned the farm where the house stood, as well as the creamery and store on the east side of the road."

Melinda had driven through the spot only once or twice, as it wasn't on her usual routes. But she remembered the slight dip in the road, just as it approached the creek, and an iron-frame bridge over the waterway. The structure was apparently historic, too rare to be ripped out and replaced, but she couldn't recall anything else of note in the area. No signs, no buildings, just a few lonely field driveways.

And now, a potential crime scene.

"When we bought our farm, the former owner's grandson had mentioned something interesting about that place." Adelaide stirred her tea with one hand and shuffled the papers with the other. "But I'd forgotten what it was. We were so busy moving and getting our retirement ducks in a row. Then they found that body, and I was sure the two were linked. And I was right. Here." She passed another printout across the table. "This is a list of former post offices in the county, noting their exact locations. It's a perfect match."

Melinda stared at the document, amazed at how many sites were noted there. It was a startling reminder that every place had a history, held its own story. And, that as the years went by, those stories could be easily lost.

"Did you call the sheriff? I don't know if it would really matter, but what if it did?"

"I sure did. On Friday. The receptionist said she's lived around here her whole life, but had never heard of Hawk Hollow. We chatted for a bit, and then one of the deputies called me back. I told him what I'd found, and where I'd found it. He was tight-lipped, as I knew he would be, but seemed curious about it. Anyway, I did my civic duty."

"What happened to the house? To that farm?"

Adelaide shook her head. "Don't know for sure. But the deputy told me they think the whole place was bulldozed sometime in the 1960s."

"So they were already looking into Hawk Hollow, before you called. Very interesting."

"That's what I thought."

Adelaide crossed her arms suddenly as if warding off a chill, despite the sleepy warmth of the kitchen. "Maybe the location was a factor, but not in the way we're thinking. There's no other farm within a half-mile of that spot, so it's pretty remote. And there's the old bridge, and the creek ... I guess if you were going to dump a body, you'd pick a spot as far away from civilization as you could."

"They say the remains have been there a long time." Melinda searched for something comforting to tell her friend. "It's not likely that ... there's still any kind of a threat. But even so, how can you stand it?"

"Barely, that's how." Adelaide took a bracing gulp of her tea. "We keep the doors locked, of course. Never gave a thought to being outside after dark, not until this happened. It was easier, once the crews all left. But now they're back, and we don't know why."

"I think I'll make a phone call tonight." Melinda arranged Adelaide's research into a neat pile and returned it to the folder. "I happen to know a local historian with a sharp mind. Let's see what Horace has to say about all this."

* * *

Horace had some of the answers Melinda was seeking, but each one seemed to raise more questions.

The Schermanns had traded their milk and cream at Hawk Hollow for several decades, until their farm was finally wired with electricity in the early 1940s. Adelaide was correct about how long the store had operated, and the creamery as well. But Horace's memories of the farm across the road were far more detailed. And more interesting than Melinda had expected.

The house was a grand structure, and Horace thought it might have been built by a relative of the man who constructed Adelaide and Mason's home. The post office, which operated out of the house's front parlor, closed long before Horace was born, but his parents and grandparents once got their mail there.

The property changed hands at some point, and the impressive farm started a slow decline into decay. Then the house caught on fire one night, sometime in the 1960s, and it was a complete loss.

"It was too bad they couldn't save it," he said sadly. "It was such a grand place. But then, once the fire took hold ..."

"Wait a second. That was a long time ago, sure, but still in the modern era. Wouldn't the fire department get there within, what, fifteen minutes or so? Was no one home when it happened?"

"Well, that's where it gets interesting. You see, the place was half gone before anyone called it in. Word was someone was there. People thought the fire started in the kitchen, but it was rather odd. Seems like an official cause was never found."

First, a mysterious grave on the property. And a fire ... could it have been arson?

Everyone thought the house would be rebuilt, but the owners suddenly left the area about a month later. The ruins were bulldozed, and the barn and other outbuildings eventually torn down. Across the road, the one-story building that used to house the creamery and the store fell into disrepair, too, and was eventually demolished. A schoolhouse had once stood on the other side of the creek, but it closed in the 1950s and was hauled away to serve as some farmer's storage shed. After that, the iron bridge was all that remained of Hawk Hollow.

Horace had one other tidbit to share: The creamery had glass bottles stamped with its name. Even though Melinda's farmhouse was combed through by the Schermanns before the auction last spring, there was always the chance a few might be lurking in the basement, or hiding on a forgotten shelf in the machine shed.

The mystery surrounding Hawk Hollow stuck with Melinda on Monday as she puttered around the house, trapped inside by the steady rain that started to fall Sunday night. It was still dark and dreary when she started for Prosper Hardware Tuesday morning, but she was eager to see what else she could find out.

"Whew! It's damp out there!" Doc shrugged out of his waterproof jacket and added it to the coat tree by the sideboard. "I had an early farm call, and man, that mud! It about took me down."

"Watch those boots," Frank warned him. "It's a good thing Miriam's not here."

"Just leave them there on the mat," Melinda said. "We're not open for another hour, anyway. And don't worry about Miriam, I'm the one who usually scrubs the floor. You'd have to deal with me."

"Nice socks." George snickered.

Doc looked down and sighed. "So what, one's black and one's brown? I was in a hurry, and I don't think that pig cared. Besides, they're warm."

George kicked out one foot and lifted the leg of his jeans. "Got the wool socks out yesterday, myself. They'll be in style until March, at least."

"When you are done with the fashion show," Auggie said, "the coffee's ready. And Jerry brought cinnamon rolls."

Once everyone was settled, Melinda was quick to steer the conversation. "I heard something interesting this weekend. That field where the body was found? It used to be a little community, of sorts. Hawk Hollow. That ring a bell with anyone?"

She waited, almost holding her breath, but soon saw she would be disappointed. Only Frank seemed to have heard of the place. "Hawk Hollow, you say? I might have seen it on some old maps, when I was going through those boxes and files at city hall. Never much there, seemed like. But that name! It's got a ring to it."

While the men didn't have the information she'd hoped for, they were certainly curious about what she knew. She told them about the post office, the creamery and store, and the grand house and its mysterious demise. "That old iron bridge, over the creek? That's all that's left."

"Is that the haunted bridge?" George suddenly looked up from his cinnamon roll. "The one where people see the lady in white? You can hear her wailing as she paces back and forth."

"Wait, I know this one!" Doc was trying to control his laughter. "If you park on the bridge and say her name three times, does it feel like someone is pushing the car?"

Jerry rolled his eyes. "Why are those ghostly women always in white, and always wearing a gown? They're never dressed appropriately to be pushing vehicles across bridges, or over railroad tracks."

"So?" Bill shrugged. "If they're dead, they have superhuman strength. Doesn't matter."

Auggie shook his head. "No, no, that's all wrong. That's not the bridge where the haunted lady hangs out. She's at the railroad trestle over the river, way out north of town. See, her boyfriend jilted her, and ..."

"She's not haunted, herself," George snapped. "The *bridge* is haunted. By *her*! And it's the one by Melinda, because ..."

Melinda threw up her hands.

"Guys! Enough already! Hawk Hollow is what I want to know about. Horace remembered a few things beyond what Adelaide discovered, and I'd hoped maybe one of you knew more. But I guess not."

"There's nothing left, other than that iron bridge." Jerry shrugged and took a sip of his coffee. "I had no idea there was ever anything else out there. The bridge is architecturally significant, but it barely passes inspection these days. I think the county tried to get it on the national register, find some money to spruce it up, but no luck."

Doc treated himself to a second roll. "Hey Auggie, is that other cat still hanging around the co-op? I was in a few days ago, and Dan was telling me about it."

Melinda saw Auggie flinch, but wasn't sure any of the guys noticed. "Oh, sure, I see him from time to time."

"Dan says he's been there for over a week now, and it's a big, fluffy male," Doc explained to the rest of the group. "He let Dan pet him the other day. Have you tried to make friends with him yet?"

"I'll talk to Karen about it." Melinda jumped in, as Auggie seemed to shrink into his chair. "He needs to be neutered and have his shots. If they can't squeeze him in at the next community clinic, maybe he could just come to the vet's office?"

"That should work." Doc turned to Auggie. "We'll take care of him, one way or another. You might as well take on a third shop cat, as long as he makes friends with Pebbles and Mr. Checkers. I'm sure there's enough mice to keep them all entertained."

George snickered. "Mr. Checkers, what a name! But Auggie, I guess we have to give you a pass on that. After all, you never had a cat before those two came along."

"Well, I better get things ready to open." Melinda saw it was time to change the subject. "Jerry, when's that walk-through of the potential sites for the community center? Nancy's asked me to come along and help wrangle the media."

"The media?" Frank's eyebrows shot up. "Who invited them?"

"Reporters from the Swanton and Charles City papers have asked to join us," Jerry explained. "It's technically a public meeting, so we can't keep them away. It's on the twentieth," he told Melinda. "Noon sharp. We'll start our tour at city hall."

Just as the men were finishing their coffee, Doc and Jerry's phones beeped within seconds of each other.

"This can't be good." Jerry reached into his pocket.

"Oh, my God," Doc gasped.

"What?" Melinda's broom stopped mid-sweep.

"There's two more bodies." Jerry's voice was barely above a whisper. "This is from Tony. He says they just found them, only a few feet from the first one."

"What?" George was out of his chair. "Why now? I thought they ..."

"Detectives have been out there again." Melinda hurried to look over Jerry's shoulder. "Adelaide said they came back, late last week. But no one stopped at her house this time. No calls, nothing."

Auggie glared at Jerry. "Did you know about this?"

"Guys, look, you know sometimes I have my mayor hat on, and sometimes I'm just Jerry. The sheriff wanted us to keep things quiet, especially after what happened the first time around."

"That was his own fault." Frank crossed his arms.

Doc whistled as he scrolled through the message. "Well, the sheriff better get it together. Tony says it's more skeletons, but one of them has a cracked skull."

"Head trauma." Auggie looked around at his friends, letting his words sink in. "You know what that means."

* 13 *

"Murder!" The woman dropped her gallon of milk on the oak showcase with a definitive thud. "They say the larger one suffered from blunt-force trauma. That, right there, tells you everything you need to know!"

"If I were a betting man, I'd go with a baseball bat." Glenn Hanson, Prosper's postmaster, was on his early lunch break and loading up on bags of candy. He said they were for Halloween, but Melinda knew much of it would end up in the bowl on the post office's counter. And in Glenn's stomach.

"You never know." The man behind Glenn shook his head. "It could be even worse: an axe. And that other one they just found? Why, it has to be a kid! They said it was smaller than the first."

The woman was nearly in tears as she paid her bill. "Some poor mother, trying to protect her child. I'd do it, in a heartbeat!"

Melinda wasn't quite sure which body was supposed to be the mom in that scenario. Was it the one with the skull fracture, or the remains found a few weeks ago? Did the mother get axed in the end, or did she pick up whatever was handy to save her child and herself? But Melinda couldn't get a word in edge-wise to ask.

"Home invasion," Glenn said solemnly as Melinda gritted her teeth and double-bagged his candy. "Some intruder came along, middle of the night. Got the whole family. Mom, dad, kid. You know, there's that unsolved axe murder down in Villisca, from way back. Something like seven people, I think."

"Yes, of course." The woman hadn't been able to tear herself away from the conversation. "There were children involved there, as I recall. Over a hundred years ago, and still no closure. And they say that house is haunted."

Melinda knew Glenn loved to gossip, but thought he had more sense than to fan the flames of fear. There already was enough of that to go around. She smiled and reached for the other man's hand basket. "If the remains are very old, like the first one, I'm sure whoever is to blame is long gone."

"Could be." Did Glenn sound even the slightest bit disappointed? "But there's no statute of limitations on homicides. Even if the killer is ninety-nine years old, justice can still be served. And even if they're dead, there'd still be closure for the lost souls and their descendants."

"Jerry says there's no similar cold cases in the area." Melinda was talking to Glenn, but she made sure to look the woman and the other man in the eye. If they wanted to discuss this with everyone, let them share that fact, too.

The woman reluctantly lifted her canvas bag off the counter. "I don't know. They could have been killed anywhere, and then brought there to be buried. To throw off the law. I mean, that's what I'd do."

"Well, Sarah, you don't seem like a serial killer to me." Glenn waved as she started for the door. He turned back to Melinda and raised his eyebrows. "I'm just saying, the killer could still be at large. Well, I better get on back. Stay safe."

"Will do," she called after him as the bell announced his departure.

Aunt Miriam was on her way up the main aisle with a carton of canned soup. "Nothing to worry about," she told the other man before he left. "All this fuss, people jumping to conclusions. Next thing you know, it'll be a zombie apocalypse, or an alien invasion."

She set the heavy crate on the counter with a sigh, then leaned toward her niece. "Between you and me, this actually has me rattled. Before, once we knew the remains were old, I wasn't so concerned. But now, I don't know what to think."

"I feel bad for Nancy. I bet the phone is ringing off the hook again. And Jerry had errands to run this afternoon, so I know he's not there to help field the calls."

"Tell you what. When I get the grocery aisle restocked, I'll run over and see if she needs help. I know they say they'll run tests on these bodies, too, but they can't get that done soon enough."

* * *

Darkness came earlier every day, and Melinda was glad to have her chores completed before sundown. She made a pass through all her buildings again, just to ease her mind, but didn't bother to barricade the doors this time. Whatever had happened in Hawk Hollow, it was done and over with long ago.

While most area residents could leave the past buried if they chose to, members of Prosper's emergency crew found their lives upended again. This discovery renewed interest in the case, and volunteers from all around the county were needed for barricade duty while investigators made what were hopefully their final sweeps through the field. Miriam insisted she could spare Bill during the day, so he wouldn't have to sign up for a night shift, and Karen kicked in additional overtime to cover the clinic while Doc did his part.

But what happened the following night made Melinda almost forget about the mysterious remains. Sunny was suddenly missing.

She called and called, and banged the old spatula against the plastic bucket, but only Stormy ran into the grain room when it was time for supper.

"There you are! I've got some gravy as a special treat. Where's your brother? It's foggy tonight, I can't imagine he'd be out roaming around in that soup."

Hobo helped her check the haymow before she fed the sheep. On the way to the chicken house, she searched the shadows for any flash of orange. Sunny rarely missed a meal, but dry kibble was always available in the barn, as was fresh water, and both cats knew it.

"He'll be along, I guess," she finally told Hobo. "Let's go find your supper, and get Hazel and Grace settled."

Melinda fixed herself a plate of leftovers, and lingered at the kitchen table with the catalog that arrived in the mail. It was packed with parkas and wool sweaters, the models frolicking in a faux winter wonderland. "The holiday season comes earlier every year. Can't we have Halloween first?" she asked Hazel, who was sniffing the closed basement door. "No, you can't go down there. I know there's mice, but don't give me that look."

The yard light was already on by the time she took her dishes to the sink and looked out into the back yard. The fog was thicker now, smothering the dead grass and erasing the drifts of leaves banked against the garage. The picnic table, one of the cats' favorite hangouts, was too far to the left for a good view. She reached for her shoes and a sweatshirt, and slipped out the back door.

Sunny wasn't on the picnic table, or under it, either. "He's probably already gone to the barn. He's fine." But suddenly, she knew it wasn't true.

Something was wrong. She ran back to the house.

"Hobo, do you want to help me look again?" He was in the living room, sprawled out on the rug, "Come on!" She reached for a flashlight, and they started out.

"Sunny!" She turned this way and that as the driveway's gravel crunched under her sneakers. "Sunny, are you here?"

The sheep were startled by her return. Sunny wasn't in the grain room, or under the stairs with Stormy, who was already snuggled in their bed of loose straw. She ran through the back of the barn, her heart pounding in her chest and her ears, and searched every lambing stall. No sign of him in the haymow.

Melinda ran outside, Hobo at her heels. She rolled the machine shed's door wide, checked the corners and under Lizzie. As they came across the yard, tears rolling down her face, Hobo barked and ran to the bushes behind the garage.

"What are you doing in there!" She shined the flashlight in Sunny's direction. "I've been looking everywhere!"

He was huddled along the foundation, hiding as far back as he could go. He didn't leap out and rub against her leg. And in the faint beam of the light, she saw a thread of foam dripping from the corner of his mouth.

"Sunny!" She set the flashlight in the grass and dropped to her knees. "Oh, no, are you hurt?"

He made a weak, guttural sound and slowly turned his head. It was like he was in a trance, but she could see the pain in his eyes. The branches scratched at her face as she crawled toward him. There was no sign of injury, no blood, but something was clearly wrong.

"What is it? What happened?"

He dropped his fuzzy head into her hand, but didn't get up. Melinda rolled back and on to her feet, then pulled out her phone. Living alone in the country, she never left the house without it.

The vet clinic's emergency line rang three times before Karen answered. She quickly confirmed what Melinda suspected: Sunny had likely ingested something he shouldn't have. He needed help, and fast.

"I'm out on an emergency call now, just got here." There were agitated voices in the background, and a cow in obvious distress. "Doc and Anne went to Mason City when he finished his shift at the crime scene, they won't be back for a few hours yet. It's not likely Sunny has any broken bones, there'd be signs of trauma. Can you get him in a carrier?"

Melinda was already sprinting across the yard, Hobo at her side. "Yes, I'm sure I can. He's so limp, I don't think he's got any fight left in him."

"Oh, I wish I could get away! But this can't wait. Do you have the addresses for the emergency clinics? Mason City's going to be maybe five minutes' closer than Waterloo, I'd head that way if I were you."

"Yes, I have them saved in my phone." It was her only option, and Melinda burst into tears. Both vet hospitals were over thirty miles' away. And in this fog ... She wrenched the back door open with her free hand, and dragged a carrier out of the porch closet.

"I know you're panicked, but please be careful," Karen begged her friend. "The visibility is terrible, you'll have to go slow. I'll call Mason City and tell them you're coming in. Sunny will need his stomach pumped, they can be ready for you. Wait, I just thought of something! Bundle him up to keep him warm, and get him in the car. I'll call you back in a few minutes, OK?"

Sunny didn't protest when Melinda gently lifted him out of the bushes. She caught an unmistakable odor as she swaddled him in an old towel, and noticed his hindquarters were dirty. Even the confines of the carrier weren't worth a reaction from Sunny. They'd made it as far as the picnic table when Karen called again.

"I have good news! Josh is home, he's going to meet you at his clinic. Do you know where it is?"

"Yes! Oh, yes, I do! It's not far from my parents' house." Even in this fog, she might be able to get to Swanton in fifteen minutes. And every minute would count.

She turned west on the blacktop, going as fast as she dared. No one else was out in this fog, and the silence in the back seat made her heart break.

"Hold on. Please, Sunny, just hold on. Josh is going to help you. We're almost there."

A familiar truck was parked in the clinic's lot when she pulled up, and the lights were on inside. Josh burst out the side door before she made it to the sidewalk. He was in sweatpants and a faded long-sleeve tee shirt, an old ball cap smashed over his hair. She almost didn't recognize him.

"In here. I've got the table set up, ready to go. When did you find him?"

Everything was a blur. "I don't know, maybe half an hour ago? Thank you for being here. I was going to go to Mason City, but ..."

"No way was I going to let you do that, not when I'm so close." Josh held the door and pointed into the first exam room. His calm demeanor helped her heartbeat slow, just a bit. Sunny was in good hands. She set the carrier on the table. "He's breathing, obviously, but see the spittle? And his back end?"

"Mr. Sunny, I guess you're having some loose poop." Josh was suddenly rather cheerful. "That's a good sign, actually. Maybe he's passed some of whatever's making him so sick. But I'm still going to pump his stomach, and that means he has to be sedated."

He studied Melinda's messy hair and tear-stained face.

"Neither of my techs are here, but I know you're handy in a pinch."

She tried for a smile, and Josh tipped his head at a metal sink in the corner. "Scrub in, and we'll get started."

Sunny was too sick to give more than a flip of his tail as Melinda petted his back, afraid to touch his flank. All she had to do was hold Sunny steady while Josh gave him the sedative. "Excellent. He'll need a few minutes before I can insert the tube, so I'm going to take a few quick X-rays."

They carefully lifted Sunny on to a small rolling cart, and Josh opened a side door.

"You might as well have a seat out front. Light switch there on the left. There's a water fountain, some magazines. Your parents live here in town, right? They can come over, if you like. Just have them use the side door."

Diane arrived minutes later, and wrapped her distraught daughter in a warm hug. "Oh, honey, don't worry. From what you've said about Josh, he's got this under control. Your dad sends his love. Said to tell you that a barn cat like Sunny? He's tough, and he's got nine lives."

"That's what I'm afraid of." Melinda wiped her face with a tissue, glad Josh's waiting room was well-stocked. "I don't know how many he has left. Sunny and Stormy only showed up a few weeks before Horace left, and Doc and Karen say they're both about three years old. But we don't know anything about them before that. I just feel so helpless."

Just like the other night, the bad memories came back, and Melinda was too exhausted to push them away. The night Oreo was suddenly sick, the crowded waiting room at the emergency clinic in Minneapolis. How she stood at the exam table, Oreo already limp in her arms and struggling to breathe. The way the vet shook her head ...

Her anguished thoughts circled back to Sunny. "What did he get into? I keep everything put away! The weed killer's on a top shelf in the garage, as is the antifreeze, and the oil for the lawnmower. I'm so careful, I always check to be sure I didn't spill even a drop, that the lids are screwed on tight."

"It's not your fault." Diane put her hands on her daughter's shoulders. "Look at me. This is not your fault. He roams all over, who knows what he found?"

"I don't like that at all! I worry about him, and Stormy, too. Being an outdoor cat is so dangerous. Between the road, and the weeds and the wild animals, I don't know which is worse."

"Well, four cats in the house might be too many. Besides, Sunny's a free spirit, so is Stormy. Can you really see them lounging on the sofa, or content to stare out the window?"

"I know, I know. Grace would clean their clocks if they tried to take over her couch." Her mom was right. Many cats preferred an indoor home, and that was the best thing for them. But not all had the temperament for it, and that included her boys.

Josh came into the waiting room. "The scans showed some small bones in his system, probably from a mouse or gopher, but I don't see any blockages. He's pretty sick, but he has a very good chance of full recovery." Josh's smile was cautious. "He needs to stay here for a day or two, I want to be sure there aren't any side effects from whatever it was he ate."

"You don't think he got into poison, then?"

"No, thankfully. We'd see more foaming at the mouth than what he showed, or convulsions. That diarrhea was a good thing, it means he was already starting to pass what made him ill. But we don't know how long he was sick before you found him. I'll start him on medicine to soothe his stomach, and extra fluids to help him along."

Josh turned back down the hallway, and Melinda reached for her mom's hand. "He's going to make it! I don't know what all this is going to cost, but it surely would have been more at an emergency clinic. And Sunny's worth every penny."

"I was surprised Josh's office is open in the evenings. When you called us, it was almost seven-thirty. He only does small animals, right, not like Doc and Karen?"

"Oh, no, he was at home." Melinda reached for another tissue, but she was smiling now. "Karen called him, he lives only a few blocks away. In this fog, it could have taken me an hour to get to Waterloo or Mason City."

Diane was impressed. "Josh opened up just for you? For Sunny?" She was silent for a moment, as if considering something, then patted her daughter on the arm. "Well, you volunteer at the spay-and-neuter clinics, so I suppose he was returning the favor."

* 14 *

Melinda hurried to Swanton after work the next day, slipping in time with Sunny before she went home to face Stormy and Hobo's confusion over their absent friend. Her parents had stopped in to see Sunny as well but, even though their faces were familiar, he was far from a model patient.

He slowly regained his strength, and his appetite rebounded as well. Emotionally, though, Sunny was a wreck. No matter how clean his kennel was, or how many of those new-to-him fleece blankets were at his disposal, he was still trapped indoors. Even worse, there were strange people, dogs and cats all around him.

"The best thing will be for him to get home," Josh told Melinda when Sunny was discharged. "He's an outdoor cat, through and through; this isn't the life for him."

When book club rolled around a few nights later, Melinda saw a silver lining to her cloud of worries about Sunny: His unexpected illness was the perfect excuse for why she hadn't finished the October selection. She'd been too busy to reach the end in time, but that wasn't the whole truth. Between the unnerving episode with Auggie and Chaplin at the co-op, and her own wild imagination, the horror classic had simply hit too close to home.

"I'm guilty, too," Karen admitted as the members gathered around the library's conference-room table. "Sam, how could you do this to us? Given my line of work, I've managed to avoid that book all these years. I tried, I really did, but it was too upsetting for me. I only got halfway, and I had to stop."

"Sorry about that." Sam seemed genuinely apologetic. "Yes, I can see how being a veterinarian would make that a tough go. But the author was perfect for the time of year, and some of his books clock in around a thousand pages. This one was shorter."

"I made it through, but barely." Vicki passed around squares of a walnut-apple dessert. "But Arthur said to tell all of you: no more books as scary as that one! Either I was up half the night, unable to put it down; or I kept waking up, and making him investigate every little noise and check the locks again, just to be sure."

Amy shook her head. "I enjoyed the book, but I have to say, I was glad when it was over. It was a relief to bring it back to the library. Every time I walked past it, there on the coffee table, I started thinking about it again."

"Sam, what's your verdict?" Nancy leaned down the table. "We all know you don't believe in the supernatural, so any change in that?"

Sam was busy adding sugar to his coffee. "Well, I didn't exactly ... look, I couldn't finish it either, OK? Baxter, our dog, loves to sit by my reading chair in the evenings. I swear he was watching me as I read it. It made me nervous."

"So, you were scared." Bev nodded knowingly. "Baxter picked up on your emotions, he was just worried about you."

Sam raised a hand against all laughter that echoed around the room. "Look, there's no such thing as animals coming back from the dead! Or people, either. But there's still the undeniable fact that all our dear pets will pass away, one day. That book reminded me of that, is all. Baxter's getting on in years."

"Well, this will shorten our discussion a bit." Nancy shrugged as she added some grapes and cheese to her plate. "But that's fine. We can always find plenty of other things to chew over, and so what if we adjourn a bit early tonight? Halloween's only two weeks' away, and I'm sure everyone is busy."

A few of the women shared knowing looks, but said nothing. Sam pulled a folded sheet of paper from his jeans' pocket.

"Nancy, I didn't want you to be disappointed. I picked the book, so I'm supposed to guide our discussion. I found these online. There's some themes we can talk about, at least. Let's see. Story structure, symbolism, and then there's fear, loss, tests of faith ..."

"Sounds like fun." Karen raised her eyebrows. "Let's get started."

* * *

While Amy, Shelby and Sam left soon after the lively discussion ended, Melinda and Vicki offered to help Nancy clean up the conference room.

"Have a good time," Karen whispered to Melinda. "If I wasn't so exhausted, I'd join you."

"I'll let you know how it goes. I have no idea what's going to happen."

Bev turned to check the others were gone. "Oh, girls, it's fine, you don't have to be so secretive." She was repackaging her cheese and cracker tray with surprising gusto. "I've decided to hang around and see what all the fuss is about. Nancy, don't you worry. We'll be with you every step of the way."

"I know." Nancy let out a deep breath. "I'm so grateful you're all willing to go on this wild goose chase with me. I would never attempt it on my own."

"Wild ghost chase, you mean." Vicki's brown eyes twinkled with excitement.

Melinda would have preferred this investigation take place during daylight hours, but that wasn't possible. It was important to Nancy to keep this walk-through on the down-low. Main Street was nearly deserted at night, except for the cars clustered in the next block by the Watering Hole. And book club was the perfect excuse for why the ladies' vehicles were still in front of the library. If anyone asked, they'd simply stayed behind to help Nancy with something. After all, that was the truth.

"I really hope we get some interaction down here." Melinda reached for her knit hat and gloves. City hall's upstairs had no heat. "So then, maybe we won't even need to go up there."

Nancy shook her head and sighed. "We must. I need to. I have to face this. I won't force anyone to join me upstairs, even if you just wait at the bottom."

"We'll go." Melinda patted her on the arm. "Whatever it takes so you can feel safe here."

"It's too bad we don't have real equipment," Vicki said, "like you see on those haunted-house shows. They can track subtle changes in temperature, record sounds beyond normal human frequencies, that sort of thing."

"Well, I can't do any of that." Bev reached into her tote bag. "But will this help?"

Vicki shrieked and stepped back. "Get that thing out of here! Where did you get it?"

Bev held up the Ouija board. "Oh, not sure. One of my sons got it years ago, as a lark. Bunch of silliness, if you ask me. Just nudge the pointer, and it slides around."

Melinda gasped. "But if you don't think it's real, why did you bring it?"

"Don't they use these, on those shows?" Bev shrugged. "Never watched them, myself. If you all can wait a second, I'll just take it back to the truck."

"Gladly." Nancy tailed Bev out of the room, as if prepared to follow her outside to make sure the board left the premises.

"Why did she keep it?" Melinda whispered to Vicki as they walked through the library. "How can she have it in her house? She ought to burn it or something, get rid of it."

"Oh, that makes things worse," Vicki said ominously. Melinda was about to ask more, but Bev had returned.

"Here, we'll need to see where we're going." She had two battery-powered lanterns under her arm. "That makes three, with that flashlight."

"Nancy, we are at your command." Vicki snapped on one of the lanterns. "Lead the way."

They stepped through the opening into city hall, leaving the bright lights of the library behind. "We'll go to the kitchen," Nancy whispered, as if someone might be listening in on their conversation. Melinda, who had an uneasy feeling in her stomach, hoped that wasn't true.

With the ceiling lights still off, they settled around the battered metal table. The room was silent except for an occasional grumble from the scuffed refrigerator, which the previous mayor had purchased from a friend's garage for a few twenty-dollar bills.

Nancy gathered her courage. "If someone is here, we want to connect with you. Can you tell us why you're here, what you want?"

"Here's your chance to speak up." Bev looked around. "There's no need to keep scaring this poor woman half to death."

"Don't antagonize it!" Vicki hissed. "Or him. Or her."

They waited, leaning close to the comforting glow of the lantern.

Nancy flinched. "What was that?"

Melinda heard it, too. An eerie, scratching sound, on the wall behind them. No, wait. "It's under the sink. Just a mouse, or maybe a few."

"Mice!" Vicki lifted her legs and sat on them. "Oh, I hate mice more than anything!"

"I'm sure you have some at your shop," Melinda told her. "All these buildings are old, and it only takes a tiny crack for them to get in."

"Haven't seen one yet." Vicki gripped the edge of the table with impressive force.

"Traps are on sale right now. Come over tomorrow and we can get you ..."

A rattle echoed from the back hall. Bev was about to speak, but Nancy motioned her to stay quiet. They waited, barely breathing, and heard it again.

"It's the doorknob!" Vicki whispered.

A cold draft brushed past Melinda's legs, but was gone as soon as it came. By the terror on Nancy's face, she'd felt it, too. But the back door never opened. No one, even Bev, was brave enough to shine a light into the hall.

Several minutes passed, and nothing else happened. Finally, Nancy got up. "Ladies, I don't know what that was all about, but we've got one more stop to make." She swiped the lantern off the table and gripped it tight. "This is the real test, both of what might be in this building, and our own courage. Anyone who wants to go home, I understand."

"I'm going up with you." Bev rose from her chair. "We have to put a stop to this. It's not right that you have to deal with this ... visitor."

Vicki had the other lantern. "I thought you were a skeptic."

"I am. But that, what just happened? I heard it with my own ears. And a draft passed right behind me, shortly after. I don't think we're alone in here. Not tonight."

The stairwell was only unlocked when someone needed to access the storage area above. That wasn't very often, and the person was usually Nancy. Even though she'd done this many times before, her hands shook as she turned the key.

"Are you sure?" Vicki was concerned. "We already had one thing happen. Maybe it's enough. It proves something. I'm not sure what, but something."

With a wail and a creak, the old door's hinges finally moved. Far above, in the thick darkness, there was the unmistakable flap of velvety wings. This time, Melinda was the one who cringed.

"Oh, no! You have bats up there?"

"I hope that's all we have." Nancy aimed her light toward the narrow wooden treads. "I mean, other than the mice and the squirrels. Hold tight to the handrail."

They climbed silently, slowly. Melinda recalled Nancy's chilling story about the time she was making her way up these stairs, and a sudden draft brushed past her. A draft very like the one they'd just felt in the kitchen.

City hall's upstairs was much different than the first floor, with one massive room taking up most of the space. A row of tall windows stared out at Main Street, and a handful of smaller ones sat high in the wall that rose over the library's roof below.

Uncle Frank's project had made a dent in the stacks of stuff, but there was still an overwhelming collection of odds and ends: holiday decorations, busted-down office chairs, dented file cabinets, even traffic cones. But tonight, the random, everyday items were rather comforting.

The far end of the space, however, had always given Melinda the heebie-jeebies. The raised platform had served as a stage decades ago and, while the rest of the room was crammed with stuff, those floorboards were eerily empty. Both backstage doors were closed, and Melinda hoped they stayed that way. So many people had passed through here, so many years ago. The possibility that one of them, or more, had never left ...

"This spot is as good as any." Nancy stopped in a sort-of-clearing in the center of the room, and set her lantern on the floor. "Pull up a mangled chair. One of you might sit on this desk here." They formed a rough circle around the lantern, and Bev and Vicki reluctantly turned off their lights.

The shadows crept in and the women waited, as still as they could be. The wind was rising, and an eerie whistle advanced toward them from the front wall.

"Oh, that's not good," Bev said sadly. "Those windows would need to be replaced before anyone could run heat and air up here. And then there's the steep stairs, the lack of restrooms ..."

"It'd cost a fortune." Nancy sighed. "I've been telling Jerry that. But people love this building. It's historic, it's the heart of our little town."

"I'm scared." Vicki's voice trembled. "I don't want to see anything, or hear anything."

"But that's why we're here," Bev reminded her.

"I'm scared, too." Nancy rubbed her hands together. "But I need some closure, I guess. The worst is better than not knowing."

Bev shifted in her seat. "Oh, girls, there's so much in this world to be afraid of. Things far worse than a wayward soul."

Nancy fidgeted in her chair. "True, but that tops my list right about now."

"This ghost, or whatever it is, isn't the only thing that scares me," Vicki admitted. "I'm so worried about my shop. What if it's a failure?"

"You had great crowds for opening weekend." Melinda was grateful for any distraction from the darkness that surrounded them. "That was brilliant to sign up for that craft tour! Those ladies will tell their friends. Word will get around."

"What if my prices are too high?"

"Then run steep discounts," Nancy suggested. "Or change them completely. The holiday season's just around the corner, this is the perfect time of year to get started."

"I just don't want to be a failure." Vicki sniffled. "Ben's off at college, Arthur has the bank. What would I do with myself?"

"You'd come up with something else," Nancy said confidently. "Some people have snickered at your ideas, sure, but most residents think your shop's a great addition to our town. My nest is going to be empty in a few years, too. Ryan's a senior, and Kim's a sophomore. I'm divorced, as you know. I'm going to be alone." She was silent for a moment. "Really alone."

No one said anything. Melinda didn't know what her friends were thinking, but her mind found something, and wouldn't let it go. It was hard to say the words, although they'd been welling up inside her the past few weeks. Like a pesky poltergeist, they wouldn't leave her alone.

"If it helps any, I'll probably be alone, too." She took a deep breath. "I don't think Chase is the one."

"What did he do?" Vicki's tone was sharp.

"No, no, it's not like that. It's just that the more time we spend together, the more I think about the future. But I'm not sure I can see him in it."

"He's in the present," Nancy said gently. "Is that enough? Does that have to change?"

Melinda almost expected to burst into tears, but they didn't come. "I don't know when, but it will. I care about him, so much, but I don't know if we really belong together. And he lives an hour away. That's hard enough, and winter's coming."

"What are you going to do?" Bev asked.

"I don't know." Melinda sighed. "Nothing, right away. I guess I'll wait for some sort of sign. We don't really talk about the future, I'm not leading him on about that. We just ... are what we are. But maybe that's all we're ever going to be."

"Nothing wrong with that." Vicki patted the arm of Melinda's coat. "Take your time. But if things are the way they are, I'd say, you're better to face that now then fool yourself into thinking otherwise."

Bev shifted in her chair. "We all have to face reality. Even me. If we're going around, saying what we're scared of, I guess it's my turn. I had my mammogram last week, and they found a lump."

Gasps of sympathy echoed around the circle.

"Oh, Bev," Nancy said, "why didn't you say something sooner?"

"Well, I wasn't sure Sam wanted all the details." She tried to laugh. "All I know is that it's early. Just a spot on the scan, if you will."

"That doesn't have to mean much," Melinda reminded her. "It might ..."

"Be benign, yes. That's what they say. I go back next Thursday. I'm not panicking, not yet, but there's going to be some long days between now and then."

"Is someone going with you?" Nancy was worried.

"I'll be fine. My hubby hates hospitals and such, and the kids are all busy with their own lives."

"Tell me the time and place," Vicki insisted. "I'll go along. My part-timers are doing great, they can watch the shop." She waved away Bev's protests. "No, no. I am not letting you face this alone."

"Neither will I," Melinda promised. "None of us will. You need anything, anything at all, you just ..."

The lantern blinked off, then back on. Vicki screamed.

"What just happened?" Melinda gasped. As if on cue, the light vanished again, then reappeared.

"Are the batteries old?" Nancy grasped for an answer.

"Fresh this morning." Bev said, but her voice wavered.

The flashing was deliberate, measured, not the flicker of a dying energy source. It was as if someone had turned the lantern off, then on. Twice.

"OK, now we're cooking with gas." Bev was the first to regain her composure. "We need some answers."

"Oh, Bev, I don't know ..." Nancy groaned.

"We have to try." Bev tried to sit up straighter in her swivel chair, which wasn't level and was missing one arm rest.

"Now, listen. We know you're up here. The mice and the squirrels and the bats can't make that light flip. Nancy's been afraid of you for quite some time. She's just doing her job, and they don't pay her enough to put up with any more of your nonsense. We've got some questions. Flip the light once for 'no' and twice for 'yes.' Do you think you can ..."

The lantern blinked twice. Melinda tried to swallow the panic rising in her throat. What was happening? She felt small and exposed in the dark, wide-open room.

"We can't leave now," Vicki said, as much to herself as to anyone else.

Bev stared at the lantern. "Did you die in this building?"

They waited. Finally, one blink of the light.

"But why are you here?" Nancy leaned forward. The shock had worn off a bit, and this was her best chance to face her fears. "Do you like this place for some reason?"

The lantern flipped three times. Vicki whimpered and crossed her arms, as if trying to comfort herself.

"OK, so you love it then." Bev let out a low chuckle.

"Did you own this building?" Melinda asked. One flash.

"I don't get it," Vicki said. "If they didn't own the place, and they didn't die here, what's the big deal? What's so special about it?"

From across the room, there came the unmistakable sound of footsteps. Everyone held their breath as the sound moved from the edge of the platform all the way to center stage. No shape was visible, there was no sign of light or form. But Melinda could feel, in her bones, that someone was there.

"Oh." Vicki let out a breath of wonder. "Oh, it's the stage they love. A performer!"

The lantern blinked twice.

"Are you a man?" Bev blurted out. "Or a woman? Once for man, two for ..."

Two blinks.

"She might be stuck here." Vicki glanced back at the stage.

"Or maybe she chooses to stay?" Melinda wondered. "Maybe she was happy here."

The lantern didn't blink again, but Melinda sensed she had the answer.

Nancy made a guttural sound and soon, she was weeping. Bev put an arm around her. "Honey, I know this is scary, but I tell you what. After all this, I'm starting to become a believer. This place might be haunted after all. But if she's telling us the truth, then she's not out to harm you."

"I've just been so scared." Nancy wiped at her eyes. Bev reached into her coat pocket for a fold of tissues. "Until tonight, every time I've heard something, felt something, I've been here alone." She raised her chin.

"If you're still here," Nancy said in a loud, clear voice, "I want you to know, I'm not a threat to you. We've been cleaning up, as you know, moving stuff around. I'm sorry we've messed with your space. But I'm going to ask you to leave. Or at the very least, to not interact with me again."

The lantern blinked once, and they all held their breath. And then, finally, a second flash.

"Is she leaving, or just agreeing to behave?" Vicki wondered.

"I'm not afraid of you." Nancy reached for the other lantern and flipped it on, shined it right at the empty stage. "I won't be, ever again."

"You know," Vicki said, "sometimes, on those shows? They bring a psychic in. And sometimes the psychic says the ghost isn't telling the truth. What we just experienced was pretty crazy, but rather positive, in a strange way. What if ..."

"What if it's just messing with me?" Nancy got out of her chair. "If someone's here, and it's just some woman who dreamed of being an actress, then I say, let her stay. This space would be really expensive to renovate into a community center, hopefully it will come off the list. And then, she can roam around up here all she wants, I guess. Either way, I'm done being afraid."

They gathered up their things and picked their way to the stairwell. It felt good to be downstairs again, and even better to be outside. Maybe there was a rational explanation for what they'd witnessed.

The women traded goodbyes as, both relieved and excited, they prepared to head home. Melinda happened to glance up while she was unlocking her car, and a slight movement caught her eye.

What was that? Was someone standing there, in the second window from the left? She blinked, and looked again. Only darkness.

* 15 *

Nancy had made her peace with the presence that apparently roamed city hall, but one of Melinda's other friends was still struggling with his doubts. With the rush of harvest finally over, Auggie could turn his full attention to getting Chaplin the medical care he needed.

Melinda dropped Lizzie's tailgate, then reached for the wire cage she'd borrowed from Doc. "We'll make it so he can go in and out, for now, so he's not afraid of it. Then the night before the clinic, you'll set the spring so the door will close behind him."

"Looks complicated." Auggie was about to cross his arms, but instead pulled his canvas cap fully over his ears. It was a sunny afternoon, but cold, with a brisk breeze. The battered metal of the truck's bed was icy under the knees of Melinda's jeans.

"No, really, it's not that hard. Here, you take it; there's a handle on the top." She reached for the stack of old blankets and the cans of tuna, and they started for the shed beyond the grain bins.

Chaplin had quickly warmed up to Dan, but only allowed Auggie to touch him a few times. The chances he'd climb right into a carrier, even if there was tuna inside, were slim to none. Setting out the humane trap now would give Chaplin the privacy he needed to make this decision on his own. If only Auggie would let his guard down and fully participate in the process.

"Maybe he's not home." Auggie peeked through the cracked-open rolling door and stepped back. "Guess we'll have to try some other day."

Melinda sighed and took the crate out of his hand.

"He doesn't have to be. Just as long as he shows up later. And he will. You're feeding him, why wouldn't he? Besides, the clinic's in three days; we have to do this now. Otherwise, you'll have to ask Doc and Karen to work him into their regular schedule."

"Geez." Auggie stuffed his hands in his pockets. "You don't have to be so crabby. That's my job."

Melinda pushed the shed door wide with an elbow and went inside. "I'm tired, OK? Had a long day yesterday."

"Well," Auggie teased, "if your boyfriend didn't live an hour away, maybe you'd get more sleep. Besides, I bet Hobo hates it when you're gone so much."

Melinda didn't answer as she slid a few old buckets aside to make room for the crate on the dirt floor. Last night, at least, Chase had stayed at her place, saving her the commute, but next time ... There was no way around the fact they lived an hour's drive from each other, and neither of them was going to move. But it wasn't just the physical distance that had Melinda worried; sometimes their emotional worlds were far apart, too.

The ladies' investigation of city hall had been unsettling, for several reasons.

Unlike Nancy, who had resolutely decided to ignore any future thumps and bumps, Melinda knew she couldn't sidestep her situation with Chase forever. She still enjoyed spending time with him. But when she'd blurted out her fears, there in the faint light of the lantern, it was as if something had shifted inside her heart. The thought of breaking up with Chase made her want to cry. The thought of being with him forever made her restless and, she hated to admit it, a little suffocated.

Auggie was a good friend, but Melinda wasn't about to discuss her personal life with him. Especially right now, when there was a more-pressing task at hand.

"Actually, I got to stay home last night. Chase came to see me. But yeah, Hobo hates it when I'm away. And Grace and Hazel do, too, even though they pretend that ... hey, look!"

In the far corner of the shed, Chaplin was watching them from behind a pile of busted shovels and rusted rakes.

Auggie nervously wrapped one hand over the other. "Oh, he's here. Why doesn't he just come to me?"

Melinda's shoulders dropped. "Well, when you stand there like that, stiff as a board, and talk in that tone of voice, it's not exactly a warm welcome. And, you have to 'speak cat.'"

"Here, kitty, kitty."

She crouched down and motioned for him to join her. "You have to get on his level, first."

Auggie groaned, but started his descent. "If I get down, I may not be able to get up."

"The trap's distracting him, for sure," Melinda whispered. "Here, use these." She pulled a package of treats from her coat pocket. "Now, put a few in your hand. There you go. Just talk to him a little. And relax your posture."

Chaplin's furry moustache wriggled comically as he caught the scent of the treats. But he stayed where he was.

"See, he's too scared." Auggie sighed. "He doesn't like me, I don't know why."

"Just keep your hand out a little longer. Give him a chance. He has to study you a bit, get comfortable with you being here."

Auggie looked down. "I've sure changed in several decades. But he looks the same. Just exactly the same."

When Chaplin was still rooted to his post a few minutes later, Melinda decided to get to her feet. It was cold and damp, and Auggie's knees weren't the only ones starting to protest. "I'd suggest coming out here, several times a day, for even ten minutes at a time," she told Auggie once he was upright again.

"I know Dan has taken some of the feeding shifts, but I think you should start doing them all."

"What am I supposed to do? Sing show tunes?"

"Just be still. Tell you what, bring the newspaper out with you, or a catalog or something. You could sit over there." She pointed out an upturned five-gallon bucket. "Read to him, so he gets used to the sound of your voice." A smile crossed her face. "Better yet, bring some baby food. Chicken, no veggies. That's what I did with Sunny and Stormy, how I got them to trust me. They ate it right off the spoon."

Auggie was speechless for a moment. "Well, I suppose I can try. But I don't know if it's going to work."

"Why are you so quick to give up? If you decide it's over, then it's no use to try at all! There's no way it can happen, or even have a chance."

Melinda stopped short and looked away, suddenly grateful for the gloom. Tears were forming in her eyes, and she didn't want Auggie to see them.

He wasn't the only one who needed to find the courage to open his heart a little more. Here she was, rambling on about not giving up and being open to change and whatever, and she'd almost shut the door on having any kind of a future with Chase.

She was as stubborn as Auggie. Sure, she'd had her heart broken before. But what if this time was meant to be different?

Auggie shifted his weight. "Oh, my hip's getting to me." Melinda expected him to start for the office, where he was in charge and everything was just the way he liked it. But to her surprise, he crouched down and held out his hand again.

"Well, I guess I can get over to Swanton tomorrow to get that baby food."

Chaplin blinked slowly, which Melinda knew was a good sign, and padded a few inches closer to Auggie. But then the cat stopped, and settled back on his haunches again.

It wouldn't happen today. But maybe tomorrow, or the next.

Melinda reached down to give Auggie a hand. "On your feet. Sorry, but I've got to get home. If we're going to get our first frost tonight, like you say, I need to cover some things in the garden. Let's put out the tuna." She pulled the tab on the can, and had to smile when Chaplin's eyes widened at the unmistakable aroma. Didn't they say the way to someone's heart was through the stomach?

"When he gets home from the clinic, where are you going to put him? This shed is cold and dirty, it's far from ideal. He should spend that first night, at least, somewhere better than this."

"I'm going to make him a nest in one of the storage rooms in the main building. He's going to hate being confined, I'm sure, but I don't want him running around until he's healed properly. Oh, he really needs to go! I want to do the right thing for him."

The concern in Auggie's voice made Melinda's heart melt. If Auggie could try, so could she. She didn't have to give up on Chase. Not yet.

She handed one blanket to Auggie, and began to unfold another. "We'll cover the whole trap, except for the front. Cats like to hide, and these will make it safe and warm."

* 16 *

A tour of the community center's potential sites seemed like a simple activity, but there were still so many ways it could go wrong. That's why Nancy and Jerry asked Melinda to join the council for their walk-through, and why Melinda felt a bit nervous the next morning as she rushed to apply make-up before starting for town.

Her public-relations skills were a bit rusty these days, but she'd probably need them, one way or another. This was essentially a public meeting, so members of the local media would accompany city leaders on the tour. Random residents could also tag along, although Nancy hoped people were too busy this time of year to trudge through old buildings and visit vacant lots.

Jake was sure to create a scene, one way or another, and Melinda sighed as she unplugged the curling iron. The rest of the council members were a good bunch, even if they were often low on tact and full of opinions. Jerry, at least, was rather thoughtful, and should be careful with his comments around the public and the media.

But these days, he was rankled any time Jake was around. To add to the tension, the clock was ticking on Delores' contribution. City elections were now only two weeks away. If Prosper's leaders wanted that two-hundred-thousand dollars, they had to reach a consensus soon.

The first frost had arrived overnight, just as Auggie predicted, and Prosper Hardware was bustling with shoppers eager to prepare for colder weather. Hats and gloves were popular, as were packages of window plastic and even a few of the season's first order of snow shovels. Esther came in at eleven to take over the register, so Melinda could dash upstairs to eat an early lunch. At ten to twelve, Uncle Frank met her in the office.

"Are you ready for this circus?" He frowned. "What?"

"Well, that hat ..."

He patted his navy-wool topper, which was lined with fleece and had a flap that folded down around the back and sides. "Just call me Elmer. But my ears will stay warm this way. Miriam insisted on it, I have strict instructions not to get sick."

"Oh, I know it's warm, but it just looks so ..."

"Backward, or do you mean hillbilly? I know, we're supposed to try to make a good impression, but it's cold out there!"

Melinda reached for her purse. "Let's go. Looks like Lucas and Walter are here." She tipped her head toward Main Street. "And there's Nancy, and Jerry."

Jake pulled up just as Melinda and Frank reached city hall's front steps. He bounded out of his SUV and waved grandly, as if at a campaign rally, to the small group on the sidewalk. Melinda put on a smile, but she was groaning inside. Jake appeared to be wearing every piece of purple-and-white spirit gear he owned.

"Might as well put in a good plug for the school district for the cameras." Jake slapped Frank a little too hard on the back as he sauntered by. Jerry, who was wearing one of the high-school's knit caps, crossed his arms but said nothing.

"I don't see what all the fuss is about." Walter spit on the sidewalk, and Melinda cringed. "We're just going to walk around." He was a retired farmer and, true to form, was decked out in an old pair of coveralls that had faded from blue to gray. At least Lucas, who'd taken a long lunch from his pharmacy job in Swanton, had on a nice pair of khakis and a clean coat.

Clarence was the last to arrive, wearing a windbreaker embroidered with his auto-body shop's logo. His canvas cap was clean, but his calloused hands carried traces of motor oil. "Sorry." He shrugged when Nancy gave him her best "mom" look. "But I've got one up on the hoist right now. Guy wants it back by four, so I can't stay too long."

Most of the city's leaders, including Uncle Frank, seemed more interested in catching up on sports scores and local gossip than guiding Prosper's future. Jake and Jerry kept to opposite sides of the huddle, and wouldn't look at each other.

Two unfamiliar vehicles were coming down Main Street at once, a rare occurrence that meant at least one of them held a member of the media. This was Melinda's last chance to say something, anything, that might keep this tour from turning into a public-relations disaster.

"Um, guys, just keep in mind ..." No one looked her way.

She clapped her hands. "Hey! Over here, now!"

Finally, she had their attention. "Walter, you're wondering why Nancy and I are making such a fuss? That's because this isn't just a walk around town. It's a public meeting, same as when you're all sitting inside. Jerry will ask for motions to open the meeting, and from then on, everything you say is on the record. If you'd cringe to see it quoted online, I'd suggest you keep it to yourself."

"So, we can't say what we think, then?" Clarence frowned.

"You are allowed to speak freely, like always." Nancy's voice carried a layer of frustration. "But just remember, anything you say is fair game. Lucas! Please put away that phone."

"We're going to go upstairs here, first," Jerry told the council. "Then check out those two lots that've been discussed. We'll circle back to Main to see the former drug store, then finish up at the old bank." Both building owners, in a gesture of small-town goodwill, had provided Nancy with keys in advance.

A local inspector had evaluated each option last week, and Nancy handed out copies of his report. "I know you all got this by e-mail." Nancy didn't seem confident the men had done their homework. "But these are for your reference."

She lowered her voice, as the woman from the Swanton paper was coming up the sidewalk. "You may ride together from site to site, but you'll be on the honor system to not discuss or debate the issue unless the entire group is together."

"It's a good thing the locations are only a few blocks' apart," Jerry added. "There won't be much time for that, anyway."

"What about you?" Jake crossed his arms. "But I guess it doesn't matter, since you're mayor and all. Besides, I know you have your mind made up." He briefly raised his gaze to city hall's second floor.

"As do you." Walter glared at Jake. "Which is a shame, since we need to keep an open mind. Jerry doesn't get a vote, anyway, so it's not like ..."

"Hello, everyone!" Sharon Myers, the editor of the Swanton Times, was in her early sixties, and wore her long white hair pulled back in a bun. She shook hands with great enthusiasm, and Melinda was glad someone understood the significance of this event.

"My, these are interesting days! Mayor Simmons, before we start the tour, I'd like to get a few comments on how the community is reacting to the shocking revelations in the human-remains case. I'm doing a follow-up."

Jerry glanced at Melinda, who shook her head in a barely noticeable "no."

His comments in the Des Moines newspaper's coverage had been well-received by most local residents, but the county sheriff had been far from pleased. He'd called Jerry and, in terms Nancy could hear from her adjacent desk, demanded Jerry keep his mouth shut.

"I'm sorry, Sharon." Jerry's voice had the perfect mix of regret and refusal, and he followed the script Melinda had given him to the letter. "But I'm not at liberty to speak about the investigation. The site in question is outside our city limits, as you know, and the county is in charge. Perhaps you might call the sheriff's office for an update?"

Sharon nodded, but the grim line of her mouth said she'd already done that, and only received a boilerplate response about "lab tests" and "waiting" and "no need to be concerned."

The young reporter from the Charles City paper had just arrived, and he flipped open his notebook with a grim shake of his head. "I called them again this morning. Got nothing new. You know, I'm getting really tired of local officials holding out on the public." He stared at Jerry.

"Well, Clark, I'll be happy to hang around after and answer any follow-ups you might have from our walk today." That seemed to appease Clark, at least for now. "Nancy, let's get started."

The group was just about to go inside city hall when an expensive black car parked in front of Prosper Hardware. A silver-haired man in a well-cut overcoat raised a hand to Jerry. It was as much a "halt" as it was a "hello."

"Mayor Simmons." The man extended one leather-gloved hand. "I'm Winston Drake, Delores Eklund's attorney."

Jerry tried to smile. "Yes, we've spoken a time or two."

"Three times." Winston took in Jake's garish outfit without so much as a blink. "Mrs. Eklund's getting along in years, as you all know, so she's not up to walking around town. But it's such a nice day, I decided I'd just drive down from Mason City and follow along."

Melinda and Nancy exchanged wary glances. No one ever came to Prosper on a whim.

"Go on with your discussion as if I'm not even here." Winston mounted city hall's front steps. "My only role is to serve as eyes and ears for Mrs. Eklund, to see that her wishes are carried out."

Clarence narrowed his eyes. "We still get the money, right?"

Sharon scribbled furiously in her notebook. Nancy put a hand over her face.

"Yes, you will 'get the money,' as long as you follow the rules. Mrs. Eklund has given me no indication she intends to revoke her support for this project." But there was a note of doubt in his voice.

"However, she has instructed me to make sure your discussion today is cordial, professional and open-minded. I understand there is a mayor's race to be decided for your little town in just a few weeks, and things have been rather ... contentious at times." He looked squarely at Jake, then Jerry. "Well, let's get started."

Jerry regained some of his composure as they began the tour. "The council is well aware of this, but I'll just inform our guests. This is an historic building, and the stairs to the second floor are not up to code as it is currently used for storage. Please take a firm hold of the handrail, and watch your step."

Melinda fell behind to walk with Nancy. "I knew stairs would be expensive, but look at that estimate!"

"I know!" Nancy whispered but was unable to contain her glee. "Isn't it great? They'd have to move walls and everything! Lisette just might get her way. This rehab would blow the budget, even if there's no surprises."

"Lisette?"

"Oh, I just made it up. I decided, if we're going to have to get along, she might as well have a name." Now that she'd faced her fear, Nancy's outlook was rather rosy. "I even put in a little request for, shall we say, an impromptu performance this afternoon. That'd fix things for good."

There was barely space for the group to cluster at the top of the stairs. Jerry turned sideways into a narrow path through the clutter, and the others reluctantly followed.

"So." He looked around at the dusty chaos with an expression of embarrassment mixed with pride. "This is option one. Way back when, we believe this was Prosper's first community center." He gestured toward the stage.

Melinda held her breath, but there was no indication they had an additional "person" on this tour.

Lucas sneezed, then did it again. "Sorry, my allergies."

Winston stuffed his hands in his overcoat's pockets. "This is a rustic choice."

"Rustic isn't half of it." Jake stepped out of the pack, then stubbed his shoe on a wooden crate. "It's a real dump, right? Every window needs to be replaced, and the wiring's a fire waiting to happen." He pointed at a dusty ceramic fixture above their heads.

"We'd need restrooms and an elevator, along with new stairs," Jerry admitted. "Some of the brick could be left exposed, to keep that historic character. And there's already a stage for performances and programs. It needs work, but it has a great feel."

Nancy's face said she disagreed, but she kept silent.

"I don't know," Clarence hedged.

"I like the idea," Frank said, "but can we execute it? What if we start work, and come across something really scary?"

Melinda looked away to hold back her laughter.

"There could be structural problems." Walter flipped through the report. "Says here the building's limestone foundation is solid, but using this space for events would put significant stress on the support beams. There goes a big chunk of Delores' money, and we'd barely be started."

Jerry said nothing, but was clearly deflated.

"Well, let's head to the next location," Nancy said brightly and gestured toward the stairs. "Four more to see, and everyone's time is valuable."

The field on the northeast edge of town was a clean slate, and the landowner was willing to look at an offer from the city. Jake reminded everyone they could start fresh, make the site energy efficient, and have plenty of parking. But some officials worried it was too far from Main Street, and it would require a significant investment to run utilities to the site.

The second vacant lot was just a block off Main, and was reasonably priced. But it wasn't as large as the first, and area homeowners had already raised concerns about event traffic and noise.

"I'm starting to feel like Goldilocks." Walter sighed as they reconvened in front of the former drug store. "This one's too big, that one's too small."

"There's some potential here." Nancy gestured at the dusty windows. "Let's just take a look."

This building was only one story, but the front was lined with plate glass. The long-vacant storefont was in the block west of city hall and Prosper Hardware, and Jerry pointed out that revitalizing it could be a catalyst for improvements along this stretch of Main Street.

The site was in terrible condition, however. The concrete floors were cracked, and the cheap drywall added forty years ago was buckling and crumbling in several places. On the flip side, the building was owned by a Waterloo-based development company that had been trying to unload it for several years. And the corner that used to be the town's soda fountain still had the needed utility hookups for a kitchen.

"I can't believe anyone sold anything in here, even twenty years ago." Lucas crossed his arms against the grime. "Much less dispensed medication."

"It's rather gloomy," Frank added. "All windows in the front, sure, but would anyone want to have an event here?"

"We'd have to create some rooms, too." Clarence pointed this way and that. "It's just one huge space now. And framing costs money."

The former Prosper Savings Bank stood grandly at Third and Main, kitty-corner from the post office. It was another place Melinda had always wanted to explore, but never had the chance.

Tall, narrow windows lined the street sides of the two-story brick building, which had a turret-shaped feature above its wide steps. Melinda flipped through the inspector's report, and was pleasantly surprised by what she found.

"It has great character," Jerry admitted as he unlocked the entrance. "Mechanicals are in decent shape."

"There isn't an elevator," Walter pointed out. "But we could use only the first floor to start. Have to get a wheelchair lift, that could go at the side door."

Winston said nothing, but Melinda sensed he was intrigued by the former bank. She wondered what Delores had told him about this location. Delores, and her substantial check, held significant sway in the community. Any positive or negative comments she made about the potential sites could turn public opinion on a dime.

Melinda stifled a gasp when they passed through the vestibule and into the front of the building. It was grander, and in better condition, than she had imagined. Oak woodwork, surely original to the vintage building, was still attached to the walls and windows. The plaster was in passable condition, and the wood floors were sturdy.

"It's a little musty," Frank admitted. "But then, the bank closed a decade ago."

"Just needs a good cleaning." Lucas nodded slowly as he looked around. "Lots of paint, of course, but that's to be expected." He stepped back quickly as a distinct scurrying sound echoed from behind a partition. "And lots of mousetraps."

Jerry gestured to a grand set of tall, paneled doors. Behind they found a few offices, a pair of tired restrooms, and one space that had been converted years ago into a kitchen for bank staff.

Clarence approached a metal door at the end of the hall. "I wonder if this is the stairs?"

"Watch out," Jerry warned. "Page twelve says there's quite the bat colony up there. I'm not sure if there's anything else up there worth seeing. But the roof is decent. Inspector thinks the chimney is where the bats are coming in."

"Melinda, what do you think?" Jerry put her on the spot. "You've got an eye for creative things."

Jake glared at her, but she turned away. "Well, it's not bad. There's lots of light. Like Lucas said, cosmetic changes would take it a long way. I could see people hanging out here, having family gatherings, community meals, that sort of thing."

"It has good flow." Walter looked around with a wide grin. "There's already a kitchen, bathrooms. It needs work, but we'd have that anywhere."

"We don't own it yet." Jake frowned. "Just because the guy gave us a key doesn't mean he's eager to sell. It's still old. The fixtures are outdated. And we need to see the heating and cooling bills, you know it has to be drafty."

Melinda was pleased, and relieved, to see the council members being professional and practical. Even Jake had been rather subdued. Maybe he wasn't so bad, after all, if he could do more thinking before he started talking.

Winston cleared his throat once the debate ebbed away. "Well, gentlemen, am I to conclude this site might get on your short list? If that's the case, I have a bit of news to share." Sharon and Clark visibly perked up at this comment.

"Delores has already spoken to the owner. She impressed upon him the significance of the community center. Now, he's not about to donate the building." Winston quickly shot down the question Frank seemed poised to ask. "But let's just say he's a motivated seller."

Frank had told Melinda the owner lived in Minnesota and acquired the building through a random family inheritance. Houses in Prosper had a modest-if-steady resale value, given the little town's charm, but commercial buildings passed hot-potato-style from person to person for very little cash.

What if this was the place? She felt a thrill as she looked around the grand front area, where the sun was beaming in the numerous-if-dusty windows.

And there was Prosper Hardware, just past the intersection. This was her family's hometown, had been for over a hundred years. Her plate was already full, but she'd be eager to pitch in on this project.

After Winston made his proclamation, he shook hands with Jerry once more and abruptly departed. The meeting officially adjourned, and both reporters left. Winston's tidbit about the bank's owner had apparently provided Clark all the scoop he needed. At least for now.

"If this guy told Delores he'd sell cheap, that could be a game-changer," Jerry said as soon as the reporters were gone.

"His other choice is to risk Delores' wrath." Walter shook his head. "I wouldn't."

"We have a lot to think about." Jerry reached into his coat pocket for the bank's key. "Our meeting is Monday, and I expect a full house. Nancy, we'd better stock up on coffee. I think we'll be there for quite a while."

* 17 *

Aunt Miriam answered Melinda's knock at the side porch's door. It had been a tricky walk up the brick pavers at the Langes' Victorian on Cherry Street, as her senses had been assaulted every few steps by Uncle Frank's garish Halloween displays.

"I see you ran the gauntlet." Miriam gestured for Melinda to come into the kitchen. "And there's that blood moon to face down, too. Auggie's been in a fit about that for days, says this is a night that anything could happen. So, is the wicked witch on duty tonight, or just the evil pumpkin man?"

"Both. But the dead guy in the coffin seems rather lifeless to me."

"He's not very reliable, even though he doesn't have anything else to do. His cord must be shorting out again. It's just as well, as Frank threw a breaker the other night with all this nonsense." She reached for Melinda's slow cooker, which was filled with sausage-and-potato soup. "Here, let me get that. Watch your feet, dear."

Melinda carefully wiped her shoes on the mat. "I changed out of my chore boots before I came."

"Oh, sorry. I mean, watch under your feet. We've got a snake in here somewhere."

Melinda froze. That was more frightening than anything lurking in the yard.

"There's no snake!" Uncle Frank shouted from the living room, where he was supposed to be tidying up but was distracted by the television. "Miriam's seeing things."

"I sure am," she called over her shoulder. "It's black, and two feet long."

Frank popped in, a dust cloth in his hand. "I've checked every corner of the basement. No way one could get in."

Miriam wasn't about to accept her husband's explanation. "Well, I doubt he came right up on the porch and knocked on the door."

With a dismissive flip of his dust rag, Frank returned to his duties in the next room. Melinda checked the shadows under the kitchen table, and the awkward spaces between the stove and the sides of the cabinets. She had made peace with the mice and the spiders at the farm, but still feared finding even a small garter snake when she was mowing the lawn. And if one was ever in her house, even in the root cellar ...

Miriam pulled a tray of ham-and-cheese sandwiches from the oven. "I got up overnight last night, came down the back stairs half-asleep, flipped on the light, and there he was, right there in front of the refrigerator. Well, I scared him as much as he scared me. He slipped around the fridge and, poof! he was gone."

"Trick of the eye!" Frank called out.

"Do you think he went right through the wall?" Miriam asked sarcastically. "Maybe it's a ghost snake, you know, one that someone whapped with a broom back in, oh, 1903."

Melinda searched for a more-rational explanation. "Is there a crack in the floor, maybe behind the fridge?"

"That's my guess. I bet he comes and goes as he pleases, once we're in bed at night. But Frank can't move that refrigerator on his own to check, and I don't want him to overdo it, so ..."

The doorbell buzzed in the front foyer. "Oh, thank goodness, your parents are here." Miriam lowered her voice to a whisper. "I think Frank's scared to death, to be honest. Maybe your dad will be kind enough to check it out."

The immediate family gathered for Sunday-night supper twice a month, rotating between the three homes. And tonight, there was a bit of family business to discuss.

Prosper Hardware was fully under Frank and Miriam's control, and had been for decades, but Miriam still liked to include her sister in major decisions. The holiday season was fast approaching, and there were several choices to be made about special sales, store hours, refreshments and activities.

"Last year's open house was a great success," Diane said as they tucked into their meal. "Melinda, do you think George would play Santa again this year?"

"I think he'd be upset if we didn't ask him. Mary made her own costume to play Mrs. Claus, and I know she still has it."

"There's still time to order more of those small tool kits we tried last year." Uncle Frank passed around the relish tray. "I recall some shoppers saying they were buying them for their wives and daughters, in particular. They're reasonably priced, and serve a cross-section of customers."

"What about the branded stocking hats?" Roger raised his spoon. "Those went over like wildfire for freebies. But now they're stocked as regular merchandise."

"They're a top seller, now that the weather's turning." Frank paused for a bite of his sandwich.

"How about we put them on sale, but find something else to hand out to the early-bird shoppers during the open house?"

More ideas were bounced around for several minutes, and then Miriam raised a hand. "Well, while we're here, I suppose we should talk about some other decisions as well."

"Do you still think the store's roof needs to be replaced in the spring?" Melinda served herself a second helping of soup. "You know, those steel panels are really nice, less maintenance. The farmhouse's shingles will have to be changed in a few years, and I'm giving those some thought."

"I like those, too," Frank agreed. "And there's so many colors we could pick from. But ... there's something else we need to discuss."

Melinda noticed everyone staring at her. She set down her spoon. Did Aunt Miriam look a little nervous?

"So," Diane began, "Miriam and I have been talking. And your dad, too, and Uncle Frank."

"We're so glad you came back when you did." Frank picked up the conversation. "And you seem to enjoy working at the store. I guess we just wonder if you see this as a permanent career move?"

"Well, sure." Melinda blinked. She hadn't expected to be on tonight's agenda. "I guess I haven't thought years down the road, but, really, I do love it."

"This isn't about taking over Prosper Hardware," Miriam quickly added. "I mean, someday, that will come up, but not for some time yet."

"What my sister means," Diane explained, "is you'll be prying the broom out of her hand when she's ninety. No, honey, we're not trying to pressure you to promise to take over the store. But since you're back, and there's no one else of your generation living close by ..." Frank and Miriam didn't have children. Melinda's sister was in the Milwaukee area, and her brother in Texas.

Frank's brown eyes lit up with anticipation. "We've got an offer to make: How would you like to become a board member?"

"It's one you can refuse, of course." Diane said. "You know the store is incorporated. Frank and Miriam are the entire board right now. I stepped aside when they formally took over from our parents."

"We'd like to add you, if you want." Miriam smiled. "As it stands, Frank and I have to agree on everything major, as we can't have a split vote."

"That's not always easy." Frank rolled his eyes.

"Rarely does the board have to make a formal decision." Miriam patted Melinda on the arm. "It's just that, well, none of us are getting any younger. With you on the board, if and when something happens to us, Prosper Hardware could continue as-is from day one."

"Until you decided to do something different," Frank hastily explained. "You're already involved, in so many ways. We'd just like to make it legal."

"And you'd be the fifth generation," Miriam said proudly. "The fifth generation of our family running this business."

Melinda didn't know what to say. She was touched and overwhelmed by the offer. It had crossed her mind a few times whether she'd want to manage the store someday, or even be its owner. In truth, she wasn't quite sure.

Miriam reached for her hand. "We're not asking you to promise to keep Prosper Hardware going indefinitely. Retail's a hard business, and running a company is no piece of cake, either. But this way, when things change someday, you would be free to do as you saw fit."

"That's our problem," Frank added. "Someone will have to do something. Keep it, sell it. Close the store, or lease the building. There's several ways this could go. Our attorney's been on us for years, actually, to do something about this. To find someone younger that we trust to be on deck when the time comes."

"Mom, did you know about this?"

"Miriam and I've talked about it. We wanted to be sure you planned to stay around here, at least for the near future."

"Someone will need to drive the bus." Frank gestured for Roger to pass the pumpkin pie, as if he considered his work done and could move on to dessert. "Prosper Hardware is the heart of this town. If it passes out of the family, that's fine. But Prosper still needs the store."

"What about Bill?" Melinda frowned. "Have you talked to him?"

"Not yet," Miriam admitted. "We wanted to talk to you first. If you weren't interested in this plan, I think we'd reach out to him next. But you're family, and you love the store as much as we do."

Roger raised his fork to speak. "That might be your easiest out, if you didn't want to keep the store going yourself. Maybe you could turn it over to Bill."

Melinda sat back, her mind reeling. A member of the board. The future of Prosper Hardware passing into her hands one day. It would be a big responsibility, but what an honor!

"I'm stunned, but I guess I shouldn't be. It makes sense. I mean, that you'd need to do something, and that you'd ask me." She looked at the collage of family photos on the wall.

"The fifth generation." A smile spread across her face. "I think it's a good idea. I mean, I don't knowwhat I'd do ..."

Frank smiled. "The Good Lord willing, it won't be an issue for a long time to come."

"But you'll do it?" Miriam's eyes brimmed with happy tears. "You'll join the board?"

"Yes." Melinda nodded emphatically. "Yes! Put me on it! Why not?"

"Excellent!" Frank pushed back his chair. "I'll call our attorney tomorrow, we'll get the papers drawn up. I say, this calls for something extra-special to go with this pie. If I remember right, there's a bottle of brandy around here somewhere. It's been a few years since we've had a reason to bust it out."

A shout soon came from the kitchen. Miriam dropped her fork and shook her head, but she was laughing.

"Our liquor cabinet, if that's what you call a shelf with three bottles, is down low, next to the refrigerator. Ten bucks says Frank found more than the brandy."

* 18 *

Auggie settled into the empty folding chair next to Melinda and eyed the packed council chambers with barely suppressed glee. "Looks like it's going to be a real barn-burner."

No matter what happened next, the coming hours would provide days' worth of fodder for Prosper Feed Co.'s gossip mill. Auggie had successfully escorted Chaplin to last week's community clinic, and the former stray was warming up to him a little more every day. That meant Auggie could return his focus to what was happening around town.

"Is it true that when you went into the bank, a whole family of bats came flying out of the old vault?" He hurried on before Melinda could correct him. "I heard one of them attacked poor Sharon. And the piles of droppings! There must be hundreds of bats in that place!"

Melinda rolled her eyes. She'd heard this story several times from customers wanting to weigh in on the community center options. Aunt Miriam had threatened to add a sign to the project's donation jar that required people to drop in a dollar if they wanted to voice their opinion, but Frank had quickly quashed that idea. It was hard enough for him to be on the council when one of his best friends was running for mayor, much less keep Prosper Hardware out of this debate.

"We didn't see even one bat." Melinda answered loudly and slowly, hoping those around them would hear it, too.

"There were a few deposits, if you will. But those were small; the mouse kind."

She held up a copy of the inspection report, which Nancy had offered on a table just inside the council chambers. "There's only a bat issue on the second floor. And no one was attacked last week. Besides, bats have sonar-like capabilities. They wouldn't run into anyone, even if they were around."

"They would if they're rabid." A woman behind them inserted herself into the conversation. "And this is the time of year when they really get active."

"Well, Halloween is their favorite holiday," Auggie chuckled. "Same as the ghosts and goblins and the assorted undead. Now, if you ran into any of those on the tour," he told Melinda, "tonight's your chance to speak up. People will want to know."

"Nope, not a ghost in sight. Anywhere."

"That's not what I meant." The woman swatted Auggie's arm with her rolled-up report. "Winter will be here before you know it. The bats will be looking for somewhere to roost. More will be coming in, what's there now is just the start of it. Jake's got the right idea. We build new, start from scratch. So what if it takes a little longer?"

"No, that's not right." The man on Melinda's left turned in his chair. "Where's the rest of the money going to come from? Martha, are you going to let them double your taxes to pay for it? No, we need to fix up city hall, keep everything right here."

Another woman chimed in. "Or better yet, tell Delores to take back her check and forget the whole thing. Between the mayor's race and all of this drama, our town's about been torn in two."

Jerry soon called the meeting to order. The panel quickly ran through a few housekeeping measures, voting with little discussion, then opened the floor for public comments. More than twenty people made their final pleas, and then the council members debated the issue for over thirty minutes. This was the last meeting before Election Day, and they had to make a decision.

Winston had been right. The bank's owner quickly came through with an agreeable price for the building, which seemed to tip plans in that direction. But Jake's continued push for a new facility brought claps and cheers from his loyal supporters, and Lucas in particular seemed to still be on the fence about what was best for the town.

Finally, Jerry held up a hand. "It's nearly nine," he said wearily. "We could talk for weeks, but we don't have that long. Does anyone want to make a motion for ... anything?"

"They only need a simple majority," Auggie whispered to Melinda. "Somebody's going to walk away unhappy. This is going to be good."

Everyone waited. Melinda expected Jake to jump in, but he had suddenly turned quiet. Maybe he knew something his supporters didn't: The other guys weren't willing to support his idea. Finally, Walter suggested they choose the bank building. Clarence seconded the motion, and then Nancy asked the council, one by one, to state their opinion.

Jake's defiant "no" brought a few cheers from the crowd, but it wasn't enough. By a vote of four-to-one, the bank site was chosen. With the weeks of debate finally past, the room erupted in applause.

"Folks, we got ourselves a deal!" Jerry's smile of relief said it all. "Watch your email tomorrow, as we'll be looking for people to join the steering committee."

As soon as Jerry brought down the gavel, Glenn Hanson stood up in the audience. "Everyone, please," he called out. "I'd like a minute before we all head home."

"You're welcome to join the committee," Jerry told him.

"I just might, but that's not it. No, I have something else to say."

The chatter and laughter ebbed away, as Glenn suddenly seemed nervous. Jerry motioned for his friend to come to the front of the room, and Nancy handed Glenn the microphone. He gripped it tight, and took a deep breath.

"I just wanted everyone to know, to hear it from me." Melinda couldn't be sure, but was Glenn about to cry? "I filed my papers today with the public employees' union. Come spring, I'm going to retire."

Gasps echoed around the room. Glenn had been a postal carrier for almost forty years, and Prosper's postmaster for the last twenty.

"But you can't!" one woman said. "What will we do without you?"

"You're a fixture in this town," a man called out. "What will happen then?"

Glenn motioned for everyone to take their seats. "They'll just have to get someone else, that's all. Look, this shouldn't be a surprise, really. I'll be sixty-two in February. I can't do it forever, much as I'd like to."

Jerry was the first to recover from the shock of Glenn's news, and he put out his hand. "Congratulations, my friend. It just won't be the same without you." Someone began to clap, and soon the entire room was filled with appreciation for Glenn's decades of service.

"That's for sure." Glenn looked at the floor and wiped his face with the back of one hand. "No, Carmen and I have talked this over. My health is all right," he added quickly, "it's not that."

Melinda shook her head. Glenn knew this community well. This sort of announcement would have him on death's doorstep if he didn't clarify things right away.

"It's time to pass the torch, to slow down a little, you know? Well, Jerry, thanks for letting me say something. I wanted everyone to hear it from me."

Jerry reached for the microphone, as it was clear Glenn was too emotional to say any more.

"Tell you what, we get this community center fixed up, and we'll have a huge party for you, right down the street." That brought a ripple of laughter from the crowd, and Glenn smiled.

As the residents filed out of the council chambers, several people asked Auggie if he would be the next one to retire.

"Are you kidding? Glenn's so much older than I am." In

truth, the gap was less than three years. "Nope, I'm at the co-op to stay. They'll be carrying me out feet first."

* * *

John brought Melinda the first straw bale, and Dylan was right behind. The Olsons were following their routine from last fall, which called for Melinda to be in charge of lining up the bales along the north and west sides of her farmhouse's foundation. It was quite a haul from the trailer in the driveway, and Melinda knew she wouldn't be able to keep up with the guys for long.

"Sounds like it was quite the show last night." John dropped his load at Melinda's feet. "I have to say, I've been rooting for the bank, myself."

"That was my choice, too." Melinda set the bale tight against the concrete blocks, and reached for the one Dylan was waiting to pass her way. "It's going to be a great space when it's done. And then, there's Glenn's news."

"Now, that one I didn't see coming," John called over his shoulder as he started back toward the trailer.

Dylan paused long enough to offer his hand to Sunny and Stormy, who were supervising from a safe distance away in the brown grass. There was always a chance all this activity might flush a mouse or mole out of the decaying flowerbed along the foundation.

"We go months around here with nothing happening," Dylan lamented. "And then, wham! Delores is flush with cash, those dead bodies turn up, and now Glenn's quitting. But you know, they say things happen in threes."

Stormy wasn't sure about Dylan, but Sunny was quick to lean over and accept a pet. Now that he was healthy again, he'd regained the disposition that came with his name. Hobo was stationed by the trailer's ramp, where he could collect attention every time someone came by. But he quickly broke rank when Ed's truck pulled up by the garage.

With John's other son away at college, Ed had volunteered to round out this afternoon's quartet. Melinda had already arranged to return Ed's favor by helping stack bales around the Bauers' foundation later in the week. Given Ed's talk about moving to town, she was always looking for opportunities to help her neighbors stay in the country as long as possible.

After greeting Hobo, Ed approached the trailer and was about to navigate its steep step. But Melinda wasn't the only one wanting Ed to take it easy. John already had a bale positioned on the edge of the trailer's floor, where it could be lifted with less effort.

All three of the guys reached Melinda at roughly the same moment, which meant there was time for a quick pause to shoot the breeze. She didn't mind. This was hard work, but it was also a chance to catch up with the neighbors. Ed had missed the council meeting as well, and wanted a full recap.

"So it was a big night, then. You'd almost forget we had those human remains turn up." He set his bale down with great care. "I'd think we'd be hearing something soon."

"Well, at least they haven't found any more." John shrugged. "Maybe that's the end of it."

"That's what the killer wants." Dylan was grim. "See, everyone had forgotten all about it, decades went by. And then, the discovery made everyone take notice all of the sudden. I bet he's just waiting it out, waiting for the scrutiny to die down. Then he'll strike again."

"Oh, thanks." Melinda rolled her eyes. "That's just what I wanted to hear. I've slept well for at least a few weeks."

"You could always get a gun," Ed said mildly. "I've offered to give her lessons," he told John.

"No, no, you know that I won't!"

"Just ignore him," John explained when Dylan turned away. "He's hooked on those podcasts, the ones where they profile unsolved murders. He says they don't scare him, but I've gotten up overnight more than once lately and seen the light still on, under the bedroom door."

Once the straw bales were stacked along the foundation, John backed his truck and trailer around to the barn so he and Dylan could unload the rest of the straw, as well as the hay Melinda had ordered. Prices had come down a bit after the drought ended, but they were still higher than she liked to pay. Bedding and feed were necessities, so she'd gritted her teeth and wrote the check, making sure to include a generous tip for delivery. This was one farm chore she couldn't handle on her own.

She offered to help move the rest of the load, but John waved her and Ed on to the house.

"We can take it from here." John smiled and shrugged, as if this wasn't dusty, backbreaking work. Melinda was relieved. Not for herself, but because she didn't want Ed to overdo it. Dylan was quick to catch on.

"We'll be there in a few minutes," he told Ed. "Don't eat all the cookies, OK?"

Ed pointed out the pots of mums that still glowed by the back steps. "Nice and bright around here. You'll get a few more weeks of color out of them before they're done."

"I wish I could say the same for the garden." She held the porch door open and watched to make sure Ed didn't miss the last step, as it was a bit higher than the rest. "I need to clear everything off. That hard freeze the other night was the end of it."

"I should get the lawn tractor out again." Ed lowered himself to the porch bench and began to unbuckle his chore boots. "One more pass, and I think the leaves will be done for the year, too."

Melinda's lawn was also littered with reds and rusts and golds. Even though it was customary in the country to allow some of the leaves to drift away on their own, she still had several hours' worth of work to come with her lawn tractor and a rake. But she spoke up anyway.

"I'll be around. Let me know if you want me to give you a hand."

John and Dylan soon came in, leaving their dusty gear on the porch. Room was made for them around the square kitchen table, and Melinda brought out the cookies and filled the coffee mugs. She passed John his check, but knew better than to offer Ed anything more than an afternoon snack. He'd wave away any payment, claiming his efforts gave him an excuse to ignore the stationary bike the Bauers kept in their spare bedroom.

The talk soon turned back to last night's council meeting, and Glenn's stunning announcement.

"Wonder who they'll send us now?" John dunked part of a molasses cookie in his coffee. Their neighborhood was miles from town, but the Prosper post office was still home base. "Glenn's had a good run, but the guy before him, I think, was postmaster almost thirty years."

Ed came up with the name. "That was Wayne Burberry. He was from over by Eagle River, if I recall, drove for that office for years before he took the gig in Prosper. I wonder if one of our current drivers would want the promotion?"

"You never know." John shrugged.

"But our population base is so small, I doubt the job pays great. Glenn would have made out OK, given the seniority he had built up, but ..."

"I'd think they could get it if they wanted it." Dylan shifted in his chair to make room for Hazel to plant herself in his lap. "I mean, would anyone really want to move here? At school, all anyone talks about is how bad they want to go away as soon as they graduate."

John's face fell and he looked away. Melinda knew he and Linda missed Tyler greatly, now that Tyler was off at college. At least Tyler wanted to take over the farm. Dylan was only a sophomore, and she wondered what he might want to do with his future.

"Well," she said brightly, trying to lift the mood around the table. "City life can be exciting and full of opportunity, but there's a lot to love here, too. Sometimes people have to move away and experience new things," she told Dylan, "and then, sometimes, they decide to come back."

"Like you did. Are you glad? Are you happy that you stayed?"

"Yes, I am. But if I had never gone away, and saw more of the world, I don't think I'd appreciate things as much as I do." She smiled at her neighbors and took in the cozy kitchen, which was filled with warm light despite the dark clouds moving in over the barren fields. "A few years ago, sitting around an old table like this, in dirty chore clothes and my hair full of straw, wouldn't have sounded like much fun. But the company makes it worthwhile."

"And don't forget, the satisfaction of a job well done," Ed added. "There's nothing better to soothe those aches and pains that come from hard work." It was a small movement, but Melinda saw him rub his right knee.

"I can see where Glenn's coming from." Ed looked out toward the barn. "He loves what he does, but he's put in his time. The day comes for all of us when you have to decide: is it time to hang it up?"

John gripped his mug. "I don't like where this is going."

"Me, neither." Melinda shook her head. "Mabel said something earlier this fall. Are you serious about moving to town? Why can't you just stay out here? Sell the rest of the cows, if you have to. I just wish you wouldn't go!"

"What's all this?" Dylan raised his eyebrows. "Are you serious?"

Ed looked at the table. "We've been kicking it around, yeah."

"You mean, you have," Melinda said. "Mabel's not ready, she told me."

"OK, OK, I've been kicking it around, and Mabel's been countering me at every turn. We'll be out here this winter for sure. I'm just saying, maybe by next fall. Last winter was terrible, I don't know if we can do another one of those."

"Your kids would help you more, I'm sure of it." John had gotten over his shock, and turned his efforts toward persuading his neighbor to stay.

"And I'm in town five days a week," Melinda chimed in. "I could bring you groceries if you run short and don't want to brave the roads."

"Let Nathan do the sidewalks, not just plow the driveway." John leaned in. "The lawn, too. As for the rest of it, Melinda's right. Sell those beef cows off if they're getting to be too much work, they're more a hobby than anything."

"What about the geese?" Melinda pointed at Ed. "Why did you bring Hector and the girls home from the sale barn, if you're thinking about moving to town?"

"Oh, I just couldn't leave them there. They're fun to have around. Mabel wouldn't agree, not when they flap their way through the garden and trample everything. But she loves them, too, I know she does."

"You can't retire." Dylan had been checking his phone, but put it down. "You're way too young for that. When I get old, I mean really old, like you, I want to still be farming, too."

Ed laughed. "Oh, but I'm not a farmer anymore, not like your dad. The fields are all rented out, and we sold off our equipment."

"So what?" Dylan gave the shrug of the young and determined. "I say, if you live in the country and you have even one animal to look after, you're a farmer. For example, I've got my 4-H lambs. That makes me a farmer, too."

Ed hesitated. "Well, nothing's been decided yet. You know, Dylan, maybe you can buy me out one day."

"It's a deal." Dylan reached for another cookie. "But I've got two more years of high school and at least four of college, too. So, see? You gotta hang on, at least until then."

John reluctantly pushed back his chair. "We need you around here. Mabel, too. But since every single one of us is a farmer, that means we all have chores to do. I think we better start for home."

Once her kitchen emptied out, Melinda cleared the table and set the dirty cups on the counter.

She looked out the small window over the porcelain sink, to where the almost-bare branches of the maple tree swayed in the rising wind, and waves of fallen leaves skipped over the sleeping garden. All of the sudden, she hurried to the calendar waiting on the wall by the refrigerator.

"Oh, it is! I thought it might be." She scooped up Hazel and hugged her close. "Exactly one year ago today, I decided I wasn't going back to Minneapolis. You weren't around then," she explained to the purring kitten in her arms. "Or even born yet. But that day changed my life, and for the better. I knew what I had to do. My mind was made up."

Sometimes, change comes along slowly; and other times, it arrives out of nowhere, but you know it's right.

It was clear to Melinda that Ed, for all his ruminating about the future, wasn't quite ready to move to town. And there was plenty of time before autumn came around again to convince him to stay.

What there wasn't time for, Melinda decided when she glanced at the clock, was any more dawdling.

"I'm a farmer, too," she told Grace, who was stretched out on the linoleum next to the floor register. "Dylan said so. And this farmer needs to feed the chickens and the sheep before it gets dark."

* 19 *

Hobo went ahead, but turned every few steps to make sure Melinda was following him down the stairs. Or maybe, to check it really *was* Melinda.

"It's OK." She smiled, her twin braids nodding along. "I'm still here, I just look a little different tonight. I bet you're glad Chase is basically himself, if a little pale."

"Hey, I heard that." Chase was lounging on the couch, half-listening to the evening newscast and flipping through the Swanton newspaper. He was wearing all white, in a half-hearted bid to be a ghost, and held the ink-coated newspaper as far away as possible. "Gee, I don't see anything in here about this party we're going to. Are you sure it's happening?"

She rolled her eyes at the hint of hope in his voice. "Yes, Karen's party is happening. It's just a few friends, but it'll still be a good time." Outside the living room's picture window, the trees trembled in the raging wind as the skies darkened toward night. It was the perfect weather for Halloween, and Melinda shivered despite the warmth pouring out of the iron floor register.

She made a slow turn. "So, can you guess who I am?"

Chase sat up and brushed at his pants. His efforts to remove the cat hair left traces of newspaper ink behind. "Hmm, let's see. That blue plaid skirt's very ... country-like, and the braids ... You're Dorothy, right?"

"Nope. But the farm reference is close."

He studied her white blouse and eyeliner-drawn freckles. "Oh, that girl, on the side of the dessert boxes. Little Susie!"

Melinda was laughing now. "That's not her name, honey. And I'm not her, either. Look, I'll give you two more clues." She reached into her tote bag, draped a blue tablecloth over her shoulders, and fastened it with a safety pin. Next came a stuffed animal, a fuzzy lamb that caused Grace to widen her eyes in wonder.

"OK, I give up," Chase sighed. "You know I'm not big on this costume thing, anyway."

"I noticed. I'm not either, usually, but I didn't want to disappoint Karen. I'm Little Bo Peep!"

He laughed and hugged her. "Now I get it. And it's perfect! Wait." He reached for the lamb. "Is this supposed to be Annie?"

"I wish, but I don't think she'd follow me anywhere, ever. No, I guess that's little Clover." She pocketed the plush toy in her canvas tote, which was also blue but stamped with the logo of a Swanton grocery store. "I can't carry it around all night, I'll want my hands free. So this will have to do."

Hobo bounced back and forth, sniffing their costumes. "Have you been outside lately? Let's make a quick visit while Chase loads the car. I'm going to lock you in before we leave."

"I would, if I were you," Chase intoned in a low, creepy voice. "It's the night when the undead roam the earth, it's not safe for man nor beast." He snapped off the floor lamp before starting for the kitchen. "But seriously, I swear I saw some huge thing watching me from the peak of the barn roof when I came up the lane."

"That's my great horned owl. They're around more nights than not. I've only seen one at a time, but who knows how many there are? I used to be freaked out, but not anymore. Those pointed ears and wide eyes let them find the mice, so I've learned to tolerate their presence. Eeek!"

Hobo had already barreled through his doggie door into the back porch, but Melinda stopped short by the table. "Oh, not another one! Grace and Hazel Foster," she called over her shoulder, "which one of you brought me a dead mouse?"

The corpse had been carefully laid out on the rag rug in front of the kitchen sink. Melinda rolled a wad of paper towels around one hand before picking the remains up by the tail, then opened the kitchen door. "Can you check the basement door's latched tight? I don't want them to bring up another before we get back."

Chase set down the pan of brownies and started for the corner of the room. "What makes you so sure they caught it in the cellar?"

She froze. "Oh, no! Don't even suggest that."

"Trick or treat." He raised his eyebrows. "You never know what's lurking in the depths of this old house. All sorts of creepy, crawly critters."

"I thought you weren't big on Halloween. You're sure getting in the spirit of things."

He gallantly took the mouse out of her hand. "I think it's the company. That, and being out in the country on the most-dangerous night of the year."

"Speaking of dangerous." She slid away from him, but she was laughing. "That thing needs to get outside, and fast."

Melinda was used to living alone, but was relieved Chase was with her as they started for town. Folklore claimed this was a night when anything could happen, and there was a charge in the air that made her uneasy. Heavy clouds were rolling in from the west, and the headlights of Chase's truck caught a few pairs of glowing eyes in the scraggly, dead grasses on the edge of the gravel.

At least there was plenty of merriment on display when they reached Prosper. Auggie had a string of orange-and-purple lights in the front window of the co-op's offices, and several of the houses along the west end of Main Street were decked out with inflatables, synthetic jack-o'-lanterns and lights.

"Remember when we were kids?" Chase mused as they reached the tiny business district. "How all we had were real pumpkins, and if you carved them too soon, they were rotten before Halloween ever arrived?"

"Kids these days, they're missing out. Look at those fancy costumes!" They were waiting for a group of children to cross Main Street. "My sister and brother and I were happy with one of those plastic masks and whatever outfits Mom could whip up on her sewing machine."

Chase laughed. "My brother and I went as hoboes, more often than not. Easiest costume ever."

Unlike Uncle Frank's motley crew, Karen's Halloween yard decorations leaned more toward the natural and sophisticated. But strings of purple lights were wrapped around the entryway's posts, and lengths of faux cobwebs trembled in the corners of the windows and along the edges of the porch's railings. The ranch house was on the edge of town. A cornfield, now shorn of its crops and barren, wrapped around the lots at the end of the street.

When they opened their doors, a fierce gust of wind threatened to trap them in the truck. "Wow, it's wild out here." Chase reached back for the brownies. "Watch out with that cape, you might get airborne if you're not careful."

Karen met them at the door, her blonde hair hidden under an unruly black wig. "Greetings," she snarled, "dare you enter the castle of doom?" She noticed Chase's clothes and started laughing, as she was in all black compared to his totally white ensemble.

"If I'm a ghost, then you must be a witch." He held out the brownies. "Where would you like these?" Karen pointed to a table loaded with appetizer plates and slow cookers, and a punch bowl shrouded in a spooky mist. Pumpkin, her collie, sported a set of black cat's ears on her tan-and-white head. The dog was stationed at the side of the table, waiting for one of the guests to drop a cheese cube or cocktail sausage.

"Nice punch." Melinda nodded her approval. "Dry ice, I'm guessing."

"Well, what good is it to have a medical degree if you can't work a little chemical magic? No, seriously, it took five minutes to set up." The doorbell rang, and Karen peered out the front window. "Great, I think Nancy's here!"

Melinda introduced Chase to several people she knew. Doc's wife, Anne, was dressed as a flapper. Doc looked like, well, himself.

"Never know when we might get an emergency call," he explained. "Cows are skittish enough when they see a stranger, I don't need to be in some crazy costume."

Vicki and Arthur were in one corner of the living room, talking with three people Melinda soon learned were Karen's neighbors. Josh was there, dressed as a pirate, and hanging out in the kitchen with a man Melinda didn't recognize.

Karen soon pulled her aside. "Have you met Eric yet? He's talking to Josh right now."

"I wondered if that was him! He's cute." Eric was a teacher at the elementary school, and Amy had arranged an introduction. Karen and Eric had only met for coffee a few times, but Melinda had high hopes he might be a good match for her friend. "Oh, did you hear about Bev? Turns out that lump was benign. I'm so relieved."

"That's great news! I was thinking about her the other day. Waiting for test results is the worst." The doorbell rang again. "I better get that. No rest for the wicked, you know." And with a comically evil laugh, Karen was gone.

Chase's offer to drive to the party left Melinda free to sample the wine-spiked punch. It was deceptively fruity, so she had to monitor her portions. But it wasn't long before she was having a great time, and her costume received several compliments. Chase seemed to be enjoying himself, and she was glad to see him so comfortable among her friends and other Prosper residents. Most people at the party knew each other, and had for years. Josh was a newcomer, too, and the two of them were soon engaged in conversation, allowing Melinda to make the rounds on her own.

Karen needed to restock the snack table, and she offered to help. When she went into the kitchen for more punch, she found Chase leaning against the counter, checking his phone.

"Great party, huh?" He rubbed her shoulder. "Karen really went all-out. And there's a nice cross-section of people here, older, younger. I'm glad I came."

"I told you it would be a great time. I saw you talking with Josh, I thought the two of you would get along. He's new around here, just moved to Swanton in ... is something wrong?"

Chase barely glanced up, all of his attention on his phone. "Oh, no, everything's fine." He was sending a text. "A friend's trying to get everyone together tomorrow night, sort of a post-Halloween party. You know, back in high school, we all had so much free time. Now, everyone's got so many responsibilities. Heather's trying really hard to work around everyone's schedules."

Melinda opened the refrigerator. "Heather ... have I met her yet? She must be a high-school friend, then?"

"Yeah. I told you about her. She's the one that moved back."

"That's great you've stayed in touch with so many old friends." She found a spoon in a drawer and stirred the punch. "I've not done a good job with that over the years, and now that I've returned, I've ..."

Something about the way Chase wouldn't meet her gaze made her stop. She put down the spoon. "Oh, that's right. You said someone moved back to Meadville a few months ago. I guess I don't remember the name, is all."

"I told you." Was he a little defensive? "It's not a secret."

"No, of course not." They had the kitchen to themselves. "Why would it be? She's an old friend, no big deal. I guess I assumed the friend that moved back was a guy, and never thought any more about it."

"Well, she's not. What? Don't tell me you're jealous, why are you looking at me like that? I never pegged you as that kind of girl."

"I'm not." A chill passed between them. Someone must have opened the front door, and the wind forced its way inside. "Not jealous. And I'm not a girl anymore, actually."

"Good. Just because we dated in high school, doesn't mean ..."

"She's an old girlfriend? You didn't say ..."

"Does it matter?" He eyed her carefully. There was something in his expression she couldn't quite read.

Karen came around the corner. "Hey, there's the punch. Oh!" She sensed the tension between Melinda and Chase, and quickly reached for the pitcher. "I'll just refill it."

"You tell me if it matters." Melinda kept her voice low, mindful of the laughter and chatter in the next room. "Does it?"

"Why are you acting like this?" He stepped away. "God, Melinda, it's not like I'm sleeping with her or something. We're just friends, OK? We hang out a lot. It's no big deal."

But his face told her it might be. Maybe not now, but in the future.

"Well." Her voice was sharper than she would have liked it to be. "If you say so, then I guess I have to believe you."

This was his chance to deny everything. To ease her suspicions, tell her he wasn't interested in Heather, or anyone else. All the things that, right then, she needed to hear. But Chase only shook his head and, his phone still in his hand, went out to the deck without a word.

For a second, she couldn't breathe. And then, she was so angry she could hardly see. What was true, and what wasn't? She had no idea. But the ounce of doubt that had been in the back of her mind for weeks now manifested itself and spread through her whole body, and she gripped the counter for support.

"Is something going on?" Karen whispered when Melinda met up with her in the hallway.

"No. Well, I don't know." She gave Karen the play-by-play. Karen narrowed her eyes and leaned back to peek out toward the deck, where Chase was still a white shape in the dark, and still busy with his phone. "Hmm. He seems distracted, to say the least. And I know you've been ... maybe not sure about ..."

"I know." Melinda covered her face with her hands. "But is this enough to end things? Some mixed signals? Honestly, I'm not convinced he's cheating with her. Not yet."

Chase and Heather had a long history, and now she was back in Meadville. It all made sense now, the missed calls and the "I'm so busy" and the "getting together with friends." She was busy, too, and hadn't given it much thought. Until now.

"Do you need an excuse to walk away?" Karen raised an eyebrow. "Sounds like he just gave you one, if you feel the need to use it."

Melinda wandered into the living room and began to chat with Nancy. Chase trailed in a few minutes later, and settled next to Melinda on the couch as if their tense conversation in the kitchen never happened. He didn't check his phone the rest of the night, but Melinda hated herself for watching him out of the corner of her eye.

What was she going to do? Start monitoring his every movement, dissecting every word of every conversation, every text? High school was so long ago, in more ways than one. Melinda was a grown-up now, and she didn't have the time, or energy, to obsess over things. Either she could trust him, or she couldn't.

She dreaded the ride home, and hoped to put it off just a bit longer by helping Karen clean up. What might she say? What might Chase say? Her mind was still reeling, and even a few extra minutes might help her choose the right words. But Nancy had already offered, so Melinda and Chase gave overly cheerful goodbyes, then settled into a stony silence once Karen's front door closed behind them.

The wind was still howling, and the heavy skies were spitting an angry, icy rain that soaked right through Melinda's makeshift cloak. She'd left her coat in the truck and reached for it eagerly, trying to get warm. Then she closed her eyes for a moment, and wondered what to do.

She shouldn't say a word. A vicious fight was likely to break out, one that would push Chase to change his plans to stay the night. She didn't want him out on the dark, empty back roads in this frightful weather. It was already after eleven, and a long drive to Meadville. Whatever happened, whatever she would say, it would have to wait until morning.

Chase chattered all the way back to the farm, and she decided she wasn't the only one trying to delay a tough conversation. There were plenty of other things to discuss, as he'd met so many new people, and Melinda was quickly preoccupied with filling in the gaps.

She'd been back to the punch bowl more than once after their argument, and her mind began to loosen its knots as they turned off the blacktop. It felt good to spot her farmhouse at the end of her lane, several warm lights shining out its windows.

Maybe Chase hadn't told her everything. Maybe there wasn't anything else to tell. Chase was with her tonight, wasn't he? He had been less-than-thrilled about the costume party, but gamely went along with her plans. Come to think of it, he'd been especially attentive lately, more willing to make the drive to her farm so she wouldn't have to come his way so often. Maybe they could still make this work. If he could keep meeting her halfway ...

The guilty look on his face had come and gone so fast. As she yawned and rubbed her tired eyes, Melinda was no longer sure if it had actually appeared, or she'd just imagined it. After all, it was Halloween. Maybe some things weren't quite what they seemed.

Hobo was glad to see them, and rushed outside. Chase offered to watch over him from the back steps. Eager to ditch her costume, Melinda pulled off her tablecloth cape and hurried upstairs to change into sweats and scrub off her fake freckles. No dead mice were on display in the kitchen, and Hazel and Grace were snuggled in the large bolstered bed they shared with Hobo.

Melinda downed a glass of water, and had started another by the time Chase and Hobo came inside.

"Want a brownie?" She snapped the lid off the pan and helped herself. Suddenly, she was starving.

"Absolutely. They're really good." Chase reached for a kitchen towel, as the wind had pushed the cold rain under the hood of his sweatshirt. "Thanks for forcing me to go to the party. You know, it was a lot of fun. Maybe I've been too much of a ... I guess you'd say, a Grinch about Halloween."

Melinda laughed, despite her worries and exhaustion. "Hmm, fine. Apology accepted." She finished her brownie and brushed the crumbs from her hands into the kitchen sink, then reached for the hairband that gripped the end of one braid. "Ugh, these things are driving me crazy. I was afraid they'd come loose, since my hair's in layers, so I wound them really tight."

Chase leaned in. "Hey," he said softly, "let me help you with that."

* * *

Melinda stared at the ceiling, listening to the wind as it wailed around the corner of the house and rattled the bedroom's metal storm windows. She really needed to get the plastic sheeting on before it got any colder. And clean the chicken house, and ...

Even her never-ending to-do list couldn't calm her circling thoughts. Her head was pounding, and her throat was dry. She'd had too much spiked punch, but that wasn't what was really keeping her awake.

She rolled over and watched Chase as he slept. He was right there, yet so far away. She wondered what he was dreaming about, if he was even dreaming at all, so at peace while her nerves were so on edge. She had no way to know for sure. And if she asked, would he even tell her the truth?

That feeling of dread came back. Maybe it was better if she didn't know.

Once again, she replayed their conversation in her mind as she laid there in the dark. There was nothing specific she could put her finger on, no one thing that told her he was cheating. But something was missing. And soon, she figured out what it was.

This wasn't about Chase, about what he'd said or done or thought. No, it was about her. She'd been shocked, and angry, and for good reason. But jealous? No.

What about now? She waited. Nothing.

And then, she knew why. As much as she cared about Chase, maybe she didn't want him badly enough to worry about Heather coming back into his life.

Tears formed behind her eyes, but maybe they were tears of regret, not heartbreak. Sure, he should have told her the truth; and she was almost sure that he hadn't. But she'd kept quiet, too, in her own way.

That night at city hall, when her friends shared their fears around the lantern's feeble light, she'd confronted something that had been lurking in her heart for weeks. Maybe she should have said something to him, been upfront about her own doubts. But it had been easier to just go along as they had before, wait to see if her feelings would deepen, if something would change for the better.

And now ... was this a sign that it was time to end things? Then, she remembered what Karen had said: *Do you need an excuse to walk away?*

"No," Melinda whispered into the dark. "No, I don't."

The clock said it was almost three. The middle of the night. Chase needed his rest, and so did she. But in the morning ...

More tears came. And this time, her heart felt like it might rip in two. Oh, how she was going to miss him! Miss having someone special in her life, even if it wasn't every moment of every day. But it was time to let go. She'd learned the hard way, more than once, that she was better off alone than in a relationship that made her feel this lonely.

Melinda pulled the covers up to her chin and, haunted by long-gone loves and too many regrets, waited for sleep to pull her under.

* 20 *

Melinda hoped to get through breakfast before she had to end things. But as soon as Chase settled across from her at the kitchen table, her puffy, tear-stained face gave her away.

He didn't yell or argue. Instead, he sat motionless as she explained how she'd been feeling, and why it was time for them to part ways. Chase wasn't expecting this, that was clear. And he was so shocked and hurt that for a moment, she wondered if she'd done the right thing.

But then, she asked him if he had feelings for Heather, and he looked away. That told Melinda everything she needed to know. He slowly pushed back his chair and went upstairs to finish packing his overnight bag. His eyes were red when he returned to the kitchen, and he gave her a hug and told Hobo goodbye.

"I'm really sorry." He swiped his keys off the kitchen counter for the last time.

"So am I."

Melinda didn't watch him go. She left the scrambled eggs on her plate and, her hands shaking, hurried into her chore gear. The wind had blown itself out sometime before dawn, but a storm of emotions still raged in her heart as she trudged down the back steps. It was November now, and her world looked as dreary as she felt. A thin film of ice covered the shallow puddles in the gravel driveway, and dead leaves lay in soggy clumps along the north side of the barn. Hobo stayed close to her side, unusually subdued for this hour of the day, and sat patiently in the barn's main aisle as she threw herself into her morning routine.

She managed to feed the sheep and the barn cats before the tears arrived. Lowering herself to the wooden crate in the grain room, Melinda tried to cry it out, as much as she could. Stormy and Sunny crawled into her lap, delaying their breakfast in an effort to purr her hurt away.

A few minutes was all she could spare right now. It took a great deal of effort to gently set the cats aside, and get to her feet. She had to keep moving, even if she was only going through the motions.

The coffee guys assumed she'd had too much fun at Karen's party, and were too engrossed in their usual dissection of Prosper's comings and goings to wonder if there was another explanation for why Melinda was so quiet and withdrawn.

She decided to break the news to Karen and her mom that evening, but everyone else could wait until she felt more like herself again.

Each day blended into the next. Melinda's phone never rang, never beeped. Chase was gone out of her life as quickly as he'd arrived. She wasn't about to call him, as there was nothing left to say. Sunday and Monday were her usual weekend, and she threw herself into her winter-preparation checklist with renewed determination. By Monday afternoon, she found herself smiling at Sunny and Stormy's antics as they helped her clean the chicken house.

It was dirty, nasty work to empty the shed down to the bare boards and disinfect every surface. Once everything was sanitized and dry, a thick bed of fresh straw would be added back in and the hens allowed to inspect their freshened home. They didn't seem to mind their banishment to the run, especially since the day was bright and almost warm, but Pansy occasionally strutted over to the row of ground-level windows to check Melinda's progress.

"Yes, Pansy, I'm almost done. I hope it's up to your lofty standards."

The roar of heavy axles interrupted the peaceful afternoon, and a cloud of dust appeared on the road. Melinda leaned her pitchfork against the chicken house's weathered boards, adjusted her dust-crusted knit hat, and sighed.

"Snarky Steve is here," she told Sunny, who was lounging in the wheelbarrow of clean straw outside the coop's open door. "Let's see how much judgement he brings with the propane this time around."

Her first run-in with Steve occurred almost a year ago, when he'd arrived unannounced to top off the tank behind the house and evaluate Melinda's efforts to keep Horace's little farm afloat. Steve knew everyone, and everyone's business, too. Once he backed in his rig and had the hoses connected, there was ample time to shoot the breeze with his customers or, if they happened to not be home, study their properties for any signs of improvements or change.

His spring visit, thankfully, had come on a day Melinda was at work, and he'd simply left the bill behind the back porch's storm door. Propane was expensive, but Melinda wanted to make sure her tank was full before winter came again. She'd scheduled this stop well in advance so she could get the financial pinch, and Steve's pointed commentary, out of the way as quickly as possible.

Melinda pulled off her grimy gloves, tossed them in the dead grass by the chicken house, and started across the yard. Steve blared the horn when he saw her coming. She forced a smile and wave, then held her breath as he angled across the farmyard and expertly backed his tanker truck between the house and the picnic table. Horace had told her that in over ten years, Steve had yet to miscalculate that tight turn.

"Howdy." He jumped down from the cab and offered a firm handshake. "Hey, Hobo! How are ya, buddy?"

Hobo's affection for Steve seemed genuine, but the dog biscuit that suddenly appeared from one coat pocket certainly tipped the scales in Steve's favor.

"Nice day, huh?" Steve strolled leisurely to the back of his rig, giving himself several moments to look around the yard before he reached for the hose. "Won't be many more like this, for sure. I take it you're trying to clean the chicken house." Was that a sneer? "I'm sure there's lots to do around here before winter sets in."

"It's a dirty job, but it needs to be done." Melinda crossed her arms over Horace's old chore coat. "I was going to run the mower around, bag up the rest of the leaves, but that big wind we had yesterday carried most of them off into the fields. Guess the rest can wait a few days, then."

"One of the benefits of country living. Sometimes Mother Nature makes the work much harder, but sometimes she does it for you." Steve was about to drag the hose around the back of the house, but the fire-scarred portion of the pasture caught his attention.

"Wow, just look at that." He let out a low whistle. "It burned farther than I thought." Of course, Steve had long ago heard about the brush fire.

"Yeah, it was pretty bad. I'm glad the back section greened up a little, earlier this fall. It's a good sign the grass will come back strong in the spring, I'm told."

"You're really lucky. Could have taken the rest of the pasture, the barn, even the house. But I'm sure it's been hard, anyway. Sorry you had to sell off so many of your sheep."

Private detectives had nothing on this guy. But Steve seemed sympathetic. Maybe he wasn't so bad after all.

"Thanks. It's been rough at times." She reached down to give Hobo a pat. "And to top it off, I broke up with my boyfriend last week. Had to do it, but ..."

Steve put down the hose and leaned against the truck. "Well, I gotta say, he's a real loser. You don't need him. You can do better than that."

Melinda couldn't let that one slide. "I don't think ... how would you ..."

"Oh, I don't have any idea who he is." Steve snickered. "But it seems like good advice. That's what my wife always tells her friends when they're going through a breakup. I'm guessing some of it applies, at least."

She shrugged. "Yeah, maybe."

"Besides, you've got plenty to do around here." Steve gestured around the farm. "If he's not good enough for you, then he's not worth wasting your time on. Look, you made it through last winter, right? One of the worst we've had in years. But you're tough, you stuck it out." He shook his head with admiration. "I gotta bet Horace is proud."

Melinda was suddenly filled with emotion. "Yes. Yes, he is." And as she looked around her little farm, she was proud, too.

"Well, I'll get the tank topped off. Have five more stops to make yet this afternoon."

The life-coaching session was clearly over, and Melinda guided Hobo to the sidewalk and out of the way. She returned to the chicken house, where Sunny and Stormy were inspecting the bare floorboards, and went back to work with a grateful heart.

"I know you don't like Steve," she told the cats as she reached for the pitchfork. "His truck's big, and it growls, and he doesn't bring you treats like he does for Hobo. But he's not so bad." For the first time in days, she began to laugh. "He's the last person I'd ever ask for advice, but he's right. And that's just what I needed to hear today."

✳ 21 ✳

Melinda was pleasantly surprised to see several vehicles already parked in front of First Lutheran on this frosty morning. The country church's lawn was as peaceful as ever, but a "Vote Here" sign was posted along the front sidewalk. As the only public building in Fulton Township, the church's longstanding offer to host a polling place saved area residents a ten-mile drive to the nearest county maintenance shed.

Living outside Prosper's city limits meant Melinda couldn't vote in the mayoral and council election, but there was a contentious Hartland County supervisors' race on the ballot. Further down were two uncontested seats on the Fulton Township panel of trustees, a group of volunteers whose role was mostly limited to mediating fence-line disputes and maintaining public cemeteries.

With few of the first and none of the latter, Fulton's group was a rather-casual lot, and it wasn't unusual for one of the seats to be vacant at any time. Ed had taken his turn, more than once over the years, as had John Olson. But there was one name Melinda recognized: Mason Beaufort, Adelaide's husband.

Prosper's city hall sported a patriotic swag as well as a sidewalk sign. Melinda breathed a sigh of relief as she lifted a pan of treats out of her car. After all these months, the grudge match between Jerry and Jake would be over by tonight.

The guys were already gathered around the sideboard, eager to try Melinda's updated version of cherry squares. Half of the fruit had been replaced with blueberries and, with the usual drizzle of white icing on top, the bars were as festive as they were delicious.

Jerry, however, could only manage one bite. "I'm sure they're good." He stared at his paper plate. "I just don't have much of an appetite today."

Auggie brushed the crumbs from his face and went back for seconds. "They're fantastic! Come on, Jerry, I can't believe you're letting this get to you. How have you handled the pressure of being mayor for four years?"

"Well, normally, there isn't any. The council makes the decisions. I just do the research and present it to them, make a suggestion here or there."

"Then look at it this way," Bill said, "if the mayor's job is mostly for show, it won't be the end of the world if Jake gets elected. I mean, how much damage can he do?"

"You're going to win," George put in quickly. "But in some ways, Bill's right. Jake can't vote on stuff if he's mayor, unlike he does on the council. He thinks it's some big promotion, but really, it would sort-of move him to the sidelines. He'd just be a mascot, if you will."

Frank started laughing. "There you go, Jerry. George just summed up your last four years in one fell swoop. All you need is a costume, and you're set."

"I hate to admit it, but he's right." Jerry finally tried another bite of his dessert. "Being Prosper's mayor is a cheerleading role, most of the time. OK, fine. If Jake wants it so badly, maybe it's not so bad if he gets it."

Doc refilled his cup. "Well, your fate is in the voters' hands now, there's nothing else you can do."

"That's just it." Jerry glanced anxiously at the round clock above the refrigerated case. "I just wish it was over. What am I going to do all day?"

"Can't you find some paperwork over at city hall?" George suggested.

"Nancy banned me from the building. Said it's too distracting to have the candidates skulking about. Jake's teaching today, of course, so he's out of the way."

Melinda finished her coffee and went behind the counter. "Why don't you get out of town? Maybe go to Charles City, or even Mason City. Get some early holiday shopping done. The stores won't be crowded."

All the men groaned.

"Well, I guess there's one thing worse than waiting to hear if you're in or you're out." Jerry shook his head. "And that's shopping."

While Jerry was on the edge of his seat, Vicki's outlook was the opposite. She strolled into Prosper Hardware just before nine, accompanied by Francesca, her fashionable Pomeranian. The little dog sported a bright-red leash, and a navy-and-white sweater that kept the November chill at bay.

"My first major holiday shipments are coming this afternoon!" Vicki leaned on the counter and rubbed her hands together in anticipation. "I signed up to be an authorized retailer for those winter-village sets, and collectible figurines, too."

"You remember what today is, right?" Melinda raised an eyebrow and laughed. "Do you have any comments prepared just in case you get elected? Between being a write-in candidate, and the first woman on the council if you win, I'm sure your phone would start ringing right away."

"Oh, that's not going to happen. So what, I put up a few signs? Lucas and Clarence have been on the council for years. I bet a third of the people in town still don't know me, and some of them think I'm a flake. Maybe next time, I'll take it really seriously. For now, I better get more mousetraps. Between the store and at home, the cold-weather invasion's already started."

"Still in the third row, toward the back. And let me know how many are left. They're selling like crazy."

The day turned out to be sunny and pleasant, and several citizens walked to their polling place. The iron benches in front of city hall quickly turned into an impromptu doggie day care, as people tethered their pooches to the braces before they went inside to cast their ballots.

Melinda and Esther enjoyed the evolving crowd of socializing dogs from their vantage point across the street, but Nancy was less than thrilled. When Melinda strolled across Main on her lunch break, Prosper's city clerk was trying to block a four-legged resident determined to breach the front door.

"Service dogs only!" she told one disgruntled man, then turned to Melinda with an exasperated sigh. "I love dogs, really, I do. But they can't bring them in here. The county auditor would have my head on a plate!"

Melinda pointed to a small table of baked goods inside city hall's front window. "Speaking of plates, how's the fundraiser going?" All the proceeds benefitted the Catholic church's plan to restore the sanctuary's stained-glass windows.

"Oh, some people don't like that, either," Nancy muttered. "Separation of church and state, and all that." She jerked her head toward the council chambers, where residents were casting their ballots.

"It's the parish's turn to provide the volunteers. Next time, the Methodists will do it, and then the Lutheran church here in town, after that. It's tradition. These people donate their time to make sure our democratic process runs smoothly. Why can't they sell some brownies, or a few pies?"

"Is it really going that badly?" Melinda felt sorry for her friend. "Can I help? I'm off at four, and I could come over."

"Oh, no, I appreciate it, but we'll manage. It's not so awful, most people are patient and well-behaved. I'll just be glad when it's over."

"Speaking of behavior." Melinda looked at the ceiling. "Have things been quiet otherwise?"

That made Nancy smile. "They sure have! Whether it's because a different site was chosen for the community center, or because I put my foot down, I don't know, but something's changed. And for the better. Oh, look, there's Jessie! I told her she didn't have to walk my lunch over." Jessie and her husband operated the Watering Hole.

"I thought it would be hard for you to get away." She handed Nancy a sack. "Cheeseburger, extra fries and a side of ranch. I bet you could use a glass of wine, too. Sorry I couldn't sneak one over here."

"No, no, I can't drink on the job." Nancy reached for her purse. "But believe me, I'm going to enjoy one when I finally get home tonight."

* * *

While the months leading up to Prosper's election were full of drama, the final results were just what many people expected. Jerry beat Jake by a two-to-one margin, and Clarence and Lucas regained their seats on the council. Vicki got her wish, as her half-hearted candidacy gathered only six votes but accomplished her true goal: raising awareness for her new business.

The mood at Prosper Hardware the next morning was especially jubilant. Not only was Jerry re-elected as mayor, but he drove into Swanton before sunrise to fetch store-bought doughnuts to celebrate with his friends.

"I think we're the real winners here," Doc said after he took a bite of a glazed confection. "This is the perfect way to get my day started."

Jerry's laughter rang out through the store. "Jake called me right after the tally was posted online, offering his congratulations. You know, I can't be certain, but I think I detected a hint of relief in his voice."

"Well, now he can do what he does best." Frank reached for the doughnut that seemed to have the most frosting. Aunt Miriam wasn't around, and Melinda pretended not to notice. "And that's spout off at meetings and rail against the establishment. Serving as mayor takes diplomacy and a thick skin. I never thought he was cut out for it, anyway."

George heartily agreed. "After that train-wreck speech at

the homecoming game, I think he lost some of his supporters. And when the rest of the council wanted the bank building for the community center, that took some of the wind out of his sails, too."

"Speaking of the community center, I have a decision to make." Jerry reached for a second doughnut. "I need to pick someone to lead the steering committee. Frank, I'd like you to take it on."

"Me? Are you sure? I understand that someone on the council needs to do it, but ..."

"That's exactly my problem. Jake's too hotheaded, and he didn't want that location, anyway. Walter only moved to town just a few years ago, so he doesn't have the sway you have with residents. I'm all-but-certain Clarence and Lucas had Delores as a teacher, and so many of her former students seem to still find her intimidating. You went to school in Swanton, so I guess it has to be you."

"Well, I can't think of a more enthusiastic endorsement," Frank said sarcastically. "But if I'm the last man standing, I guess I can take it on. You know, Melinda's been talking about paint colors and light fixtures and grand-opening activities."

"The panel's going to need lots of volunteers." Jerry turned in his chair. "You might as well say you'll help. Frank's going to wrangle you into it, anyway."

Melinda looked out to where the bank building waited just down the street. She could already see its potential. How could she say no?

"Fine, twist my arm. Put me down."

Jerry grinned and looked around. "Anyone else?"

"I think it's going to be a fantastic space." Doc leaned back in his chair. "But the holiday festival's going to be here before you know it, and I've got to round up the critters for the live nativity."

"Why not just get the same ones?" George frowned, then started to chuckle. "Oh, that's right! Yeah, you might want to replace a few of your actors."

Auggie had been unusually silent. "You know, all this drama and debate about the community center? I'm not buying it."

"What do you mean?" Frank leaned over. "It's about all anyone's talked about for the past two months. I mean, other than those human remains. Personally, I'm relieved we had that deadline. If not, we'd still be fighting about it."

"That's just it." Auggie rubbed his chin. "Delores stirred everyone up, waltzing into that meeting with that check. Telling the city they could take the money and do as they saw fit, other than meeting her deadline. She had it all planned out; I know she did."

"The council got to pick the location." George shook his head. "It was up to them to decide."

"Well, sort of." Jerry said slowly. "Auggie, I see where you're going with this. City hall's upstairs needed too many repairs, that was obvious to most people. And the vacant lots were just that. Nothing to start with. The old drugstore's pretty trashed inside. But then the bank ..."

"Was owned by one of Delores' great-grand nephews," Frank finished the thought. "Which wasn't discovered until after the council made its decision. Someone ready to sell at a bargain price and make a fast transfer. Is it true the city's getting permanent access even before the sale is final?"

"Yep. Her attorney's bringing the keys tomorrow."

"I don't know how we missed it." George seemed genuinely disappointed as he turned toward Auggie. "That this guy was actually related to Delores."

"Well, he's never lived in Prosper." Auggie shrugged. "Nor have his parents, who would be Delores' ... oh, it doesn't matter. It's hard enough to keep tabs on everyone right here in town, day-in and day-out."

Doc smirked. "It makes sense that she kept that part quiet. Now, if she had offered the money, but then told the city which location to choose, people would have been furious. Some of them might have demanded the council refuse the donation."

"Exactly." Auggie crossed his arms. "Oh, Delores, she's a sly one. You don't spend decades teaching hundreds of teenagers and not pick up some street smarts along the way."

"I swear, is anything around here what it appears to be?" George topped off his coffee. "I guess it all works out in the end, if we finally have a community center."

"I'll take it however I can get it." Jerry's phone buzzed, and he carefully set his cup on the hardwood floor and reached into his pocket.

"What is it?" Auggie leaned over and tried to read the screen. "Is it Jake again, wanting to stay on your good side?"

"Yeah, I wish. No, the test results on all those remains are back from the state crime lab. They pushed the last ones up in the queue, so they could get some closure on the case as soon as possible."

Everyone held their breath as Jerry scanned the message. He gave a whistle of surprise, then began to laugh.

Frank frowned. "What's so funny? People have been wound up about this for weeks."

"And all for nothing, if this is correct. Has to be, it's from the sheriff's department. Those bodies? They're really old."

"So?" Doc shrugged. "We knew that."

"What do you mean?" George raised his chin. "How far back are we talking here? Postwar era, or even the Great Depression?"

"Older yet. Pioneer days." Jerry picked up his coffee mug and got to his feet. "They're calling in the state historical society. Well, looks like the first action of my second term will be attending this press conference. It's at noon, over at the courthouse."

Auggie reached for his coat. "I better get to the co-op, there's going to be a lot to discuss. Jerry, my heartiest congratulations on your re-election, but I'd bet those dead people are going to push you right off the stage."

* 22 *

Adelaide slowed the car as it started the gentle descent into Hawk Hollow, then shifted to the shoulder of the gravel road.

"We'll hoof it from here," she told Melinda. "That field drive has too many ruts and tall weeds in it, I don't want us to get stuck. If Mason hadn't taken the truck to town, I'd get us closer, for sure. Either way, we'll have to climb that gate."

"Fine by me." Melinda pulled on her gloves. "Won't hurt us to hike in. Besides, who knows what else might be out here that's historically significant? The less this field is disturbed, the better."

Tests had revealed all three victims died in the mid-1800s, which placed their deaths around forty years before Prosper ever existed. Even Swanton, which was now the county seat, hadn't been more than a village until just after the Civil War.

The smaller skeleton was that of a child, as many had suspected. As for the pronounced skull fracture on one of the larger sets of remains, several possibilities had been raised that didn't involve murder.

With modern medicine still decades away and few, if any, doctors in the area, life in the county's earliest days had been dangerous and too-often short. Something as simple as a bad fall, or a swift kick from a spooked horse, could have caused the head injury.

"They're saying DNA shows all three were of European heritage." Adelaide got out of the car but didn't bother with the locks. "Mostly a mix of German and British."

"Very common for early settlers in this area." Melinda pulled her knit cap down against the sharp breeze. "Just think, pioneers! And here everyone was so worried, terrified a killer was on the loose."

"We gave ourselves a good scare, didn't we? What is it about this time of year that has people looking over their shoulders so much?"

"Fall is a beautiful season, but it has that underlying feeling of decay and loss. Add in Halloween, and you've got the perfect recipe for people frightening themselves."

Adelaide stepped on the gate's bottom rung. "I'm so glad the mystery's been solved. Just so you know, we're out here on official business, since Mason's a trustee. The board's going to take over the cemetery once it's formally recognized, and they'll have to get a committee together to work with the historical groups. The guy that owns this field gave me permission to come out today."

"Glad to know we're not trespassing. I guess I hadn't thought about that." Their boots crunched through the dry grass as they aimed for the creek. "So, he's going to sell off this little plot, then?"

"He's donating it, which is wonderful. It's about the best ending we could have hoped for. You know how scared I was there for a while, like everyone else. But I have to say, I wondered about this very thing, once the sheriff said they thought the remains were really old. Hawk Hollow wasn't ever a town in the usual sense, but it obviously was a gathering place in this part of the county."

"Maybe it was a stagecoach stop." Melinda picked up the story as she gestured across the empty meadow. "Before that fancy house was built, there must have been something here."

"Probably a log cabin first, then a smaller house." Adelaide stopped a respectful distance from the disturbed earth along the creek. Yellow caution tape still surrounded the burial site's modest perimeter, which was marked by a series of metal posts. "These people could have been passing through, and something went wrong. Or maybe they lived nearby, even right on this land. It's likely we'll never find out what really happened, or when. The state didn't start keeping death records until 1880."

"From what Ada and Horace have told me, the Lutheran church didn't form until the late 1870s. Before then, there wouldn't have been a cemetery anywhere around here. People did what they had to do."

A few brown leaves still clung to the trees along the bank, and they shivered in an unexpected gust of wind. "Just think of it," Adelaide whispered. "Your child gets sick, and there's nothing you can do. Or your husband is terribly injured. You try everything you can think of, but you lose him, anyway."

"Those women were tough." Melinda shook her head with admiration. "They had to be. And sometimes, we think we have it hard! Can you imagine spending the winter out here, in a cabin?" She glanced around the windswept field. "It wasn't just difficult, it was dangerous. Disease, accidents, anything could happen."

There was a sudden movement in the dry grass along the creek. Melinda expected a wild animal to appear, but nothing showed itself. She and Adelaide were only visitors to this remote corner of the township, and not worthy of acknowledgement. Fire, decay and neglect had wiped away all traces of human existence, and nature reclaimed this sacred spot long ago.

"You'd never know anything had ever been here," Melinda finally said. "A farm, a family, that grand house. The creamery across the way." She crossed her arms against the wind and stared at the three gaping holes in the ground. "You know, it's the stuff of nightmares, in some ways. These unmarked graves, forgotten and neglected. And everything else gone. But really, it's not so much scary as it is sad."

"It haunts you, for sure." Adelaide sighed. "But in a different way."

"So, what happens now?"

"Well, the township's going to make up for lost time. A sturdy fence, a sign. The grass will be kept under control. They might even replant it to native prairie. We don't have names and dates for the deceased, so I don't know about grave markers."

"There still could be something. One for each, or at least a group monument. And what about the rest of Hawk Hollow?" Melinda turned to admire the iron bridge, whose rusted angle beams created their own work of art against the gray sky. "A sign, maybe, for the creamery and store site? And Jerry said the bridge is historically significant."

"Just because Hawk Hollow is long gone, doesn't mean it has to be forgotten." Adelaide rubbed her gloved hands together. "Heck, it *does* still exist; we're here, right now! Oh, can you just imagine how it was?"

Melinda could. "We have to do something to preserve what's left, and remember what used to be."

"I knew you'd agree." Adelaide elbowed Melinda and grinned. "That's why I wanted you to come down here with me today. Not much can be done yet this year, before the ground freezes, other than replace the remains. The rest will have to wait until spring. But that gives us plenty of time to raise some money."

"Another committee, huh? Why not? I'd be honored to help out." The possibilities made Melinda feel warm inside, but the deepening cold was threatening to seep through her layers. "The light's about gone, I suppose we should go."

Shadows were gathering at their feet and they took their time, picking their way across the uneven field.

"It gets dark earlier every day." Adelaide shook her head. "Thanksgiving will be here again in a few weeks. I don't know where the time goes."

"Me, neither." Melinda swallowed the lump suddenly forming in her throat. One day Chase was in her life, and then he was gone. She'd done what was right, but sometimes it still hurt, and regret and loss crept up on her when she least expected it. "It's been a crazy fall, for sure. Just one shock and surprise after another."

"I'm really sorry about Chase." Adelaide held the gate steady as Melinda climbed over, then started her own ascent while Melinda returned the favor. "I know you were the one to end things, but it's still hard."

"I had to do it. It was awful, but there was a sense of relief, too, once I made up my mind to let him go."

"And that was exactly the right thing to do. Oh, it's been decades since I've been in your shoes." Adelaide gave a rueful laugh. "But back then, I always knew: You can't hang on to the wrong one, even if it's the easy thing to do at the time. Because if the wrong one's in the way, the right one won't ever get a chance."

Would she ever find the right guy to share her life? Melinda still hoped so. But if not, she'd find a way to be content with what she already had. Which was, although unexpected, more than she'd ever hoped to find.

"You're right; it's best to go with the flow. Besides, I guess I've resigned myself to being on my own."

"Nothing wrong with that." Adelaide rounded the car's bumper and pulled the keys from her pocket. "But you never know what's going to happen."

Melinda settled in, glad to shut out the cold. The heavy clouds were lifting at last, and the western horizon was now painted a brilliant blend of orange and red, a shot of bright light before the day slipped away. She gazed out over the meadow one more time, and was rewarded with the sight of a hawk soaring high above the creek.

Adelaide turned the key. "Man, it feels good to get out of that wind! Do you have time for a cup of tea before you hurry home to do chores?"

The sudden warmth of the car made Melinda's cheeks flame, but she was smiling as the wheels started to turn. "That sounds perfect. Let's go."

What's next

"The Blessed Season": Book 8 will be coming your way Sept. 29, 2020. Read on for an excerpt from the book!

And then ... This series isn't over yet. Look for Book 9 in spring 2021 ... and maybe, a Book 10 later that year. After that? It's too soon to say too much, but I'm considering several ideas for a brand-new series (or more than one!) that will be rooted in the same geographical area. We'll all get to enjoy new adventures, and some of your favorite characters from the "Growing Season" series will show up from time to time!

Stay in touch: Be sure to sign up for the email newsletter when you visit fremontcreekpress.com. That's the best way to find out when future books will be available.

Recipes: Three more special dishes have been added to the collection on the website. They're filled with fall flavors, to be sure, but enjoyable any time of the year!

Thanks for reading!
Melanie

SNEAK PEEK: THE BLESSED SEASON

November: Main Street

The hum of a power saw echoed from behind the closed door, where Bill was as busy as one of Santa's elves with lumber orders for several Christmas crafts and gifts.

"I'm so glad we kept the woodshop going." Miriam paused to straighten the boxes of Christmas lights and garland that filled the end-row display closest to the register. "So many people don't have the means to cut their own, and it's one more service we can offer customers. We're on track to have a near-record month for that portion of the business."

"And Bill loves it, too." Melinda took off her apron and added it to a peg in the wall. "You should see what he's working on this morning. Pieces for a rocking horse, and a toy chest, I think."

Miriam glanced at the calendar. "Bill's really in his element this time of year. Before you know it, the holidays will have blown past, and he'll be back to cutting stair treads and shelves. Then it'll be chicken-coop frames, spring fix-up projects ... nope, it's never dull around here."

"Well, I better get over to the post office." Melinda took her purse out from under the counter, and reached for her coat. "I want to get my holiday stamps before Glenn starts to run low."

As Prosper Hardware's front door closed behind her, Melinda wondered how Glenn Hanson really felt about his plans to retire. He'd worked for Prosper's post office his entire career, and loved almost every minute. But it was time to slow down, he'd told his friends and customers, and really enjoy life.

A woman coming out of the post office greeted Melinda, then lowered her voice. "I don't know what it is, but something's wrong with Glenn. He barely said three words to me while he weighed my package, and he seemed really down. And I thought he was so excited about retirement!"

"Well, this will be his final holiday season, I suppose it's hard for him. Thanks for letting me know."

Upbeat holiday tunes greeted her when she entered the post office. But they were on a low volume, and the place was otherwise silent and empty. Except for Glenn, who was studying something on the counter with a furrowed brow.

"Hey, Melinda." He barely looked up. The woman was right. Glenn was as rotund as ever, but he was far from jolly.

"I like this garland." She pointed at the front of the service counter, searching for something positive to say. "Those red and gold balls really set off the greenery."

"Yeah, it's nice." He looked away. "I hope everyone else appreciates it, too. And the lights in the window, all of it. Because this is the last time. The last holiday season."

"I'm sure retirement's going to be a big adjustment," she said gently, setting her purse on the counter and reaching for her wallet. "But, just think, next year you'll get to enjoy the holidays. No more extended hours, lines of cranky people dragging in boxes. You can be at home, with your grandson in your lap, watching movies and eating cookies."

His face had turned red. Was he crying?

Melinda peered around Glenn toward the door into the back of the post office. It was closed. Without a word, she pushed through the half-door in the counter and put a hand on Glenn's arm. "Hey, what's the matter? You seem upset."

He elbowed the sheet of paper toward her. "This! This is what's wrong. I can't believe it!"

Melinda snatched up the letter, which was from the regional postal center. As she scanned its contents, she began to feel lightheaded. "Glenn! This ... this can't be! Can they even do that?"

"You're damn right they can!" He wiped at his face with the back of his hand. "I can't believe it, but they want to shut us down! The feds are on a rampage, trying to cut costs by closing post offices, especially in little towns like ours." Glenn slammed one meaty fist on the counter, and Melinda jumped.

"They've been planning this for months ... years!" His eyes blazed with fury. "Do you know what my regional supervisor told me this morning? He said his bosses admitted they were just waiting for me to file my retirement papers. Saves them having to lay me off, see? They knew I'd fight it, and they're right about that. They want to divide up the rest of my crew, have them work out of Eagle River or Swanton."

"What are they going to do with the building?" She looked out at Prosper's sleepy Main Street. "Who's going to buy it? And, why run drivers way out here from other towns? The gas alone ..."

"Doesn't make sense, does it? But that's the government for you. Overages, cost projections, blah, blah, blah. We're nothing to them, our little town. Nothing but some numbers on a spreadsheet."

Glenn dropped into the stool-height chair behind the counter. "We're through! This is going to end us. Not just the post office, but the whole town!"

"Hold on, you're just upset." But Glenn's gloom was contagious, and Melinda searched for any ray of hope she could find. "Wait! It's not final, not yet. Further down, the notice says this is a proposal. A *proposal*, Glenn."

He was so lost in his grief and anger, Melinda wasn't sure he'd even heard what she'd said.

"Did you see this? They're going to host public hearings. The first one's going to be sometime next month."

"It doesn't matter," Glenn said through gritted teeth. "That's all a show. If they say they want to do it, it's already done."

"But, there has to be something we can do!" Melinda's anger now nearly matched Glenn's. "This is the dumbest thing I've ever heard of!"

"All we can do is tack that letter on the bulletin board." He pointed to a frame of cork on the far wall, next to the brass-plated mailboxes. "It's an official notice, it has to be posted where the public can see it. I just can't do it." His eyes were sad again, pleading.

Melinda slipped around the counter and, with shaking hands, found a spare tack on the board. She found a space between the lost-and-found items and a notice for the Methodist Church's holiday dinner then stood back, staring at a sheet of white paper that contained such shocking news buried between government jargon about "infrastructure" and "operating expenses" and "synergies."

Glenn was now numb with grief, and had his head down on the counter. "It's going to be OK," she told him, trying to believe it herself. "I don't know how, but it will be."

He didn't answer. The holiday stamps long forgotten, she grabbed her purse and dashed out the door, barely looking both ways before she ran across Main Street.

"Nancy!" She burst into the library, searching for her friend. "Nancy?"

"In here." Nancy was behind the front desk of city hall. "Oh, my God, what happened? Is someone hurt?"

"No, no. Where's Jerry?" Melinda was panting now, from exertion and the weight of the news she carried. "We have to tell him, right now. And someone needs to help Glenn."

Nancy steered Melinda toward a chair. "Sit down, take a deep breath, and start at the beginning."

"The Blessed Season" arrives Sept. 29, 2020.
Visit fremontcreekpress.com and sign up for the newsletter
to find out when future books in the series will be available.

ABOUT THE BOOKS

*Don't miss any of the titles
in this heartwarming rural fiction series*

Growing Season (Book 1)

Melinda Foster is already at a crossroads when the "for rent" sign beckons her down a dusty gravel lane. With her job gone and her prospects dim, it's not long before she finds herself living in a faded farmhouse, caring for a barn full of animals, and working at her family's hardware store. And just like the vast garden she tends under the summer sun, Melinda soon begins to thrive.

Harvest Season (Book 2)

Melinda's efforts at her rented farmhouse are starting to pay off. But even in Prosper, nothing stays the same. One member of the hardware store's coffee group shares a startling announcement, and a trip back to the city makes her realize how deep her roots now run in rural Iowa. As the seasons change, Melinda must choose between the security of her old life or an uncertain future.

The Peaceful Season (Book 3)

As a reflective hush falls over the fields, Melinda turns her thoughts toward the coming holidays. She has a list of what will make the season perfect: Prepare her acreage for the coming winter, host her family's Christmas dinner, and use her marketing smarts to upgrade Prosper's holiday festival. But when a mysterious visitor arrives, she is reminded there is so much more to the Christmas season.

Waiting Season (Book 4)

Melinda finds herself struggling to keep the worst of winter's threats from her door. She pushes on because Horace's offer still stands: He'll sell her the farm in the spring. But as winter tightens its grip on rural Iowa, Melinda's biggest challenges are still to come. A series of events threatens to break her heart and shatter her hopes, and it will take all of her faith to see the season through.

Songbird Season (Book 5)

The first blush of spring finds Melinda filled with great expectations. But as the songbirds return and the garden's soil is turned, not everything's coming up roses. When Uncle Frank makes a shocking discovery in the town's archives, the fallout threatens to dim Prosper Hardware's bright future. As friendships are tested and family ties begin to fray, can Melinda restore the harmony in her life?

The Bright Season (Book 6)

Moving to the country's brought her a new set of skills, but does Melinda have what it takes to fix matters of the heart? It's hard enough to let the past go, and let a new love in. But when a mysterious box is pulled from her farmhouse's crawlspace, she's torn between protecting the former owner's privacy and tracking down the woman he once loved.

Turning Season (Book 7)

Melinda's sun-dappled days are disrupted when little Prosper is suddenly thrust into the spotlight. An unexpected windfall gives new life to a long-held hope, and a surprising discovery puts everyone on edge. And as the mayor's race heats up, Melinda discovers small-town politics can be worse than anything that goes bump in the night.

A TIN TRAIN CHRISTMAS

Travel back in time to Horace's childhood for this special holiday short story inspired by the "Growing Season" series

The toy train in the catalog was everything two young boys could ask for: colorful, shiny, and the perfect vehicle for their wild imaginations. But was it meant to be theirs? With a little faith and their parents' love, the boys just might discover the true spirit of Christmas.

Made in the USA
Las Vegas, NV
01 February 2024

85169239R00156